CW01622623

Urban Venus

Before children, Sara Downing was a Chartered Accountant, but she always knew her dream career lay elsewhere. She started writing in 2009 and hasn't since yearned to return to the world of accountancy.
Sara lives in Worcestershire with her husband and three children.

Also by Sara Downing:

Head Over Heels
Stage Fright
Hand On Heart
The Lost Boy

To Stephanie,

SARA DOWNING

Urban Venus

Merry Christmas!

Sara Downing

x

The right of Sara Downing to be identified as the author of this work has been asserted in accordance with the Copyright, Designs and Patents Act 1988.

All characters in this publication are fictitious or are historical figures whose words and actions are fictitious. Any other resemblance to real persons, living or dead, is purely coincidental.

Venus of Urbino by Tiziano Vecellio reproduced by kind permission of the Uffizi Gallery, Florence

© Sara Downing 2011
Paperback ISBN 978-0-9956529-1-0
www.saradowningwriter.co.uk

© Cover Design – Liz Bryan Muir 2018

For Jack, Harry & Emilia

Venus of Urbino by Tiziano Vecellio (Titian)

1

Bologna, 1541

The carriage rolls with a thief-like stealth through the sleeping streets as I take my leave of this beautiful city, my childhood home. The golden façades and porticoed passageways are illuminated by the final rays of moonlight before the cloud sweeps the nightlight from the sky; it serves to make an easier passage for the driver but reveals to me the streets and alleyways that I will see no more. Now I prefer the darkness.

The rearing Torri loom before us, the huge towers that pierce the skyline and seem to point to heaven itself, outstretched like fingers pleading for the forgiveness I know cannot be bestowed upon me. Their towering greatness serves to make me feel small and unimportant, my crime simply to love a man who could not be mine. We reach an open space, away from the narrow streets, and the driver picks up speed, whipping the horses to go faster and spirit us from this place. I pull my dark cloak around my head as the breeze cuts through me, and shiver with fear and the knowledge of an uncertain future. In as much as I know I cannot stay here, it pains me to go, and my heart pounds fit to burst from my chest as I consider what I have forgone.

How can I leave this man who has loved and cherished me more than anyone in my short life? But I have to go; to stay would mean certain persecution. The man I love had no choice but to disown me, for his own sake and for the sake of his family. I so dearly wish that he could come with me, but it is not possible. He has his reputation to consider; it cannot be hindered by his love for a woman who is not his wife. He is long since gone from me.

A sleeping pigeon, startled by the carriage wheels, flies up like a black ghost, its wings flapping in the semi-darkness like the cloak of the devil himself. This beautiful city, once so welcoming to me, now appears menacing and evil; why should I want to stay?

We speed through the Piazza Maggiore and I permit myself one last glance up at the church of San Petronio, its huge campanile cutting the shadows of the square firmly in two. A sudden spear of moonlight illuminates a stained glass window, and the image of Our Lord is revealed to me. Am I worthy of looking upon his face? I feel I should deflect my gaze, lower my head in shame, but I am drawn to see his visage one final time. As I glance upwards, his enigmatic smile is sufficient to bestow upon me his blessing and forgiveness.

I am now resolved to do what I must, despite the sinfulness of such an act in the eyes of the Lord. As the carriage makes a sharp turn into the Via d'Azeglio I pull my cloak tightly around me and throw myself onto the street below.

2

Florence, Present Day

'*Ecco, signorina,*' exclaims the *tassista*, the unfortunate Florentine taxi driver who has had the onerous task of transporting me and my luggage from the station. And plenty of it there is, too. The term 'travelling light' has yet to make it into my vocabulary, let alone my way of life, and the poor man had spent ten minutes outside the station, attempting to squeeze every last suitcase and holdall into his small, battered (and almost certainly un-roadworthy) Fiat, for the final leg of my journey.

Fortunately I've been lucky enough to have had plenty of offers of help with my heap of clobber at all the various en-route changeovers; there seemed to be a steady supply of willing passengers (usually male, so chivalry can't be entirely dead, can it?) or porters to help me disembark from one leg of the journey and re-embark on the next. And that was without employing any of my feminine wiles on them; not that I'd dream of capitalising on being a mere petite little thing, with a ton of luggage, and more than slightly challenged in the ability-to-carry-one's-own-bags department. I know I've packed too much, and that's my own fault, but there you go. I'm going to be here for the best part of a year, so I need it all! I just don't have enough arms to carry it myself, so any offers of help are greatly appreciated.

I suppose I have fared pretty well on this journey, all things considered. Flying just wouldn't have been an option for me; the check-in chick at the airport would have taken one look at my personal luggage mountain and run off screaming, not to mention the hideous amount in excess baggage charges I'd have had to pay. Anyway, I've made it now, and as I hand the driver a twenty euro note, I don't expect to see any change from it, despite the relatively short trip. The poor man has had to work hard for his money after all.

What a place this is! I've only ever seen Florence in 2D, and the 3D version is really quite overwhelming. 'Shabby chic' has to be a term that was coined for this city; my short taxi ride brought me past palazzos and through piazzas, under archways and alongside gothic churches in glorious gilded stone and marble, all teeming with history but with an unexpectedly welcoming feel to them. There's culture by the bucket-load here, no doubt about it, but none of it daunting in the way that it can be in some big cities. To me, Florence seems to beckon you to explore and enjoy; nothing is hidden away behind barriers like a museum piece, preserved for posterity but never experienced by the masses.

The streets are heaving with tourists and locals alike; the latter go brusquely about their daily business, the former trail languorously, guide-book in hand as they gaze upwards at the magnificent domes and towers, oblivious to the crowds hurriedly trying to get past them. The inevitable parties of Japanese tourists shuffle quickly from street to street, following their umbrella-clutching guides, and snapping away on the myriad high-tech bits of photographic equipment that dangle round their necks.

And here I am, finally, outside the place that is to be my home for the next year. It, too, is steeped in that same gorgeous shabby-chic as the parts of the city I have seen so far – a tall medieval building on several stories, each floor seemingly with its own style, almost as if it had been built one layer at a time by different architects, like some sort of gigantic wedding cake. No doubt it has simply been modified countless times over the centuries; some of the changes remain and others have crumbled to reveal the original detail in the structure behind them. Whatever its history, it's a far cry from my student accommodation in Newcastle, a typical little early twentieth century northern two-up-two-down 'back-to-back', complete with an original outside loo (and one indoors now too, thankfully), a back yard, and a view of the identical row of houses behind it. I'd been happy there though – at least until recent events had conspired to make me otherwise – and I hope it will be available to rent again when I return to Newcastle next autumn to embark on my final year.

With a deep breath for courage, I grab what I can manage of my bags, leaving the long-suffering taxi driver to carry the rest, and turn the heavy iron handle of the little door in the huge oak gate on the front of the building. The taxi driver steps through behind me, calling out a 'Buonasera signorina, e buona fortuna!' as he heaps my luggage in a pile, happy to leave me quickly and move onto the next (hopefully less demanding) customer, now that his job here is done. Whether he is wishing me luck for my stay in Florence, or merely with getting all my bags up to my apartment, is anyone's guess. I'm going to need luck for both, I suppose.

What greets me inside that little door is far from what I'd expected. In my head is a cool, slightly tatty but grandly marbled vestibule of a large block of apartments; instead I open that door and step into a magical garden. It's brimming with bougainvillea, roses and hibiscus flowers, and surrounded on three sides by a high brick wall, giving it an air of complete stillness and tranquility, and shielding it from the prying eyes of neighbours; a tiny, perfect and fragrant oasis within the heart of this bustling city. I can't believe how fabulous it is; the surprise takes my breath away and I stand there, rooted to the spot, trying to get my wits together.

I spy a pair of slim, brown feet with cyan-painted toenails peeping round the side of the building; presumably another resident soaking up a bit of sun and enjoying this beautiful space. I decide not to go any further for fear of disturbing whoever she is and making a nuisance of myself in my first moments here, but just as that plan formulates, the feet drop to the ground, and the person attached to them comes around the corner.

'Ciao!' the gorgeous vision before me exclaims, shaking her mane of glossy dark hair almost in slow motion, like something from a shampoo ad, and stretching her lithe form. 'You must be Lydia,' she exclaims in perfect English with only the merest lilting hint of an Italian accent. 'Benvenuta a Firenze! I am Leonora! I am your flat mate! Pleased to meet you!' and at this juncture she grabs my hand in both of hers and shakes it vigorously, whilst proceeding to plant a kiss on each of my cheeks. 'I thought I would wait for you here, help you with your bags,' she goes on, surveying the luggage around my feet. 'Good job I did,' she adds, laughing.

Leonora can obviously spot an English person at ten paces – how else could she have been so sure that I was her new flat mate and wasn't moving into one of the other apartments? I hope it's just my mountain of luggage giving me away and that I'm not letting the side down in the fashion stakes by dressing like a dowdy Brit. But one glance at Leonora's attire – perfect figure-hugging designer skinny jeans and simple but elegant black strappy top – confirms that yes, I probably do look like your typical English girl abroad, in my cropped summer trousers, pastel tee-shirt and flip-flops. And my (relatively) pale complexion probably has something to do with it too. I think I'm quite brown (for once it hadn't been a bad summer back home) and by UK standards I almost certainly am, but compared to Leonora's naturally gorgeous olive glow, I look positively anaemic.

I am as overwhelmed by this friendly, gushing welcome as I had been by my first glimpse of that walled garden; Leonora must think I am stupid, as it's a good couple of minutes before I manage to emit a single word. Although that's partly explained by the fact that she barely comes up for air She is obviously glad to have a target on which to practise her immaculate English, but at this rate I anticipate I won't be making much improvement in my own Italian linguistic skills – it's going to be all too easy to speak to her in English.

When Leonora finally stops regaling me with the joys and wonders of '*La vita fiorentina*' (she is going to have to fill me in on the finer details of the city all over again at some point, as this is all way too much too soon and I can't take it in) she grabs a few of the heavier looking bags and bounces energetically on her endless legs towards the building to escort me upstairs to our apartment.

And what greets me inside is more along the lines of what I'd expected, although it still produces a jaw-hitting-the-ground-in-amazement moment. A cool, pale and well-trodden marble floor gives rise to the most dramatic, if shabby, staircase, which coils intricately around the edge of the circular stairwell like a tangled and gnarled wisteria. The iron fretwork of the banisters is broken at intervals with metal flowers and garlands, which make the whole structure seem alive, and possibly more at home in the garden we have just left, than in here. As I crane my head upwards I imagine climbing to the top of its infinite spiral like Alice, and disappearing into Wonderland, into another space and time away from reality.

'We are on the third floor, *il terzo piano*,' Leonora informs me as we climb, giving me a little Italian lesson en route. I don't know if she's been told that I do actually speak some Italian, but I can see I'm going to have to fight for my right to have a bash at it, or I will go back home after a year out here with not much more than the pidgin Italian I possess now.

We reach the third floor and Leonora opens the door to our apartment. Another 'wow' moment as we enter the place that is to be my home; a huge room of epic proportions with a fantastically high ceiling – and a painted ceiling at that. I can't believe I'm really going to live in a building which has its own built-in Renaissance works of art! It's furnished with antiques, whose general state of repair is indicative of the fact that this is a rental property – so they probably aren't terribly valuable – but that doesn't matter as the overall effect is perfect. To fill a room such as this with a couple of cream sofas from Ikea and a glass coffee table would have been an offence punishable only by death.

Leonora shows me to my room and dumps the first few bags on the bed. Not only am I going to be living in Renaissance heaven, but I have an oak four-poster bed to boot! Leonora explains to me that this was her friend Manuela's room; she is off doing a similar thing to me apparently, living abroad for a year, only Manuela has gone to South America. She is an archaeology student and plans to spend the year researching the Inca Trail. What a relief she and I aren't doing a straight swap – can you imagine giving up all this for a single room with a faded candlewick bedspread, a view of the outside loo and those forever grey Northern skies? I hope she's been given an equally stunning room in her new temporary accommodation, wherever she is, in sight of a plethora of historic monuments or with some dramatically mountainous vista to open her shutters onto every morning.

'You settle in and have a look around,' Leonora suggests generously. 'I'll bring up the rest of your baggages.' Finally, a flaw in her otherwise perfect English. Just wait till she hears my Italian, though. Still, at least I can muster up the basics such as ordering food and drink, and making myself understood around town, so in theory I won't starve or get too lost, which has to be pretty high on the list of most important things as I settle into my new home city.

The shutters had been closed against the onslaught of the sun's heat, and the room is dark but by no means stuffy. Although it's late September, the temperature is still in the upper twenties (oh, to have that even in the height of an English summer!) and the sun high in the sky, but my room is cool and tranquil, something to do with all the marble and high ceilings, I suppose. I'd lost my directional bearings as we circled up the staircase, and as I throw back the shutters and let the warm air gush in, I am delighted to find that my room overlooks the garden and I smile with undiluted pleasure as I take it all in again. I'm not so high up that I can't appreciate the colours and aromas from up here; in fact I can smell the late summer roses that twirl round the building and reach as high as the floor below ours. I breathe in the exotic, heady scents, and shiver with excited anticipation. I have a feeling I'm going to be happy here.

I wake up in a daze, completely disorientated and glancing around the room for some reassurance as to my whereabouts. As my brain and eyes slowly come back into focus I remember I'd started unpacking, hanging my clothes in the vast armoire which is so huge I'm convinced there's a rear exit leading to Narnia. I'd been setting up my books and art materials on the huge oak table which will serve more than adequately as a desk, but then that gorgeous four-poster had looked so inviting, calling 'Try me, try me', with its creamy embroidered bedspread and huge squidgy bolster pillows, I thought I'd just have a teensy little go and see how comfortable it was. Not surprisingly, I was shattered after nearly twenty-four hours of travelling, and must have nodded off almost instantly.

I have no idea what time of day it is; there is still a gentle warmth wafting in through the open window and although the sun isn't blazing with quite the full force of earlier, it isn't yet dark. Good, so I haven't missed the evening, then. Leonora had promised to show me some of the sights by dusk; trendy bars and restaurants, the 'cool' places to 'be seen', which is a big thing for the Italians, so I've been informed. From early evening, the *aperitivo* hour comes into full force, and anyone who is anyone wants to be seen socialising at the smartest bars and bistros, soaking up the café culture and watching the rest of the world go by. It's the time of day when all the beautiful young things are out and about, gossip and confidences are exchanged, and martinis and proseccos quaffed in abundance. It sounds glamorous and exotic, and a far cry from a trudge down to the dingy old-man's pub on the corner, in coat and boots, for a 'quick one or two,' as it would be back home. I can't wait to experience it for myself.

I can hear voices coming from the living room – although that seems a pretty lame word for a room of such palatial dimensions; I think I might have to be posh and call it the drawing room. So I quickly run my fingers through my slept-in hair, add a touch of lip gloss, and venture out to investigate.

Leonora is draped gracefully over one of the antique sofas, now wearing a light blue strappy silk dress which shows off her perfectly tanned and toned arms, and sipping a tall glass of something cool and sparkling. Her head is thrown back, showing off her long elegant neck, as she laughs at someone's joke. Next to her is another girl, presumably Sophia, my other flatmate. She is equally gorgeous but in a blonder, more Northern-Italian, curvaceous sort of way. Actually, she looks more Swiss than Italian, although her dark skin gives away her heritage. She is a complete goddess as well. How am I ever going to stand a chance with the male of the Italian species with these two to compete with? At most I will be picking up their cast-offs. Although having had that thought, I sneak a quick glance at the three men who are also here and try to keep my bottom jaw from going slack; well, if they are representative of the standard, then cast-offs aren't going to be half bad. I can cope with that.

Hang on a minute, what am I doing thinking about men? I surprise myself at how soon after a broken relationship I find myself ogling these three. (I'm not really ogling, am I? More like just appreciating the scenery.) But then they are a huge cut above most of the men one comes across in the UK. Not wishing to put our dear old pale English chaps down at all, but the chances of being in a room with three UK blokes, and even one of them equalling these Italian gods in looks and style, has to be highly improbable. And here I am, merely hours after setting foot in this place, surrounded by wall-to-wall Italian male gorgeousness. How can a girl complain about that? I must have died and gone to tall-dark-and-handsome heaven…

I'd managed to put Ed and all the emotional baggage surrounding him out of my head during the journey down here, probably because I'd had too much physical baggage to contend with. There hadn't been a lot of time for contemplation, which was probably just as well. And I can see there are going to be plenty of distractions here too; that all has to be cathartic doesn't it?

Ed and I had been together for the entire first two years we'd spent at uni. We'd been one of those sickeningly loved-up couples who hook up in Freshers' Week and are glued at the hip forever after. Only our forever after had been cut dramatically short when I'd found him in my bed with my housemate, Jules. He'd promptly become my ex-boyfriend, and she my ex-friend. Fortunately we'd all been due to head home for the summer a week or two later, so I won't have to face either of them ever again – and by the time I return home from Florence to complete my final year they will both have finished their degrees and be long since gone. Good riddance to bad rubbish.

Ed and I had talked about the future, marriage, mortgage, babies, all that sort of stuff, and I'd just assumed, naively it would now seem, that I'd found 'the one'. I thought we'd just drift from uni to fantastic careers, followed a few years down the line by domestic bliss in a home of our own. How stupid I'd been. Apparently he and Jules had been at it for half of our second year. Why hadn't he just done the honourable thing and finished with me if she was the one he wanted to be with? But no, he'd decided to keep me hanging on too, to cover his options, no doubt, in case Jules blew him out. Bastard. And there she was, fully aware of his relationship with me, AND pretending to be my friend, whilst they were both making a complete fool of me behind my back. I'd had the last laugh, though, if you can call it that – I hadn't felt much like laughing – when Jules had promptly dumped him as well, before they'd left for the summer. Served him bloody right.

The summer at home with my parents hadn't done much to ease the pain of deception. I'd drifted from job to job in an attempt to distract myself as well as to save a bit of cash towards coming out here, but the diversion hadn't worked and I'd felt like I needed a complete change of scene to really thoroughly erase all thoughts of Ed (and the treacherous Jules) from my mind. Well, it looks like the local eye-candy might be able to help with that. Of course, I'm not so shallow as to think that a quick fling with a gorgeous Italian will completely cleanse my broken heart of all the torment it has been through over recent months, but it has to be a tonic, doesn't it?

Even if I'm never lucky enough to hook up with one of these gods, then looking at them alone is enough to give a girl's spirits a huge lift, from a purely aesthetic, study-of-the-male-species perspective. I'm here to appreciate the arts, after all, so why shouldn't I start with the inspiration for much of it – the male form? It certainly puts a smile on a girl's face, and it's wearing said smile that I boldly venture forth to be introduced to them all.

'Ecco l'inglese!' one of these extras from a Dolce & Gabbana ad exclaims. And it doesn't sound in the least pejorative, in the way that we English can sound when referring to another person by their nationality. No, he is clearly eager to meet me, whoever he is, and now that all eyes, both male and female are on me, I feel myself blush, which can't do anything but emphasise my blotchy

English Rose complexion, compared to my Italian counterparts' smoothly glowing ones. Let's just hope some of the men in this country have a penchant for paler skins.

I'm never great at the best of times at walking into a room full of strangers, but fortunately Leonora gets up to greet me and physically escorts me across the room to meet the others, who are all immediately on their feet and kissing me on both cheeks as though I am their long-lost English cousin. Sophia, the other as yet un-met flatmate, envelops me in a huge hug. 'Welcome to Florence,' she says. 'You are going to love this place, I know it. And we are going to be such friends!' I needn't have worried, they are all so lovely.

The three male models are introduced to me as Stefano, Dante and Lanzo. God, even their names are sexy. I just can't imagine them being half as alluring if they were called Bob, Dave and Pete. I start to wonder whether two of them are romantically linked to my flatmates, and hope to goodness that the plan isn't to set me up with the 'spare' this early on in my stay, so I immediately start watching for body language between any potential pair to see if I can deduce who 'belongs' to whom. There's nothing obvious at this stage, no chemistry between any of them beyond the usual Italian all-round effervescence, so I just hope they are simply a bunch of friends who are being generous enough to include me immediately in their inner sanctum. A large group of ready-made friends is just what I need right now; lots of lively conversation and nights out and plenty of people to show me the sights, with no strings attached.

'Allora, la bella signorina inglese,' Lanzo begins, shuffling up on one of the sofas and patting the gap where I'm now expected to squeeze in between him and Sophia. 'You are to be ours for this year. That is truly wonderful. We are honoured to have you.' Were he English, I would be thinking 'What a sleaze-bag', but he manages to carry off, with the utmost sincerity, what could otherwise be a highly flirtatious comment, without making me cringe in the slightest. 'My friends and me, we will show you everything,' and he gestures with both arms in a big sweeping movement. 'Firenze, she is a wonderful place, you will settle in very quickly, be sure of it, and you need never feel homesick or alone. Our friends will be your friends,' he says, both hands moving to cup his heart.

I'm not used to such gushy friendliness – we Brits just don't do the whole welcoming thing in quite the same way. I used to find groups of friends at uni quite cliquey and exclusive sometimes, and not very receptive to newcomers. But I'm quite glad he is so full-on, and as he's another one who, once started, doesn't quite know when to stop, thankfully I'm not called upon to say too much.

'Thank you, you're all very kind,' is all I can manage, as I grin from ear to ear, feeling relieved that I've landed where I have, and looking forward to the evening ahead.

3

Three hours and four – or is it five, maybe? – bottles of prosecco later, (who knows, the waiter hasn't left the empties lying around to be counted) and I feel as though I have been in this city for ever. I haven't even slept here yet, unless you count those few zzzz's I managed to grab on my gorgeous four-poster earlier, and already Florence is my new spiritual home. It's not even as though I've seen many of the sights, because I haven't, although it is pretty lively here in the Piazza della Signoria, and there have been plenty of 'sights' passing by to keep us entertained. Not generally of the cultural variety though.

I have a feeling of total contentment, and I'm fairly sure it's not entirely down to the relaxing effects of alcohol. There's just something about the atmosphere of this place that has already hooked me in and is making me feel as if I've lived here longer, almost a sensation that I might have been here before, a very strong déjà vu effect. Maybe it's just the fact that I've read so much about Florence, and I had pretty much committed the map of the city centre to memory. So now as I see these churches, monuments and piazzas leap off the page and become real, they are more than just buildings to me, there are the essence of the place.

Leonora, Sophia and the boys (no, they're not boys, they are definitely men) had insisted I go with them into the *centro* for the evening, and that was fine by me. I hadn't taken much persuading, and they'd waited patiently for me to have a quick shower, smarten myself up a bit and unpack something a little more glamorous to wear. Fortunately my clothes seemed to have survived the journey OK. One thing I have always been good at is packing, which is probably just as well as I always seem to travel with so much stuff in tow. My Mum taught me years ago about the virtues of packing with tissue paper, and my suitcases bear testament to her painstaking way of folding, wrapping, tucking and stacking, to ensure that everything arrives looking as though it has been freshly plucked from the wardrobe, instead of having been ferried half way across Europe. Given my glamorous companions' easy style and grace, I am eternally grateful to her that I can instantly find something suitable, and un-creased, to wear at a moment's notice.

The gang, for want of a better word to call my new friends, had planned to spend aperitif hour (which is usually about three hours long, according to them) in this bar in the piazza, then move off to a club later in the evening, should the fancy take them. Despite a level of fatigue which has left me feeling quite hollowed out and not-of-this-world, I couldn't say no – they are my entry point into the Italian way of life and I'd have been a fool to turn them down for a spot of tiredness. I felt sure I'd pick up as the evening wore on, and I seem to be doing just that.

So here we are still, sprawled over a couple of pushed-together tables in front of the Café d'Epoca, a somewhat more glamorous establishment than your average café, to the north of the square. Aperitif hour is long since over, but we have stayed, all far too comfortable with the location, the incredibly balmy evening and the relaxed company to be bothered moving on to somewhere livelier. It's pretty lively here, in any case, and the clientele largely young and trendy. Waiters buzz around us, clad in the traditional black uniform with white aprons tied around their waists, trays raised high on pointed fingers as they scoot by with their neat bottoms between the tightly-packed tables.

I am glad of this slight change of plan; I certainly don't have my dancing head on tonight. I'm not sure my addled brain could keep pace with club-land noise either; for the time being I need to be able to hear what my companions are saying if I'm to stand any chance of keeping up with the conversation. I know my Italian lip-reading skills wouldn't hold up amidst blaring music. For the moment they all communicate with me in a mix of Italian and English, which is great, but I'd love for them to feel quite soon that they don't need to explain things to me in my own language. I want to integrate here, be one of them, learn the language properly, and having this ready-made group of friends thrust upon me has to be the best way possible to blend into the Italian lifestyle.

'So, Lydia, have you left a trail of broken-hearted men back at home?' Lanzo asks, cheekily I think, seeing as I hardly know him and don't really feel I'm at the sharing confidences stage of our friendship just yet. Or maybe I'm just taken aback because he's hit on a bit of a raw nerve and so far today Ed has barely popped into my head at all. But now he's there again, damn him. I struggle to think how best to answer Lanzo's question.

'Well, I did leave someone behind,' I start, falteringly, 'but he won't be missing me. In fact it was all over before the summer. We'd been together for a long time but it turned out I wasn't quite what he wanted.' I hope the vagueness of my reply will be enough to satisfy his curiosity and avoid further questioning.

'La poverina bella Lydia,' he replies, looking genuinely sorry for me, and he pats me gently on the hand. There are no fireworks as he does that, I'm glad to note, and he doesn't give the impression that he is checking for sparks either. Although these men are all so lovely, and gorgeous to boot, the last thing I need right now is for one of them to think he has a chance with me. Not for the moment, anyway. Male attention is all very nice, and most definitely a big morale-boost, but I certainly don't want it to be at a level which is anywhere beyond just friendship.

'*Allora*, what are you going to get up to whilst you're here?' he goes on. For my own state of mind and composure I have to assume he's referring to my day to day life, and not my love life, so I start to regale him with my plans on the art front and what I want to study and get involved in. He listens with interest, so clearly I have been barking up the right tree, and not failing to interpret any 'signals' he might have been intending to send out.

'…and I'm supposed to do lots of research for my dissertation – shouldn't be too tricky with all this on hand, should it? And then the plan is that I head back to the UK with that all done and my final year should be a doddle!' He looks a bit confused at my last word. Proper, long dictionary words like 'dissertation' are clearly no problem for him, but throw something dodgy from the vernacular such as 'doddle' and he's lost, poor chap. I set out to explain the meaning of it and he laughs, begging me to teach him a few more slang words. I love how the idiosyncrasies of our complex and bizarre language are always a source of fascination and amusement to foreigners. He flashes a winning smile at me but it's a friendly one and not overly flirtatious, which is a relief.

There is a wail of sirens and screech of brakes as two *polizia* cars appear from nowhere and pull to a sudden halt just in front of the café. Two armed policemen jump from the first car and run off into the bar a couple of doors down. Whilst I follow the events with open-mouthed amazement, the others seem completely unfazed by the whole thing, and barely glance in the direction of all the excitement. Sophia explains to me that it's just the way they do things here. Chances are there probably hasn't been a murder or an armed robbery, it's just the Italian police force's way of dramatically over-reacting to some small crime such as petty theft or a disgruntled customer causing trouble in a restaurant. I can't say I'd want to be on the receiving end of it, even though I have to admit they do look pretty fetching in those uniforms. It seems I have a lot to learn about the way things are done over here, the sort of stuff the books don't tell you. It's a good job I have my new friends to look out for me.

4

Sunday morning finds me dozing lazily in my gorgeous bed, reluctant to stir, in case reality kicks in and this fabulous place turns out to be a dream. I can't believe this bed is all just for me, I ponder, as I stretch out like a starfish in the middle of it. It's practically the size of a tennis court, and sleeping under these drapes makes me feel like the heroine of a period film. By rights I should be woken up by a maid in a mobcap, tiptoeing in to open the blinds, presenting me with my breakfast on a tray and calling me 'ma'am'. But then I'm not really dressed for that – I don't think my Tatty Teddy shorts-and-cami PJ's would pass muster as the cameras started to roll.

I am quite excited about tomorrow morning – heading off to the University for the first time to meet my tutor and find out what they have in store for me. Although I do actually know that I will be pretty much left to my own devices this year, which is great. All those fabulous resources on hand, experts to consult if I need to, plus the added bonus of being completely surrounded by the art itself. What better place could there be to study, paint, and just generally immerse myself in the culture? I can't wait to get stuck into it.

Apparently I'm supposed to attend two tutor groups each week, mainly to touch base and make sure everything is going OK, then there are optional lectures and classes I can sign up for if I want to. Of course I want to – what's the point of being here if I don't seize the opportunities coming my way? I'm going to grab them all with both hands and wring every ounce of benefit from them, educational and otherwise.

As for today, Sophia has offered to take me to the Uffizi Gallery and show me round. I've done the online virtual tour, but I can't see how the on-screen version can possibly do justice to the reality of actually being there. I am in awe of it. The place sounds like heaven, room after room of Italy's artistic heritage, paintings and sculptures all there for public consumption, thanks largely to the Medicis and the other wealthy Florentines over the centuries who had the means and the passion to collect these fine things and make them available for the masses. And all that amidst the backdrop of the building itself, the corridors, the archways, the views across the Arno, the architectural splendour of everything. I can't wait.

Voices in the kitchen and a heavenly aroma drag me from the final dregs of sleep. I manage to pull myself out of my cosy pit as if led by the nose like a sniffer-dog, in search of the coffee my sense of smell has already detected. Its redolence is almost tangible and attacks all my senses in the nicest possible way, giving me a wake-up kick before even a single drop has passed my lips. Nobody does instant coffee here, which is a blessed relief after two years of stolid student-made coffee of the cheapest, nastiest sort. We always made sure we had the proper stuff in our house, but there was no accounting for what you could be given to drink at friends' places.

Sophia and Leonora are gassing away at full throttle at the kitchen table as though they have been awake for hours, which I'm sure they haven't, given the lateness of the hour we all got home last night. They look as gorgeous this morning as they did last night, even without the make-up, and as a contrast I consider my tangled and almost vertical hair, baggy eyes and blotchy skin as I catch sight of myself in the shiny fridge door. Leonora hands me a coffee without asking if I'd like one, and it disappears without touching the sides, despite its strength.

'So, what's it to be today, Lydia?' Sophia asks. 'Statues, paintings, what do you fancy? Or a quick tour round the whole gallery so that you can get a feel for it? I expect you will be spending hours in there over the next few months so maybe a bit of an introduction would be good?' she says, pretty much answering the question for me. I'd decided on a whistle-stop tour for today; get my bearings, see where the artists are that I'm going to focus on, that sort of thing. And Sophia will have a bit of insider knowledge; she knows which routes the tour parties take and how to dodge the worst of the crowds.

An hour or so later and Sophia and I are fighting our way through the hordes of people across the Piazza della Signoria. It has a totally different feel to last night, somehow more frenetic, even though today is a Sunday and in theory a day of rest. No chance of any rest here; tourist trails are in full swing, with armies of all nationalities battling it out for the right to join the queue to the Palazzo Vecchio, pushing and jostling to have their photos taken with David whilst they wait. Hercules regards them severely as they assault his statuesque companions in the Loggia dei Lanzi with their cameras, phones and camcorders. A couple of passing *poliziotti* move in on a young Scandinavian-looking family who have just settled down on the steps of the Loggia to devour their paninis, pointing to the '*Non mangiare, non bere*' sign over their heads. I spot a woman discreetly trying to breast-feed her baby, tucked up just behind Perseus, and I hope for the sake of her child that they don't spy her too and ask her to relocate.

The sky is a strong azure blue; I can't believe what a perfect day it is. If you glance upwards and away from the crowds, the magnificence of the place is astounding. Wonders of architectural brilliance jostle for the skyline, and the campanile reaches high above us like a spear, away from the crowded foot of the Palazzo to the spacious heavens above, as if pleading to be plucked from the onslaught of visitors below.

We turn the corner towards the Uffizi, squeezing past the semi-circular patches of crowds which have formed around the mime artists on the steps of the gallery, as captivating as the real statues in the alcoves. Here a white-painted, powdered man, as motionless as David himself, until an eyelash flutter gives him away as a mortal soul. There a gold-leafed, ivy-clad female, still as a corpse, unaffected by the small child desperately tugging at her sleeve in an attempt to illicit a reaction of some sort. Their collection boxes bear testimony to their brilliance; you just can't help yourself from stopping and staring, willing them to move, giggle, sneeze. And when they don't, you can't help but reach into your pocket.

Further along are the inevitable sellers of cheap copies of the 'masterpieces' within. 'Looky-looky, buy-buy! Cheaper than museum prices! Signorina, Miss, Fraulein, Mademoiselle,' they urge, guessing wildly at nationalities, as the vast majority swarm past, clutching precious gallery tickets and searching for door numbers.

Sophia has pre-booked and we sweep through a practically queue-less door and into the gallery. She drags me up what feels like endless stairs – not really what I need on the back of a hangover and a late night – and then we are high inside this huge edifice, and remarkably, away from the worst of the crowds.

'Time for coffee,' Sophia announces, I suspect in an attempt to speed up our progress through the gallery. We've been here almost two hours already and have barely seen a third of the museum. I can't help but tarry awhile, I'm an art lover, what do you expect? She's a mathematician, with a healthy appreciation for the culture of the city in which she has chosen to study, but you can't blame her for not wanting to linger to the degree that I do. Maybe I should thank her for bringing me here and send her on her way, perhaps to do a little Sunday morning browsing round the shops, but I don't want to appear rude, so I accept her offer of coffee and decide to play it by ear.

'The café on the terrazzo is brilliant,' Sophia enthuses. 'It's over the top of the Loggia, so you get all that lovely view to look at whilst you sip your espresso. That's if we can get a seat of course. If not we'll just stand and watch the world go by. Andiamo?'

'Si, andiamo,' I acquiesce. Poor girl, she's clearly had enough of culture for one day, and needs a bit more excitement; some real-live people to look at instead of wall-to-wall long-dead ones.

Sophia was right. It is busy and there are no seats, in this very bright, modern space which seems totally at odds with the antiquity of the museum. We buy our coffees and stand at the perimeter of the outdoor seating area, as close as we are allowed to get to the edge, and peer through the balustrades at the swarming masses below. A wedding party appears from the far corner of the Piazza, the bride with her veil streaming out behind her, clasping the hand of the darkly handsome groom as they float on air across the square, the crowds parting for them, and followed more sedately by family and friends in their colourful Sunday Best. They make for Rivoire, the chic café-bar on the square, which apparently sells mind-blowing chocolates at wallet-blowing prices, presumably for their wedding breakfast, which I can imagine will be very caffeine- and chocolate-orientated.

I decide to brave it with Sophia; I don't want her feeling she has to give up her entire Sunday to me. She barely knows me yet, and I really appreciate her bringing me here, but I'm sure there must be other things she'd rather be doing today. I put that proposal to her and she looks visibly relieved. It's one thing showing a regular tourist the sights, but another thing entirely when you have a serious art-lover in tow, and I don't think she had anticipated just how riveting I would find it. So I gently and gratefully release her from her obligations and after coffees have been drunk she scoots off in pursuit of a little retail therapy to perk up her Sunday.

I haul my gallery guide out of my pocket and contemplate which room to visit next, a warm feeling of relaxation and enjoyment spreading through me as I now realise I can take my time and not rush through the rest of the gallery. I stroll back along the corridor, following the path of a thousand daily footfalls on terracotta floors worn smooth over the centuries. Fewer people seem to be heading through into room twenty-five, so I follow Sophia's advice of not observing the regular, prescribed trail and duck in quickly as a Japanese tour party heads into the room next door. This leads me through to a network of smaller rooms, quieter for the moment, so much so that I can hear the click-clack of my own shoes on the polished tiles.

Through into room twenty-eight, the home of some of Titian's work. I've already singled out Tiziano Vecellio as one of the artists I want to focus on whilst I'm here, so I'm thrilled to see so many of his paintings in the one room. Even though he was a Venetian artist, there's enough of his stuff here in Florence for me to put him on my list and have plenty of material to work with. Just as well I sent Sophia on her way; I plan to spend ages in here, and the welcomed coffee break has left me refreshed and ready to do just that.

This room feels quieter and more serene than the rest of the gallery, although maybe it's only due to the current lull in the volume of passers-by. But then the comparable calm of the room is shattered instantly as the Japanese tour party I'd done so well in evading enters from the opposite doorway. I sit down on a green padded bench to wait as I cannot now get close enough to the paintings I so want to see.

They are a motley crew, this party; some listening earnestly to the guide and clearly genuinely interested in the art, others simply along for the ride, so that they can tick off the Uffizi as done on their grand tour of Europe. They fiddle and twitch at the back of the group, texting, or adjusting their photographic equipment, whose prohibited use in the gallery must be hard to bear for a race reared on recording their entire lives and adventures in 2D.

Suddenly the crowd disperses again, spirited away by their guide to the next room, and the works of art are revealed to me once more. Now I can see the beautiful Flora, fresh-faced in her youthful gracefulness, and the wonderful Madonna of the Roses.

Opposite there is Eleanora Gonzaga, a formidable-looking woman whose harsh countenance is only softened slightly by the small dog at her side; the far from aesthetically pleasing Francesco Maria della Rovere, Duke of Urbino, her husband; and between them, the beautiful and unsurpassable Venus of Urbino. Wow. A true masterpiece, even though I don't like that term very much. I try to avoid using it whenever I can, as these days it seems to be bandied about as loosely as that fickle term 'celebrity' is used back home to describe someone whose claim to fame is a mere five minutes in the spotlight. But masterpiece this is, quite undeniably. And not just because of the familiarity of it. I know it has a reputation as one of those paintings which are instantly recognisable to a good majority of ordinary people who otherwise know nothing about art, a bit like the Mona Lisa or Botticelli's Primavera. But Venus is in a league of her own, and seeing her in the flesh, as it were, I am totally captivated. Such is her popularity that she is behind glass; a real shame we cannot touch such a great work of art, but her value is too high and there are always those few who want to spoil it for the rest of us.

Just as I regret the presence of the glass, a man's hand goes out towards the Eleanora painting next to her, not for malicious means I'm sure, but because he is an enthusiast and is clearly longing just to touch the painting. An alarm beeps loudly, alerting the guard, who leaps in quickly with a '*Signore, per favore non toccare.*' His words are not harsh but his expression takes no prisoners. As they move off I sit down again in front of Venus to contemplate her more fully.

Now the room is still once more, I can properly take in my surroundings. A room that seemed a perfect cube to start with is actually slightly off-kilter, as though a small child has picked up this block-shaped room and squashed it into vague imperfection, like a chunk of plasticine. I imagine it probably hasn't changed for centuries; the only concessions to modernity are the invasive, bright red fire extinguishers, alarm buttons and wiring. All the high-tech things a historical building can't function without in the twenty-first century, particularly when it's crammed from floor to ceiling with priceless works of art. The smell is of true museum, a mix of oil on canvas and all things old, the stuffiness of a room never opened to the fresh air for fear of the damage it may do to the art within. I breathe deeply and wallow in the aroma of times past.

Venus reclines in her opulence in front of me. I know popular belief has it that the models for Flora and Venus are one and the same, but as I glance over my shoulder at Flora again, despite the similarities of facial expression and incline of the head, she has none of the wanton sensuality of Venus. Maybe it's just because Flora, in her innocence, is looking meekly to one side, away from the gaze of the onlooker, whereas Venus seems to be regarding you directly, as if challenging you not to find her beautiful. I suppose she could be the same woman; certainly the style in which they are painted is so very Titian in its appreciation of the voluptuousness of women.

So who was she, this Venus? The books all say that no one really knows who commissioned this painting, even though it eventually came into the hands of the Della Rovere family, and that link seems to be reaffirmed here by the placing of Venus between Francesco Maria and his wife Eleanora. It must have been a pretty racy painting in its day, and I wonder how the austere Eleanora feels about her portrait hanging next to the wantonly nude Venus in perpetuity, forced for ever to stare at Venus' beauty, when she herself had not had the fortune to be blessed with such charms.

I imagine Eleanora's spirit, wherever it may now reside, being totally shocked. Maybe her ghost haunts the gallery at night, trying to wreak havoc on the painting, and that is why Venus is behind glass? That random thought makes me giggle out loud, and as I raise my hand to my mouth to stifle it the guard gives me an odd look. Even more amusing if the model who sat for the Venus painting had had an affair with Francesco Maria. Imagine if this girl from the sixteenth century had come between them in life and now here she is, hanging between them for eternity! But who would ever know that sort of detail about their lives? I resolve to find out a lot more about them all.

I am surprised to find myself so intrigued with Venus, and I know I will be coming back here a lot; there's something about this room, and in particular, that painting, that I love. It seems to draw me in, compelling me to sit here and look at it. Each time I look I discover details I'd not noticed before, from the folds of the curtains to the drape of her hair. Women of that era were certainly appreciated for their curves; there's no way the skinny Kate Moss's and Victoria Beckhams of our day would have appealed to those Renaissance artists. No, in those days, they liked them a little plumper, more womanly. Not a size zero body in sight on the walls of this gallery….

He runs his fingers lightly around my jaw line, grips my chin in his thumb and forefinger and gently turns my head to one side, raising my face to what remains of the light. He glances angrily towards the window; the rapidly darkening day is frustrating his attempts to capture the hues of my skin on canvas. I recognise the feel of these caresses as entirely artistic and not in the least romantic. Not for the time being, for I know that presently I am model, not lover, as he tries to focus on his work, but the effect of his touch is to cause me to shake with mirth and also to quiver with desire. He is tickling me, I cannot help it! He scowls at me, but I know it is only from creative frustration and the knowledge that this light will give him at most another half-hour of work, before the darkness claims his brush strokes until dawn. He cannot paint satisfactorily by candlelight. He says my beauty merits reproduction only in full daylight. Dusky hues do me no justice, he insists. He is the one who knows, after all. He is the artist, I am merely his muse, his inspiration.

'Come here, my love,' I urge, as he paces the room, desperately seeking out the lighter corners that might permit him to paint for a little longer. 'Come to me,' I say again, and this time he cannot resist. He places the tools of his trade respectfully on the chest at the end of the room and with a languorous sigh, steps up onto the platform beside my lettuccio, the vast oak daybed which serves as my stage, and as the altar on which he pays homage with his brushes to my beauty. He unfastens the small buttons at the neck of his linen shirt and lifts it over his head in a deft movement, and then he is beside me, his strong chest warm against my bare shoulders. His lips seek out mine and I close my eyes as the passion engulfs me and I lose myself in his embrace.

I wake up with a small jolt – surely I can't have been asleep? No, that's not possible; I've only been sitting here for a few minutes, haven't I? Not time enough for a nap. Glancing quickly at my watch for reassurance I see that barely any time has passed at all and yet I feel like I am waking from a long sleep, as refreshed as if I had slept for hours. This tiredness is starting to get to me, and I know I haven't given myself proper time to recover from the journey yesterday, fool that I am. My mother would have something to say about that if she were here, which thankfully she isn't. Which reminds me, I must call them all later and let them know I'm still alive. I'd sent a quick text on my arrival but that was the only newsflash so far. Was it really only yesterday that I arrived? Somehow I find that hard to believe. Must be all this napping, giving me the illusion of having spent more nights here than just the one that I actually have.

Rubbing my eyes I glance across in the direction of the guard's seat. The male guard from earlier has now morphed into a woman, so I suppose I must have slept for long enough to miss that changeover. This one is a stout lady in her late fifties who looks more National Trust volunteer than scary security staff, so I don't think my oddness will result in her having me carried off to the madhouse just yet. This strange English woman who sits and giggles in front of the Venus painting and then decides to follow that moment of madness with a little nap on the bench. I am sure they get all sorts in here, not just art nutters like me, overcome with tiredness and the excitement of it all.

As my mind re-engages I have the vague recollection of a dream of some sort. Amazing how the brain can pack what feels like a fully-fledged action-packed movie into the space of a few minutes' doze. At home I used to have my best dreams in the morning, in those few precious moments before waking up properly, almost as though the subconscious which has stirred slightly from the deeper slumber of the night is more capable of producing dreams than the unconscious, dead-to-the-world state that most of us occupy for the majority of our sleeping hours. Or maybe it's just that we remember these ones more easily, as they take place so close to us waking up?

Fascinating subject, dreams, and something I want to explore whilst I'm here. After all, so many paintings are depictions of dreams, or stories of divine inspiration. It has to be a possible topic for my dissertation, as there's so much material I could use. I haven't really decided yet, but I certainly should give it some serious thought, given my own predisposition to dreaming.

I've always been a bit of a daydreamer too, which has been a constant source of irritation to parents, teachers and the like over the years. But I always counter it with the argument that you can't have a proper artistic temperament without the ability to dream. That only ever got me out of trouble in more recent years, I have to say, when my artistic skills did start to look like they might be half decent, but it was always worth a try.

I can't really get my head around what the dream just now was all about. I have a strong recollection of touch, sensuousness and a deep feeling of love between two people. I felt exposed, almost naked even, and when I came to I half expected to have to cover myself up, here in the gallery. It must have something to do with gazing at all these romantic images, I suppose, and I shrug it off for the moment as no more than the wanderings of a very tired mind. Early night tonight, I resolve. No partying in the piazza for me, just a sensible, quiet night in before I head off to my first day at the university tomorrow.

5

Monday morning dawns bright and sunny – again. Oh, to live forever in a place like this where the sun always shines, the sky is always the kind of blue a child would paint it, and the temperature is short-sleeve warm, even at this early hour of the day. And here we are with October rapidly approaching; at home it would all be grey skies, lots of rain, and we'd have hauled the winter woollies out of the wardrobe long since.

It has to be good for the soul to live somewhere like this – how could anyone ever contemplate being miserable here? I throw open the shutters in my room to an onslaught of brightness and breathe in the rose-smelling scent from the trailers beneath the window. All sad or bad thoughts seem to have deserted me since I arrived here; the change of scene, climate, culture, or a combination of the three, seems to be divesting me of my worries more than any other distraction I've tried so far. Ed? Ed who? Who was he? Oh, just some stupid bloke I once knew who didn't know what was good for him. Who needs him, anyway? I certainly don't. The course of my new life here stretches ahead of me like uncharted waters, waiting for me to pull up anchor and set sail. I can't wait.

Leonora has to go in for a lecture this morning, so she suggests I tag along with her. She's a Law student, so she can at least point me in the direction of the Arts Faculty and leave me to it. I need to go and get hold of all the forms I need, not just to register at the university but to make myself legal for living here too; residence permits, all that sort of official stuff. As we dog-leg at a brisk pace through a network of tiny backstreets whose names all blur into one, I wonder how on earth I will find my way home later. Fortunately, like the tourists from whom, thanks to my educational motivations for being here, I am one step up on the evolutionary scale, I am fully equipped with map and compass, in the guise of very clever iPhone apps, plus I do possess the ability to be able to make myself understood in the native language. Well, just about, anyway.

Finally the imposingly grand Palazzo Strozzi looms before us, and I part company with Leonora, who has a breakfast date with a friend before her lecture. I manage to locate the building in the Via del Parione, and firmly put on my best Italian-thinking head before braving it alone.

So, now I am legal. Forms all completed, in duplicate, triplicate and whatever else they were, just loads of them it seemed, all in very complex Italian with hardly any punctuation, a bit like English legal documents only they could have been in ancient Greek, for all that I understood them. I will probably find out all too late that I've signed up for some dodgy time-share, bought a car or pledged to donate my organs, instead of applying for my course and the various study and residence permits I need. I hadn't realised just how bureaucratic the Italian way of doing things would be – it had been bad enough at home filling in all the documents I needed just to get me here, and now I am here I have had to do it all over again, tenfold. So much for us all being in Europe and it being a paperless society in the twenty-first century. Ha.

Formalities dealt with, it's time to meet my tutor. Signore Tizzaro's office is Room 26a on the third floor in Block B, so I have been informed (and thankfully understood) so I grab my map of the building and head off. I must be getting near when I hear raised voices. Clearly someone is not happy; a male and a female voice are in the full throes of a pretty vitriolic argument, but I can't hear enough to decipher what is being said. Suddenly a door flies open with a bang and a very angry, but very attractive girl, most likely a student from the armfuls of books she is clutching, flies out into the corridor, flicks her hair aggressively over her shoulder with a scowl and flounces off towards the staircase.

I look around for 26a before realising it's the room the girl has just emerged from. Great, Signore Tizzaro is really going to be in a receptive mood for meeting a new student, especially one with whom there's likely to be a little bit of a language barrier, requiring him to make more of an effort to communicate than normal. Perhaps I should come back later, or tomorrow, I wonder, but as I stand in the corridor, poised either to knock or to flee, I haven't yet decided which, his door flies open again and this time, he (I assume it's him) is standing there, tucking in his shirt and running fingers through dark, dishevelled hair.

'*La Signorina Irvine, presumo di sì!*' he exclaims, pronouncing my surname 'Ear-veen-ay' as his expression softens from the taut air of post-argument tension to a more welcoming smile in a mere split-second. Either this guy is a great actor, or that fight didn't really mean much to him at all. Whereas that poor girl looked like she was about to throw herself from the campanile at sunset. I hope for her sake that she was unhappy with her grades, or something like that, rather than it being a disagreement of a more personal nature… In any case, it's nothing to do with me, and as long as he is a good tutor, then that's all that matters.

If I had been expecting a crusty old academic, then Signore Tizzaro is about as far removed from that as you could possibly get. He doesn't look that much older than me, although he has to be, I suppose, if you take into account the number of years of effort actually required to get to professor-hood. Such gravitas doesn't come with extreme youth, so he must be thirty as a minimum, I'd guess, and he'd have to be at least that old to have read half the books lining his shelves. And, I note later, to have written the six volumes of his own work, displayed in a rather prominent position on the bottom shelf near his desk. In the corner of his office there is an easel with a half-completed painting, and despite its state I can clearly see that it is of the girl who left his office just now. Model as well as student then… Hmmmm.

Signore Tizzaro invites me to call him Vincenzo. Apparently there aren't the formalities in the Italian higher-education system that we have back home, he says.

Yeah, right, try telling that to the guy on the admin desk who had me filling in fifty thousand forms not too many moons ago. Formality was his middle name. I have to say that whilst the arrays of books lining his room are impressive, Signore Tizzaro, or should I say Vincenzo, fails to make the initial impression on me that he is clearly hoping to. After my obvious exposure to the argument, he seems to be trying too hard to compensate by laying on the charm, but why he should feel he needs to is a mystery to me; he's my tutor, not a prospective lover. I've already marked his card as a womaniser, even with so little evidence to go on. Whilst my new friends Stefano, Dante and Lanzo seem to be able to carry off that very over-the-top Italian 'way with women' without it seeming offensive, Vincenzo just comes across as a bit creepy. Which is a shame, as I had been hoping for someone to look up to this year, someone I could draw inspiration from. But that's going to be tricky if I don't feel entirely comfortable with him.

During and after our first conversation, I can't help thinking back to that poor girl leaving his office; I wonder exactly what cause she had to be so angry with him, and the word 'sleazebag' keeps popping into my head. I try to divorce it from my professional opinion; we have to work together, after all. I can't allow myself to think at this stage that it was a lovers' tiff. I shouldn't be drawing such conclusions based on first impressions alone, and I resolve to give the guy a break, see what he has to offer me. I'm not normally one to judge people I hardly know so harshly.

I leave Vincenzo's office with a lecture timetable, study guide, map of the city (another one) and various other bits of paperwork to add to the green, pink and blue sheets of paper Mr Formality downstairs gave me earlier. Luckily for me it looks as though my lectures are scattered about in various parts of the city centre, and some even in the great homes of art themselves, so I consider myself very fortunate not to have to traipse off to some dull 1970's concrete lecture theatre every day. It seems the faculty like to present as many of the lectures as possible in situ, and who can blame them; it has to be heaps easier to inspire your students when you actually have the art to hand as a prop, instead of relying on PowerPoint and other mock-ups, as we had to back home.

As for today, I want to go to this afternoon's lecture on Raphael, which is being held in a side room at the Uffizi. Great, another chance to get back in there, and this time without having to buy a ticket; the uni provides us with special passes on the days we need to get in there for lectures. I must remember that – it's one way to save the Euros, to hoard up my visits for days when I can get in for free!

After leaving Newcastle with my bank balance looking none too healthy at the end of the summer term, I had worked a lot over the long holidays. Well, a lot is a bit of an understatement actually, as I'd worked all the hours I possibly could in a vain attempt to erase Ed from my mind and not be left sitting around with time on my hands, going over it all time after time. That last bit hadn't worked too well but at least the financial side of my plans was a success and I'd managed to pay off my overdraft and save up enough to see me through – hopefully – most of this year. My parents are helping me out with accommodation costs – I don't see how I could do this otherwise – but I don't want to have to put on them any more than I have to so I need to be careful, or I will end up having to work whilst I'm here too. And I'd planned not to have to do that.

The lecturer looks an interesting sort; typical 'mad professor' hair cut (although that mop probably hasn't seen a pair of scissors in two decades, more likely a set of garden shears), dreadfully mismatched clothes (aren't we in one of the Italian centres for fashion here?) and a set of teeth that could be used as park railings, complete with rust. Nothing aesthetically pleasing about him at all, although Vincenzo did say he was one of the more brilliant and inspiring lecturers, so again I need to maintain an open mind and give him a chance, and stop judging people on first impressions.

And I am enthralled from the start. Signore Di Girolamo rounds up and captures his audience like the Pied Piper within seconds of the start of his lecture, and I sit completely rapt for the full hour, not even breaking my gaze to glance around the room at the others present, or, surprisingly, the artwork lining the walls. At the end, as he starts to pack his things together, he is suddenly surrounded by a swarm of students, all wanting to ask more and get inside his brilliant mind.

'You are English, yes?' the guy next to me asks, as I'm busy observing this scrum and packing away my own notes, still in thrall to the greatness of Signore Di Girolamo. 'What did you think of our fantastic professor? Isn't he brilliant? I am Eduardo,' he says, holding out his hand for me to shake. Oh no, not another Ed, even if he is an Italian version and looks nothing like my Ed. Has he been sent here to haunt me, a flashback from my painful past? Don't be so silly, Lydia.

'Mi chiamo Lydia. Piacere,' I reply, seizing the proffered hand, and not wanting him to think that like most English people abroad, I can't have a go in the native tongue.

'How are you settling in? Have you fallen in love with our beautiful city yet?' he asks in Italian, and I manage to formulate a sensible reply which doesn't sound half bad, I think. He understands me, anyway. 'A few of us are going for a coffee now. Would you like to join us?' he asks.

I can't believe how welcoming everyone is here. There I am, thinking I stand out like a sore thumb as the English girl, but these guys are going out of their way to include me in their circle of friends. It would be great to get to know some people on my course; I can't expect Sophia and Leonora to keep providing ready-made friends and do all the hard work, so I accept gladly and gratefully. I will have to sneak back into the gallery on my free pass later and go and see the Raphael work properly, but I can't miss an opportunity to make some more friends.

'We are going just around the corner from here,' Eduardo adds. 'We no drink caffè in this piazza, too expensive,' he goes on in English, wagging a finger and smiling. 'We know a lovely bar, not far from here, well, not very lovely but caffè is good. I show you, you come with us.'

I follow him and his small band of friends, who each introduce themselves to me with a welcoming smile and a handshake. I can't recall making friends ever being this easy in my first week at Newcastle. Freshers' Week seemed to be fraught with pressure to get in with the 'right' crowd, join the 'cool' clubs, and work out where to be seen and with whom. Florence doesn't seem half as fake and pretentious as all that; everyone I have met so far has been genuinely lovely, with no ulterior motive in getting to know me other than that they would like me to be their friend. Simple as that.

Eduardo was right about the bar; it's far from lovely. It's the sort of place that if I were on my own, I would give a very wide berth to; one of those typical little backstreet cafés you see all over any big city in Italy, a bit grubby and seedy looking, with most customers standing at the bar drinking their coffee. (I hadn't realised until now that they charge you more to sit down – common mistake of the foreigner.) Fortunately one of the group knows the owner, Mario, so we do get a table, for no extra charge, and I am glad of it, as there is no lingering over coffees as compact as these, and without a table there would have been limited opportunity to get to know the rest of the crowd I have come here with. Not a latte or a cappuccino in sight at this time of day; they are the territory of the tourist, apparently. Nothing that milky should be drunk post-breakfast, so I am told. So it looks like no more long frothy coffees for me as I try to integrate myself into the Italian way of life; it's straight down the hatch with this potent blast of thick, black liquid.

I leave the café an hour later with two of those shots coursing round my veins, feeling very energised, and intent on going back to the Uffizi to have a look at the

Raphaels. Those duly visited and notes taken, I find myself again in room twenty-eight. I start with a closer look at Flora and Eleanora, then end up on the bench in front of my Venus. Funny how easily I am drawn here…

'Maria, wake up. Come quickly,' the whisper in my ear stirs me from a gentle slumber. 'He is here, he has come to see you.' Clara hands me my robe which I quickly pull around my shoulders, and locates my silk slippers tucked under the side of the bed.

I descend the staircase nervously. It is several weeks since I have seen him; I do not know what his reaction to me will be. Did I give myself to a man who will cast me aside, like the others have done, or have I found in him someone to whom I will be very special, as he is to me, who will look after me and cherish me as I long for so very much? But if so, why does he come to me in the depth of the night, if not for just one purpose?

'My darling…' I start as I set eyes on him, but he motions to me to be silent, placing his index finger gently over my lips and steering me quickly into a side room. It is cold in here, the fire long since extinguished. Only the upstairs rooms require heating at night; once the gentlemen have retired for the evening with the girl of their choice, Rosetta dampens the fires downstairs, her job for the night done, all monies collected, doors closed until the morning. She can retire to her own bed – alone.

It is fortunate that I also find myself alone this evening; tonight, for once, there is no male company for me. Rosetta is a kind mistress, I believe. She does not force us to work every night, nor will she insist we work if we are tired, or ailing, or suffering our monthly curse. Provided we succeed in earning our keep for the week, a headache or simply a wish for some peace can provide a night of respite. And the gentlemen who visit are only of the finest class; they are kind and generous to us and do not treat us in the manner our profession befits. Yes, I have been lucky here, I know that.

He places his hands gently on my shoulders and looks me directly in the eye, before lowering his head as if in slow motion and brushing my lips with the most fleeting of kisses. Then he seems to come to, out of his mesmeric state, and remembers the purpose for which he has come. 'Pack your things quickly, my love. You are coming with me tonight. My carriage awaits us outside. Clara will say nothing to Rosetta, it is agreed.' Here he gently taps his pocket to show that Clara has been remunerated for her silence. 'Go now, fetch your clothes and your possessions; I will wait here for you.'

So I am to be spirited from this place, at last! But now the hour of my departure approaches I find myself fearful. I have been happy here, despite the manner in which I earn my living, and well looked after, and I cannot help but feel a little apprehensive about what the future holds. It is one thing to make promises to one's love in the depths of night, another to bring them to fruition and to make good those pledges for eternity. Can he really keep me safe, and love me like he tells me he wants to?

With great speed I dress and pack my affairs, which are few and of little worth. Casting a brief backwards glance at the place which has been my home for all these years, I spy Clara's earnest face watching nervously from the window as I climb into the waiting carriage.

6

I leave the gallery in something of a daze. What is it about that room that sends me to sleep the moment my bottom hits that bench? I'd brought my books with me to take some notes, but barely had I withdrawn pencil from case than I was out for the count once more. It's like some weird art-hallucinogenic thing going on; just a few minutes of exposure to it and I am off. I wonder if the other rooms in the gallery, or even other paintings, would have the same effect on me, but then I haven't put that to the test and I'm not sure I want to either. One set of dreams at a time is more than enough for me to cope with.

Am I reading too much into all this? Perhaps I am just still really shattered; all the excitement of arriving, meeting so many lovely new people and being so completely and utterly overwhelmed by the beauty and culture around me wherever I go? I just need to pull myself together and get on top of it. Yes, that'll be all it is, pure lack of sleep and over-tiredness.

Another dream. This time I remember it a little more clearly. I couldn't begin to say where I was, or even who

I was, even though I know quite clearly 'I' wasn't me, but I do have a strong image of the man in the dream. He was my lover, whoever he was. His face was unfamiliar, and although the 'me' in the dream knew him, in real life I have no idea who he is. But I did recognise the look in his eye as one of sheer adoration; that look is quite easily translated from subconscious to conscious state. A bit like the look I used to see on Ed's face in the early days. Go away, Ed, stop invading my thoughts, you bad, nasty nobody. The kind of love I felt in this dream was far beyond anything you and I ever experienced.

I remember it being night time, and wearing something long, silky and floaty, a nightie perhaps? Why was I meeting this man in my nightie? I wrack my brains to try to bring some more detail from the dream back to life but at the moment it won't come. But bits of dreams tend to have a habit of creeping up on you when you're least expecting them; something you do or say during waking hours can spark off a memory from the subconscious, in the same way I suppose that the tiniest daytime thought or insignificant action can trigger a certain dream the following night. It's all somehow linked in these crazy, clever and complicated human brains of ours.

Dreams always seem to lose a lot in translation – there's nothing harder than having to try and explain a really exciting or funny dream you had to someone without it sounding like a whole load of tosh, and I know that if I voice this one, even just to myself, then its meaning will fade. Dreams are a bit like books written in your own, personal language, or code, I suppose, only to be understood by you and no one else. They make perfect sense whilst in your head, but are so hard to verbalise. Although at the moment I don't understand this one; I just don't remember enough about it and I desperately hope some of it will come back to me soon.

My phone beeps in my pocket, bringing me out of my dream-obsessed state. It's a text from Leonora. 'Hope day 1 going well. Aperos @ 6 in café Strozzi, v. del Trebbio. See you there! xx.' I text a quick reply back to say I'll be there and load up my 'Map' app for the umpteenth time today. I'm sure I'll get my bearings here eventually; I have to, I practically swallowed the guide book whole before I came out. GPS position located, I realise it's not that far and decide to walk along the Arno, then cut back up into the town. I haven't been along the riverside much yet so it gives me a chance to see a few more sights.

As I turn away from the river and into the Via de' Tornabuoni I gasp, instantly wishing I had been born to landed gentry, instead of being the daughter of a couple of retired office workers from Sussex. Even new money would do, any kind of wealth, I'm not fussy just as long as there is lots of it. This street is quite literally bulging with designer stores, their vast and opulent window displays positively oozing with gorgeousness. Salvatore Ferragamo sets the standard for what is to follow with its huge, illustrious store overlooking the Arno, delicious bags and shoes screaming 'Buy me, buy me' but simultaneously flashing their expensive price tags with a 'Ha, you can't afford me, you're only a student,' taunt. Ahhhh if only. One day I am going to be rich and come back to that shop, completely confident of my status and unabashed at my spending power like the wealthy young couples I can see inside now, and BUY SOMETHING REALLY EXPENSIVE. Or even several things.

My big sister, Evie, would love this part of town, I know that for a fact. Now there is a girl who is born to shop and has the means to do so. I must drop her a text over the next couple of days; it would be great to get her out here and show her the sights… And maybe she'd take me shopping...?

I traipse past the others; Prada, Gucci, Bulgari, Cartier – all the best names have a presence here – and swoon at the window displays. Beautifully attired shoppers, well-heeled and high-heeled, zip from one store to the next, oversized bags crammed with goodies dangling from their arms and proclaiming 'Recession, what recession?' There I was thinking we were in the middle of a global financial crisis, but quite clearly the cutbacks have not cut back their budgets.

I turn from temptation and the certainty of a lifetime of debt into the little side street and track down the café. Leonora and Sophia are comfortably ensconced in the far corner, looking a bit like they've been there all day. I wonder where exactly in their timetables the study fits in, but clearly it doesn't impact too heavily on their social lives. Dante, Lanzo and Stefano are there too, plus a couple of other girls I haven't met yet, so my social circle is set to expand yet again. Leonora is sporting a fine-looking shopping bag of her own from one of the stores I have just passed. I would wonder how she managed that on a student's allowance had I not picked up from conversations yesterday that her father is a banker in Rome, pretty high up in one of the top financial institutions. Obviously papa wants his little girl to be able to buy the odd treat now and again. Lucky thing, can't begrudge her that I suppose.

Drinks ordered and a chair found for me, everyone is keen to know how *l'inglese* fared on her first day all alone in the big *città*, and I regale them with tales of the flirty Vincenzo and the fight, the stupendously great Signore Di Girolamo and my charming new friends from my course. I surprise myself at just how much of this I manage to recount in Italian; at this rate I should be coping pretty well with the native tongue within a couple of weeks. I am walking proof that total immersion is the only way to learn a language.

'I've heard things about Signore Tizzaro,' Sophia warns. 'Apparently he's a huge flirt. Just be a bit careful.'

'Don't worry,' I reassure her. 'I couldn't be less interested in him – not my type at all. I wonder who that girl was, though. It did look like she was a bit more to him than just a student. He was painting her too.'

'Yeah, he does that, apparently. He has a real eye for a pretty girl who'd make a good model. He's a fantastic artist, though. In fact he's got an exhibition coming up at the Strozzi in a couple of weeks. I'm sure he'll tell you all about it and get you to come along,' she explains, then adds: 'You might see a few of your fellow female students on canvas!'

Once the rest of the group are deep in conversation about something else I venture covertly to Sophia: 'I had this weird dream in the museum.' Much as I want to tell someone about it I don't want her to think I'm a little bit crazy when she's only just met me – and has to share an apartment with me.

'You fell asleep – in the Uffizi!' she howls, finding it amusing that the girl who had so avidly toured the museum with her only the day before could find the time to take a little nap with all that enthusiasm bouncing around in her head. 'How did you manage that?'

I explain to Sophia that it wasn't the first time it had happened. 'I had these strange dreams; I wasn't me, I was someone else and there was this man I was in love with. I think it was the same man in both dreams. It's all a bit vague, but I think I really loved him, whoever he was. He kept looking at me with these big, puppy-dog eyes. He had this goatee beard on his chin, I seem to remember, a pointy little thing, and his clothes were odd, it definitely wasn't twenty-first century gear he was wearing. And there was a carriage and horses, I remember that now, too. He was taking me somewhere. Where to and where from I have no idea.'

'Well you seem to have remembered quite a bit of it,' Sophia replies. 'Do you do this a lot – fall asleep in strange places that aren't your bed? That could get you into all sorts of trouble, you know!'

'Can't say I do. Think it's the first time it's happened actually,' I explain. 'I do dream a lot, and I remember quite a bit of my dreams usually, too. But I don't normally fall asleep in places like that. It's all a bit odd. Maybe it's just my body's way of catching up on the tiredness of the weekend. And looking at all those paintings.' I try to shrug it off with a smile and make light of it, but I desperately want some more details of the dreams to come back to me, so that I can attempt to make sense of them a bit more.

One of the other girls in the group that I haven't met before is Francesca, a petite little doll-like thing with huge eyes and a mane of dark, wavy hair down to her waist. I'd noticed her go a bit quiet and awkward and look away from the group when I was talking about Vincenzo earlier. I really want to find out what it is that she knows, so I seize my moment when there's a lull in the conversation between her and the other girl I've not met before, Alessandra, to the other side of her. I feel a bit odd prying into someone's private life when I hardly know them, and I surprise myself too at my sudden interest in Vincenzo; after all he hadn't exactly made the greatest of first impressions on me earlier.

'What are you studying Francesca?' I ask. 'Are you an Art student too? Only you seemed to know Signore Tizzaro when I was talking about him earlier.'

'Er… yeah… no, well, no, I'm not doing Art, I'm studying Classics actually. But… um… a friend of mine used to know Vincenzo, really well. She had a bit of a thing with him for a while, but he dumped her as soon as the next pretty girl came along. He's a bit like that. Really do be careful, won't you?'

'How does he get away with it?' I ask. 'Back home, lecturers who get into relationships with students can get into all sorts of trouble. It goes on, of course it does, but it's not quite as out in the open as it seems to be here.' I've barely known this guy five minutes and already I've managed to form an opinion of him as the biggest womaniser going.

Francesca gazes off into space and doesn't go into any more detail, and I don't push it, but I can't help thinking that this 'friend' of hers is actually her, which is why she doesn't want to expand on it further. He clearly hurt her, judging by her expression when she heard his name just now, so who can blame her. All she sees is history repeating itself and yet another girl going through what she went through.

But why should I care? I'm not going to be making the mistakes these girls have made. My head isn't as easily turned by a bit of flattery and the offer to make me his next model and muse. I just want a tutor I can learn something from; any unwanted advances coming my way will be instantly rejected. For some reason he fascinates me though; must be that sheer blatant way he has of going about, taking what he wants and discarding it when he's finished. Everyone loves a rogue, don't they? Well, I don't, that's for sure. Not any more; I'm all done with rogues.

We leave the café at around eight and stroll back through the well-lit streets towards the apartment. Florence is so atmospheric by night; I think I almost prefer it once darkness has fallen. It obscures the graffiti and the other imperfections that adorn the city in places where they really shouldn't be, on walls and archways, even on the huge monuments and churches, and the subtler light seems to enhance the historic feel of the place, take us back to when it was in its prime. We pass by the majestically up-lit Duomo and the smaller but by no means insignificant Baptistry, whose gilded doors glint with an almost artificial brilliance under the spotlights.

I pause to glance in the window of a tourist-type shop selling postcards and prints of the city's great artwork. Amongst Botticellis and Giottos of all sizes I spot a small Venus of Urbino towards the back of the display, almost obscured by the other pictures. But to me it is as though she has her own personal spotlight, seizing my attention and rooting me to the spot.

The sudden jolt of seeing her hits me with a lightning bolt of memories from one of the dreams I had in the museum. Someone is painting me; I am nearly naked, reclining on a huge sofa or lounger of some sort. The man in the dream is pacing the room, angry about something, and I am doing my best to calm him down. Eventually he gives in and comes to me, and I have an immense feeling of love, sensuous touch and of being held in a way which makes me feel more cherished than anything on earth. Who is this man, and for that matter who is the woman – the one that I 'become' in these dreams? Maybe I have just been looking at too many renaissance paintings, too many reclining nudes, and my subconscious brain keeps trying to transport me back to those times?

Sophia calls to me from the corner of the street, shaking me out of my daydreams. 'Where did you go to?' she asks. 'I've been calling you for ages, you seemed to go into some sort of trance, it was a bit weird.'

'Oh, it was nothing, I think I was just remembering something from one of those dreams,' I reply, trying to pass it off as unimportant. She really is going to think I'm a weirdo if I keep doing this, so I decide to keep to myself the memories of what came back to me, quickly changing the subject as I run to catch up with her and the others, who have just disappeared around the next corner. Looks like everyone is piling back to ours, and I am glad of that as the last thing I fancy is a night in on my own.

These dreams and the memories of them are starting to give me the creeps a bit and I need a good distraction.

I can't recall having had recurrent dreams before, although these two weren't exactly what you could call recurrent; they were more like separate instalments of some bigger story, I think, like there's some crazy soap opera playing itself out in my head. All I know is that the man and the woman – me – are basically the same in both, but I don't know why and I don't know who they are. I don't know what the 'me' in the dreams looks like, although I am quite convinced that she isn't Lydia Irvine, twenty-first century girl.

That's enough for now; I don't really want to have to expend any more thought power on it, it's wearing me out. What I need is a lively night in with lots of friends.

And that was exactly what I got. Stefano, Lanzo, Dante, and my newly acquired friends Alessandra and Francesca didn't actually leave until some time well after two o'clock. They were all great company, but they left so late, and as they have all been so nice to me, I would have felt rude sneaking off to my bed halfway through the evening. Spot the would-be English party-pooper.

Oh God, my head. I know I'm a student and therefore should be used to the whole stay-up-late, get-up-late scenario, but my body clock just doesn't work like that, and never has done. I was always one of the real girly swots who actually made it to nine o'clock lectures instead of languishing in bed for another two hours, and not because I'd set an alarm clock the size of Big Ben for some unearthly hour to wake me up, but just because I seem to be made that way. And come the evening, when the bell for last orders rang that was pretty much me done too. Nights later than that tend to send me into a downward spiral of tiredness and absent-mindedness.

Still, I haven't got to go in until my tutorial with Vincenzo at twelve today, so maybe I could try going back to bed and see if I can catch up on a couple of hours… Worth a try, but somehow I doubt I will be able to. I like to sleep at sensible, grown-up hours, when it's dark outside mainly, although given my recent propensity for dropping off in the museum, maybe all that is about to change, and it could be argued that I take my rest anywhere and everywhere. Perhaps I should avoid the gallery for a while; those dreams and my attempts at interpreting them are starting to give me the creeps.

Time to resort to headache pills, I think, as I pull myself out of bed and head to the kitchen in search of water.

'Ah, la bella Signorina Earreenay, come stai?' Vincenzo greets me as I enter his office for the first of my formal tutorials, shaking my hand fervently with both of his. Which I suppose is better than him coming at me with that double-cheek-kissing thing like everyone seems to do here. I say 'formal tutorial' as he'd texted me earlier to see if I'd rather meet him in a café or bar, instead of at the faculty building, to which I'd promptly replied that I'd rather come to him this time, as I wouldn't mind seeing some of the books on his shelf. So we find ourselves in the confines of his pretty palatial office, and my excuse for meeting him on neutral territory seems to have been accepted without too much fuss. I don't for one minute think he was hoping to ply me with alcohol and seduce

me into being his next model, but given all I've heard about him in such a short space of time, I think I would rather be here.

Our tutorials are supposed to be formal, anyway, so I don't feel too bad about shunning his plans for something a little more relaxed. I am under strict instruction from Newcastle to document all my tutorials and lectures as part of my coursework, which will then count as a very miniscule part of my pass mark for this year. I think it's just their way of feeling that the cost of me being out here for a year is justified, and also it gives them some proof that I am actually turning up to things and learning from it all. Fair enough, I suppose.

There's definitely something about being in the right environment to learn, and even if Vincenzo and I had the most in-depth conversation in a bar, somehow it just wouldn't feel quite as academic as spending our allotted hour here, amidst all his great tomes and academic material. Less temptation to make small-talk, and more focus on the work. I wonder how long it will be before he thrusts one of his own volumes in my face, for me to take away and digest?

But instead of foisting his books on me, towards the end of the tutorial, Vincenzo hands me a stiff, white envelope from a pile on the corner of his desk and says excitedly, 'Open it now.' By the look on his face I suspect it is an invitation to his exhibition, which the girls were talking about yesterday. He sits in silent anticipation, hands folded in his lap like a small child who has presented a lovingly homemade Christmas present to its mother and is waiting for her face to light up with delight. He is clearly feeling very pleased with himself at the prospect of a showing at one of the finer art institutions in the city, and rightly so, really.

'You're having an exhibition!' I exclaim, feigning surprise. Can't have him thinking I already knew about it, as that might imply that I'd been discussing him with someone else and I don't want to oil his ego too much.

'So, you will come?' he asks, clasping his hands together. I prolong his agony by pulling a pensive face and producing my phone from by bag, scrolling through the calendar to find the right dates, and then finally saying:

'Oh, yes, I can come. I seem to have a free day on the Thursday.' As if I wouldn't have gone, but I don't want him thinking that his exhibition is so important that I would clear the decks to be there, regardless of any other commitments I might have. Actually, I can't wait to see his work; the little bits of it I've seen around his office are very promising. He has a strong, individual style, quite unique really, and despite the female-students-as-model dramas I've heard about, I am expecting to be very impressed. I need to give the guy a chance.

7

The crowds line the streets ten deep. I stand at the open window and gaze down from my privileged position to the masses below, whose gentle chant of 'Il Papa, il Papa' grows stronger as the Papal procession nears the piazza, and his ardent followers glimpse for the first time his lavish procession. How fortunate we are to have a visit from our Holy Father; he honours us humble Bolognese so greatly with his presence.

Whilst Rosetta gladly gives us this leisure time to feast our eyes upon the great man and his entourage, she expects us to do our duty as normal this evening. There are many visitors to this city and, despite the religious fervour which brings them here, they are but men and have their needs, and those will not be inhibited by the presence of Il Papa. Our usual clientele will tonight have to compete with gentlemen from outside the city, and whilst the disbursement Rosetta demands of our visitors will deter those whose manners are less refined, we need to be prepared for a long, tiring night of hard work, with men whose desires and wants may be unfamiliar to us.

Finally the cavalcade comes into view, and I do believe in my eighteen years on this earth that I have never seen anything so beautiful and so richly opulent. A convocation of choirboys leads the way, their red cassocks and brilliant white surplices mirrored by the crimson, lighted candles they carry before them. The carriage seems to be made from gold alone, as though hewn in one piece from gilded rock, and is studded with vast coloured gems which glint in the mid-afternoon sunshine. The horses' hooves click rhythmically on the warm cobbled streets, and the air is filled with the sweet pungency of their newly-deposited dung.

The Papal guards, in their striped blue, red and yellow uniforms, adorn the sides of the procession like strutting peacocks, the plumes in their helmets wafting in the gentle summer breeze. They march in perfect unison, almost bright enough to detract from the Holy Father himself but then… yes… suddenly I see him! He is close enough for me to glimpse his kind, benevolent face. He waves serenely to the crowd, casting his gaze first to one side, then to the other, so that all men shall be equal in the receiving of his blessing.

I cannot believe it, that I should this day gaze upon the Holy Father! I make the sign of the cross on my chest and raise my eyes to the heavens for forgiveness for the sins which I am compelled to commit daily, according to my profession. 'Please find a place for me in your heart, My Lord,' I plead, as this mortal but most holy representative of Our Father on High passes by.

It is as I thought. A steady procession of men has visited our establishment from the moment that darkness fell. I myself have been fortunate to have had only two clients thus far, both of whom hail from outside of our city, and neither has wanted to tarry in their mission. Once they have achieved what they came here for, they have departed; clearly there are wives and families to return to in their lodgings here, and they cannot give good reason for a prolonged absence. I am pleased at this; Rosetta will be happy that I am fulfilling my duties to her, and am free again to meet the needs of further visitors as the evening progresses.

I descend to the drawing room to await the next client who might choose me for his pleasure. The atmosphere within is one of excited anticipation, not only for the pleasures of the flesh which are to come for these gentlemen, but from the exhilaration of the day itself. Rosetta pulls me to one side and leads me directly to a gentleman who is seated quietly in the corner, behind a screen and away from the hubbub of the rest of the salon. He gazes out of the window as if in reflection, and as he turns to us, I note that he is greater in years than many of his fellow clients in the room. One could not describe him as handsome in the true sense, but he is a fine looking man nonetheless. His face is long and thin, tapering towards his narrow jaw-line, which is graced with a small beard. His cheekbones are high and firm, his nose a little on the large side for his face. However it is his eyes that strike me and as he turns to greet me it is as though they are looking into my very soul and I am immediately lost.

This man fixes me with his stare, taking my hand and kissing it reverently as though he has just been introduced to a lady of the finest standing. I do not move, nor do I speak. Rosetta instructs us always to let the gentlemen take the lead and thus I am not permitted to utter a word until he has first addressed me. He keeps hold of the hand he has kissed, clasping his other hand over it, and leads me gently from the room and towards the stairs, all the while regarding my profile as though he cannot take his eyes from me.

We reach my chamber, and Clara furnishes us with the necessary comforts for the occasion: some small beer and wine, and a dish of sweetmeats which she places discreetly on the credenza, before exiting the room as silently as a ghost. Still he has not spoken to me; instead he removes his outer wear, placing it carefully on the cappellinaio and comes to stand in front of me, as I busy myself with pomander and rose water, awaiting his instruction. Despite the everyday commonness of this routine, I find myself nervous in his company, like a virgin bride in the sole presence of her husband for the very first time.

Finally he crosses the room and stops directly in front of me. With a huge sigh he cups my face gently in his hands, his fingertips below my earlobes as he turns my face slowly from one side to the other. His own expression as he does this is one of sheer transfixion. He seems to be studying each of my features in turn; I see the movement of his eyes from my lips to my brow, from my hairline to the point of my chin. Finally he speaks.

'Such perfect beauty,' he says, and his voice is barely more than a whisper. 'What is your name?'

'Maria,' I reply. I do not choose, as some of the other girls here do, to change my name and give myself a false title. Maria was the name my dear, late parents chose for me, and as an infant I was blessed in God's house under that name. Besides, there must be a thousand Maria's in this city; what is there to hide when my name can neither betray me nor locate me amongst my other namesakes? In any case, I have nothing to hide; no family to come after me, no one on this earth who would give a fig as to my whereabouts, other than those in this establishment who have become my family and friends.

'Why are you here, Maria?' he asks. I consider that I have never been asked this question before. The gentlemen who attend me rarely take an interest in my own person, beyond my physical attributes and the pleasure these can bring to them.

'My parents passed into Our Lord's care when I was thirteen, and Rosetta gave me a home,' is my simple reply. 'She has been very kind to me, I have been happy here.' I do not feel I need to justify my presence in this house beyond that. What other options are there for an orphan girl of lowly status, with neither father nor brother to protect her? I believe myself fortunate not to have fallen into more disreputable hands; my corpse could now be defiled and

rotting at the bottom of the River Po, were it not for Rosetta's kindness.

He leads me gently to sit on the side of the bed. I cannot recall a client ever wishing to embark on conversation before taking his pleasure, but if that is what he desires, then I must grant him his wish.

'What say you of the visit of Il Papa today?' he enquires. How strange this man is. What reason could he have for being so interested in my opinion?

'We are greatly honoured,' I reply. 'He passed by our window and he is indeed the most holy and reverend man.'

'I have had the considerable honour of being in his presence this afternoon,' he replies, but does not expand on this any further. Who can this man be? Some kind of dignitary? But of course I am not permitted to enquire this of him. If he wishes to remain anonymous to me then he has every right to do so.

As though suddenly remembering the reason for which has come, he asks, 'May I kiss you now?' He gently pulls me to my feet, and is it as though time itself has halted as he places his hands carefully at my waist, and pulls me slowly towards him. Our faces are merely an inch apart for what seems like an eternity, as he studies me intently again, and those eyes bore into my soul once more. I feel myself quiver with anticipation at this sensation which is so unfamiliar to me.

With the utmost tenderness he kisses me and it is as though a spear of desire cuts right through my body in an instant. There is a fire burning in me that I have never felt before; this man has ignited the passion I believed I did not possess. How can I be permitted to feel passion when daily I satisfy the needs of several men? There is no room in my head or my heart for these kinds of feelings; I acquired long ago the skill of isolating that part of my brain which might allow me to experience personal pleasure from my daily occupation. But it would seem today that I do after all have the capacity to feel passion, it was simply that the spark which might set it free had never been lighted until this very moment.

His lips move from mine to my neck, behind my ears, around my chin and over my décolletage. I feel as though my legs can no longer hold me upright, and swoon with an intense longing, stronger than any emotion I have ever felt, into his arms. Responding to this he gently lays me back onto the bed, but instead of tugging at my skirts and his own breeches and continuing on as most clients would, he pulls away from me, stands up and begins to pace the room.

'What is it sir? Do you not find me pleasing?' I dare to ask, conscious that my failure to provide him with a service will not sit well with Rosetta. This has never happened to me before.

'You should not be here,' he replies. 'This is not the place for you. Your beauty and serenity place you far, far beyond all this.' He waves his arm around the room to indicate my surroundings. 'What trick of fate that I should make your acquaintance in this manner! I declare I have never set eyes on such beauty, and the respect I have for you cannot allow me to defile your body in this way. You must be mine and mine alone. Please, dear maiden, please say it can be so.' He rambles on in such a way, his sentences short and frantic, meanwhile pacing the room, and although he says these things to me, he cannot seem to look directly at me, as though to do so would break his resolve and he would be compelled to ravage my body, regardless of the convictions of his mind.

I do not speak, so shocked am I, and my silence causes him to stop his pacing and come to me finally. He takes my hands in his and says: 'Tell me, dear maiden, that you feel it too?' And clenching both hands to his heart he continues, 'There is something in here that draws me to you. I have never felt this before; please tell me you feel it too?'

So that is what I saw in his deep, penetrating eyes, when I first set eyes on him downstairs. Have we both been struck with the bolt of lightening that is love? I know I felt something when he first looked at me, a connection, a feeling deep down inside of my being, as though I knew him, or had met him before in another life. But love? I do not know how love should feel! How could I? The only love I remember was that which I had for my parents, and that is many moons ago and oh, so very different from this.

'I do feel something for you sir, but I know not what it is. But this is my place is of work, I have nowhere else to go, no family to care for me. How could I possibly leave here?'

'I will come for you,' he says. 'Soon.' And the look on his face tells me that this is no idle promise. But what awaits me beyond these walls? I do not remember much about my childhood, the only time I have not spent here, and it now seems so distant. This place has been my home for so long that it will be strange, and somewhat frightening, to leave it. And to go to what? I do not know this man, and although I recognise that he feels something for me, as I do for him, what guarantee have I that he will actually keep to his promise and come back for me? He is but a stranger.

I am torn between the need to throw myself back into my life as it was before this moment, should he not return and my heart be broken for ever, and the desire to hold these moments dear, in the hope that he will be true to his word. Only time and fate will tell what Our Lord has in store for me.

He kisses me gently on the cheek, touches his finger to my lips and with one last glance at me, leaves the room. It is only as he closes the door behind him that I realise I do not even know his name.

8

'La Signorina Irvine, benvenuta!'

Finally getting to grips with my name, Vincenzo welcomes me flamboyantly to his exhibition, with kisses on both cheeks. I manage to accept his greeting swiftly and sweep by, clutching my catalogue to my chest and leaving him to encircle himself once more with an adoring posse of admirers and groupies, queuing up to butter his ego.

In this huge salon on the third floor of the gallery, I'm momentarily too bowled over to hang around and chat to him just yet. It's not the paintings themselves which have produced such a reaction in the first instance, although I'm sure they're brilliant and I will have a look in a minute – I don't want to appear too keen, do I? But the setting itself is stunning, with its hugely high ceilings and vast windows, and an amazing feeling of light and space, despite the age of the building. Lucky man, securing an exhibition slot here; what better place to showcase your work and hopefully earn a few commissions? There's something to aspire to; I can't see my own paintings ever being good enough to command an exhibition room like this, but there you go.

I spy Vincenzo over my shoulder, making an attempt to break away from the group but being besieged once more, and I start to focus on his work at last, looking up the first piece in the catalogue as I do so. *Look busy and engrossed,* I say to myself, *then perhaps he'll leave you to browse in peace.* Although why I don't want him hanging around me whilst I'm looking at his paintings, I'm really not quite sure.

Despite my initial misgivings about him, Vincenzo has proved to be worth his weight in gold over the past few weeks. For his assistance in settling me into the course, helping me find the most useful lectures to attend, and generally keeping me on an even keel he has been brilliant. But there's still this nagging feeling in the back of my head that there's something about him that I find really unsettling, even though he has done nothing to reinforce those notions in any way. He is incredibly good looking, there's no doubt about that, and it is a bit of a distraction, how could it not be? My tutors back home were several centuries older than him and you'd have to have pretty low standards in the self-worth stakes to think about getting involved, even if your overwhelming ambition was to sleep your way to a First. And I haven't felt in any way that Vincenzo's been trying to crack onto me, or flirt with me. But the bizarre thing about all that is that I'm actually quite disappointed that he hasn't tried, despite trying to convince myself that I'm relieved he isn't setting out to 'groom' me as his next model and muse. Over the past couple of weeks I've heard more stories about his carryings-on with students and it's made me even more convinced that I'm not going to become either a notch on his bed-post, or his next model, or both. No, that's not for me. Definitely not.

So why do I find myself feeling slightly down at heel about the fact that he hasn't tried? Surely it's not just some vanity thing, or me feeling that I might have lost my touch? If a sexy young tutor decides I'm not gorgeous enough to merit his attentions, whilst he clearly isn't slow to spread it about with the rest of the female population at the university, must there be something wrong with me or am I maybe not attractive enough? I'd like to think I wasn't quite that shallow. Let's just hope he's being honourable and just doing his job, for once without the need to resort to sex to reinforce the tutor/student relationship.

I hover in front of one of his paintings, called simply, 'Girl, Nude.' Well, she's certainly that. Very nude. There is an element of the voluptuous renaissance nude reclining girl about her, and whilst the painting isn't quite shocking in the way that some pornographic images can be, it's verging on the ever-so-slightly dodgy, with just a little bit too much of her visible. God, I don't want to end up there, on display in an art gallery for all and sundry to see. I don't recognise her, which is a relief, as I'd hate to have to sit next to her at a lecture, with what I'm seeing right now! I know it's all in the name of art, but somehow when it's dead artists and dead subjects it all seems a lot more bearable. Not when they're walking the streets of Florence this very day. Call me a prude, if you like, but that's just the way I am.

Talking of nudes, I've been back to the Uffizi – same room, same painting – and I did have another dream. I'd stayed away for a while – using the excuse of too many lectures plus a multitude of essays to submit. I thought I might 'cure' myself of the dreams by giving the gallery a wide berth. I'd imagined that once I got over the tiredness, maybe the dreams wouldn't come any more. But despite my best intentions, I had to go back just to see what would happen, as though some strange power was reeling me in like a helpless little tiddler on the end of a very long line. I had to go back at some time – I can't avoid the place for the entire rest of this year, after all. It's going to be a fairly integral part of my studies. So on the very first occasion I'd been back to room twenty-eight in a few weeks, there I was, snoring on the bench again within minutes.

I remember quite a lot of the dream, too. There was something to do with a Papal procession (not being a regular church-goer, or even that religious, it all felt a bit ecclesiastical to have come from my head!) and a young girl who I think works in a brothel. I was her again, whoever she is. I have an overall impression of her occupying quite a gentle and calm existence, despite the way she makes her living. She comes across as quite a serene and graceful sort of character.

I can recall the me/her character meeting a man for the first time, a man who I felt was to have a defining effect on my/her life in the future. Again it was that overwhelming notion of being loved and cherished like no other, to the same extent that I'd felt it in one of the dreams from before. What I'm supposed to make of it, I really don't know. I wish I had even an inkling as to why I keep getting these dreams, but I have to say, they are hooking me in and I'm intrigued to find out what happens next, a bit like waiting for the next instalment in the soap opera that is the life of this young woman, whoever she is.

Bizarrely everything feels out of sequence in the dreams; I don't really feel like they've come at me in any particular order. It's more like they're random snapshots of various moments in time, with no regard for chronology. I think what I need to do is start writing them down, try to make some sense of them. I need to start logging people and places that recur, try to put the events into some kind of sequential order, if that's at all possible. But that's easier said than done; at the moment I'm not even entirely sure if the male character is the same throughout. I haven't really seen, or at least remembered, enough of him from each dream. The sense of adoration is similar every time this man is present, so I would like to hope he is one and the same and that this is some kind of disjointed love story playing itself out in my head. But what's it doing in my head and who planted it there in the first place?

'Come stai, Lydia? Che pensi della mia mostra?' It's Vincenzo, desperate to know what I think of his great works. Although I'm standing in front of one of them, catalogue in hand and looking like an authentic art buff, I'm actually completely away with the fairies and thinking about my dreams. His words, over my shoulder and out of the blue, his breath warm and fragrant against my neck, startle me with a shiver down my spine and I'm immediately back in the twenty-first century with a bolt.

Vincenzo has managed to shake off the ensnaring net of what looked to me like paparazzi, cameras swinging around their necks as they jostled for the best shot, best quote. I calculate that they must be slightly higher up in the food chain than the normal 'paps', given their desire to photograph and interview an up-and-coming young artist, instead of chasing half-baked celebrities around in their murky little lives. If Vincenzo's work is attracting this much interest, the outside world must consider it worthy of attention.

'It's fantastic,' I reply to Vincenzo, and I'm not exaggerating in the name of flattery. It really is very good. So far I have spotted only a small handful of paintings that may or may not be studies of my student contemporaries, but I'm also relieved to see that the works are not entirely a depiction of the female form in all its lush beauty. Some are landscapes, some abstract works, a real mix, even some that I would term a bit 'mass-market'. He certainly is incredibly talented, and I find myself telling him just how fabulous I think it all is, with reference to some of my favourite pieces. Whilst he's thrilled that suddenly I seem to be so impressed despite my earlier indifference, he then appears to spy someone over his shoulder that he wants to avoid, and with a downward glance and his hand firmly on my elbow, steers me into a quieter corner of the gallery, where there is a huge abstract painting which takes up two thirds of the wall space. His next comment makes me wonder if it was just a ploy to get me alone:

'This is my favourite work,' he says. 'Join me for dinner tonight and I will tell you all about it, what inspired me, and what it actually is.' And this last bit he says with a very serious expression, looking deeply into my eyes as though I am honoured to have the painting's secrets revealed to me, and me alone.

'I… um… er, OK then,' I find myself saying, all too quickly and feeling like a bit of a dipsy female, despite my earlier resolutions and the fact that I had every intention of saying no to him. But dinner can't hurt, can it? I have no aspirations of it being any more than dinner, after all. We will go to some upmarket restaurant, sit in a well-lit corner, and I will make doubly sure he has no illusions as to what buying me dinner will ultimately buy him. In any case, I probably won't have to fight him off; he's shown zero interest in me in that way before, and I'm sure he will act very honourably tonight and things will continue in the same vein.

'Lydia, you're not!' Sophia exclaims as I fill her in on my plans for this evening. 'After everything you've said, you're meeting him for dinner! Well, just be careful.' She is sprawled on my bed, alternately leafing through a magazine and chatting to me, whilst I change for my big night out with Vincenzo.

'Stefano will be disappointed. He really likes you, you know. He's just been keeping his distance after, well, you-know-who.' I like the way she doesn't like to mention the 'Ed' word. 'He didn't think you'd want to rush into anything just yet.'

'Do you know, I'd never picked up on that,' I say, genuinely surprised, but beaming from ear to ear nonetheless. All the men in our little posse have been absolutely lovely to me since I arrived here, but in my naivety I hadn't picked up on any glimmer of interest from any one of them beyond that of friendship. I love them all dearly, they are such good mates, and I wouldn't really want to get into a relationship with any of them for fear of it changing the dynamics of the group and the possibility of losing a friend for good if it were all to go pear-shaped. Still, it's nice to know I haven't lost my touch entirely. There I was, in a wasteland of male attention, then like buses, suddenly two come along at once. But Vincenzo hasn't got a ticket to ride on my love-bus, oh no, this is just a working night out. We are going to talk art and all things intellectual, and he's going to explain his work to me, nothing else. We won't stray into any areas of conversation where meanings might be misconstrued. We'll stick to the straight and narrow, and all those other just-good-friend clichés. I relay this to Sophia and she gives me a strange little knowing smile.

Vincenzo had said he'd pick me up, as the restaurant is on the other side of town, too far to walk to in heels, south of the river on the Lungarno Guicciardini. Nove, it's called. Quite trendy, and also quite pricey, so Sophia tells me. Good job the treat is on Vincenzo, then. Not the sort of place my student allowance could stretch to.

But when the taxi arrives, it's empty. 'Signore Tizzaro awaits you at the restaurant, Signorina,' the taxi driver informs me, and we speed through a network of back alleys and one-way streets before crossing the Ponte alle Grazie, which affords me a fantastic view of the Ponte Vecchio, on the side of the Vassari corridor. Now that is something I really must do whilst I'm here. Apparently it helps to have friends in high places when it comes to securing tickets to one of Florence's best kept secrets. A hidden passageway connecting the Palazzo Vecchio to the Palazzo Pitti, via the Uffizi and a network of corridors across the city, all lined with works of art not generally seen by the public. It sounds magical – note to self to talk to Vincenzo about how to get my hands on a ticket. I'm sure he must be able to pull a few strings amongst his art-world contacts.

The Arno looks beautiful by night, strings of lights along the river bank backlighting the stunning architecture and that famous skyline of domes and towers. The streets are a-buzz with office workers and shoppers heading home after a busy day, and the evening throng just venturing forth for the night. The atmosphere is as electrifying as ever and despite myself I feel quite exhilarated and full of anticipation for the evening ahead.

As the taxi pulls up at the restaurant, Vincenzo steps out of the shadows and opens the car door for me. If I didn't know who he was, I might have mistaken him for one of the doormen, as he bows low with one arm towards me and the other behind his back, saying *'La Signorina Irvine, posso aiutarti?'* It's all quite comical really; no one has ever offered me their arm before, and I feel as though I've been transported back in time to the age of chivalry – although in this country I'm pleased to report that chivalry is still alive and kicking. I can't help but stifle a giggle though, as it all seems a bit out of place at this buzzing, vibrant restaurant, whose loud music and trendy clientele spill from the bar area onto the streets around us.

The waiter shows us to our table, and it isn't in a well-lit, public area of the restaurant, as I'd hoped. No, we are outside on the covered *terrazza*, complete with amazing river view, but more worryingly, very atmospheric lighting, so much so that it's almost completely dark. It seems to be packed with young, good-looking couples, who without exception seem to be holding hands across the table and gazing into each other's eyes. Oh no, I appear to have been sucked up from the streets of Florence and transported to the set of Nightmare on Valentine's Day, The Movie. Take me home!

OK girl, stay professional, this is a business dinner, I tell myself. No need to cave in because he's brought you to such a romantic place. Yes, he is gorgeous and looks even more so than normal tonight, but you are not here to be seduced so just don't let it happen.

Vincenzo settles me at the table and doesn't seem to notice that I'm more than a little uncomfortable, or at least if he does, he doesn't let it bother him. He probably likes the feeling of control that unnerving a woman brings. With a quick click of his fingers, champagne is promptly popped and the waiter is pouring it expertly into two flutes.

'To Anglo-Italian relations,' he toasts, with something of a self-satisfied grin, and I fear he isn't referring to some football match or other. His smugness implies that, for him, the outcome of the evening is a foregone conclusion, and I will be in his bed before the night is over. Well, no way.

'To the success of your exhibition,' I counter-reply, hoping to bring the conversation back to where I want it, on safer territory. 'Did you make many sales?' I ask, hoping that if I get him talking about himself and his work, his two favourite topics of conversation, then he will be off and running.

'I did pretty well actually, and got a couple of commissions out of it too, which is great,' he starts. Fantastic, crank him up and off he goes, as planned. I try to stop looking worried, un-tense my shoulders which are currently up around my ears, and start looking interested as he goes into detail about which paintings he has managed to secure sales for, and where the commissions are to be based.

'Bologna, that sounds brilliant,' I respond enthusiastically, and he launches off into detail on what this particular commission involves.

'Not till next summer, though,' he adds. 'I can't neglect my duties here, and the university would never give me time off. Besides which, I have too many students I care about too deeply to leave behind.' He gazes at me like a love-sick puppy, and I make sure my hands are firmly in my lap so he can't reach out and grab one of them across the table.

I try again to get him to tell me some more about Bologna, but now as I attempt to nudge the conversation in the direction of his own life, he turns the subject back to me. This isn't part of the plan at all. It's going to be hard work and we've only just had our starters. So at this juncture I decide to tell him about something I had planned to keep to myself, at least for now – my dreams.

Vincenzo sits with his chin on his upturned hands, raptly attentive, whilst I tell him about the dreams. In recounting them to a third party I find I remember more detail, and I start to see some sort of jumbled story emerging. But who is this girl, and why is she trying to get into my head to tell her story? I'm not into the supernatural in a big way, I don't believe in ghosts, and I've never really paid much attention to people who claim to have had a 'past life' and all that sort of mumbo-jumbo stuff. Or so I'd thought until this moment. But right here and right now, telling this girl's story for her, I feel that there should be some sort of explanation as to why she is 'haunting' me, which really is exactly what she is doing. Have I been 'chosen' to have these dreams? I don't see loads of other people becoming semi-narcoleptic the moment they set foot in that room, so why me?

Vincenzo gives off the impression that he has been listening seriously to my stories and my attempts to interpret them, but then suddenly he gazes around the room impatiently, as though he's bored, and clicks his fingers (I hate it when people do that in restaurants – it's so rude!) for the waiter to come over.

'More champagne for the Signorina!' he commands, as I protest that, no, thank you, I have had quite enough and am perfectly happy with my San Pellegrino sparkling water for the rest of the meal.

'Well, what a fantastic imagination you have, *cara*,' he exclaims, in something of a patronising tone of voice, once the waiter has been sent packing with his tail between his legs. 'Whoever would have imagined you could come up with all that just by looking at a painting? You should put your ideas onto canvas, you know, then maybe this 'girl' of yours will become more real to you. But honestly, all this talk about you being 'chosen', I mean… Come on!'

I hadn't expected him to be so dismissive and I am cut to the quick, feeling very silly. It's too late now, I have told him all about it, so whatever he thinks of me, it's too bad. With any luck it will dampen his ardour, which has to be the upside of it all.

Sophia and Leonora seemed to take me quite seriously when I told them about the dreams. Well, at least whatever they were really thinking, they hadn't let on, and they just showed genuine concern about me and my habit of falling asleep in strange places. Plus I could see in them a growing interest and intrigue in the female character who was starting to emerge as something of a persona in her own right. They weren't dismissive like Vincenzo, far from it. It hurts, not being taken seriously, and somehow you *expect* your friends to take you seriously. And yes, I know that to the casual onlooker the whole thing must be a bit weird, but after several weeks out here, Vincenzo knows me pretty well, and I have to say I'd hoped he'd be a bit more supportive.

Vincenzo slips away discreetly to settle the bill and do whatever the male equivalent of 'powdering one's nose' is – knowing him it's probably a bit of self-adulation in front of the full-length mirror, adjusting his crotch and making sure his bum looks pert enough in his tight black jeans. Whilst he's away I decide that I'm not going to let what he said bother me; he can doubt me if he wants to, I don't care. I know something strange is happening to me here, even if he just thinks I'm mad.

When we pull up outside my apartment there is one tiny, awkward moment when I think Vincenzo is going to lean over and kiss me, and then he quite obviously decides not to, instead leaning in towards me and giving me a kiss safely on each cheek before stroking my nose gently with his finger, like you'd do with a cute child. He thanks me for my charming company and hops out to open the taxi door for me. Pausing on the pavement, he looks at me hard and chuckles quietly to himself before climbing back into the cab with a *'Ci vediamo domani!'* See you tomorrow.

Yes, see the mad-woman tomorrow.

9

'Ciao Mamma! Ecco tua figlia!' I exclaim as my Mum picks up the phone on the other end of the line. She doesn't speak a word of Italian, bless her, but hopefully it won't take her too long to work out that it's me, her long lost daughter, calling at last.

'Sweetheart, how are you? We haven't heard from you for ages.' Oh no, here come the hidden, read-between-the lines reprimands. I've had a lifetime of interpreting Mum's real meaning when she says something, so I'm used to it. I have only called home twice since I've been here, but I've sent loads of texts & emails, so it's not as though I'd disappeared off the face of the earth completely.

'I'm good thanks,' I reply. 'Course is going well, I've made some great friends, and this place is amazing!' I have absolutely no intention whatsoever of telling her about the dreams – I'm not completely stupid. Mum would be over here before you could say 'Uffizi Gallery,' whisking me back to the safety of the UK, away from all this, where she could keep a close eye on me. She'd imagine I'd been possessed or something. I might not be into all that 'supernatural clap-trap', but Mum is, and she'd think the 'voices in my head' were a message from someone, and whilst she'd find it intriguing if it were a third party experiencing it, with her young and very precious baby daughter, it would be the scariest thing ever.

So I keep calm and carry on, filling them in on all the stuff about my friends, my social life, (well, the safe-to-tell-your-parents bits anyway) and my work.

'How's Evie?' I enquire of my big sister, who I haven't had any contact with for a couple of weeks.

'She's fine – desperate to come out and see you, of course. Well, between you and me, dear, I think she's working on James to treat her to a slap-up weekend in one of Florence's finer hotels, plus a bit of designer shopping, you know what Evie's like.'

Yes, I do. There are almost two decades between myself and my gorgeous big sis. I love her to bits and have worshipped her since I was tiny, as she was always the big grown-up one, an adult already whilst I was just the annoying little kid trying to pinch her make-up and drooling longingly over all her fancy clothes. She grew up and moved out whilst I was still small, but the bond between us is very strong.

Evie and I share a Mum but have different Dads. Evie's Dad disappeared off the planet when she was tiny, and Mum was left in her late teens with a baby to bring up by herself. She didn't meet my Dad till a decade later, when she'd learnt to stand on her own two feet and thought she'd never find another man, but he had a big enough heart to embrace Evie as his own and stepped straight into the role of father to her. After years of trying for a baby together, they were just about to give up on the notion when I appeared on the scene, later than intended but oh, so wanted. So Mum has always been incredibly protective of me; I'm her little baby so it's understandable, I suppose.

Apparently Evie's early years were hard, although she says she doesn't actually remember much about life before my Dad came along. Mum had no money in those days, so when she met Dad and they had more than a couple of pennies to rub together for the first time ever, she lavished material things on Evie to make up for the lack of them early on, especially when they assumed there weren't going to be any more babies. Not that Evie is spoilt or anything, she isn't, but she does like the high life, and luckily for her (or was it a matter of careful choice?) she found herself first a well-paid career and then a husband who could maintain the lifestyle to which she had become accustomed. James and Evie have a wonderful time, and I don't resent them that in the slightest, so if they do want to come out here and splash a bit of cash around then good for them – as long as they take this impoverished student out for a couple of nice meals and perhaps a little bit of shopping…

Much as I'd love to see Evie, I need to stall her on coming out for a while yet. I can't have a family member rocking up whilst I am still in the middle of this dream dilemma and don't know what's going on. It would just worry my parents too much. So I say to Mum: 'That would be brilliant, I'd love to see her, but tell her that Florence is at its best in the spring. Before the tourists come over in full force and before it gets too hot. And the sales are on then too.'

That last bit should swing it.

'That's sensible, dear, I'll pass the message on but then I'm sure you two will be in touch again soon, won't you?' Mum, as ever, trying to get her brood together. Evie and I can go for months without so much a text or two, which confounds Mum somewhat, but we always slip back into our fabulous sister-friendship whenever we get together, so the big silent gaps in between don't seem to matter too much. Mum doesn't get that, of course, and her constant scheming to bring her babies together more often is sometimes an annoyance, sometimes a source of amusement to Evie and me.

Signore Di Girolamo is giving a lecture on Titian this afternoon – at the Uffizi – which I have to get to. It's on the symbolism in Titian's work, and I can't wait. I just hope that if he pops a copy of the Venus of Urbino up on the white board, I don't go into a trance and start having the next instalment of my dream story. I'm pretty sure my dreams do take place in the Renaissance era; having studied so much of the work from that period there's such an intense feeling of the time and place being hundreds of years ago.

I have some time to kill before the lecture starts so I decide to spend it in my favourite room of the gallery. My phone alarm is set to beep at ten to three, just in case I end up having another little nap this afternoon…

Clara unpins my headdress and releases my hair from the tight braiding which encircles my face, letting it fall across my bare shoulders and down the length of my spine; its natural curl is enhanced by the hours it has spent tightly and intricately bound and it breaks forth from its tether as though possessing a life of its own. She pulls her fingers through it, then gently works at it with the mother-of-pearl comb as I lean back to enjoy the sensation. Her accomplished strokes relax me and as I gaze upon my reflection in the gilded looking glass before me, I see the tension of the day lift from my shoulders, and my humours at once become more serene.

I am beautiful, I know that, and I recognise the good fortune I have to be blessed with an attribute which, in giving me a means to earn a living as I did until so recently, has probably saved my life. God has blessed me with a face which men adore and which women aspire to, and for that I am grateful.

Once established here in my new home in Venice, I sent for my dear Clara to follow me and join the employ of my casa. *I confess I feared more than a little for her safety, when I left her behind in Bologna. After all, she had been party to my plan to escape with my love and had been instrumental in facilitating it for me. I could not abandon her to the wrath of* Rosetta*; whilst my patron had been so kind to me for all these years, I would not wish to imagine her capabilities, were she to decide that revenge for losing me was a necessity.*

My ablutions complete, I rise and walk towards the window which gives out onto the canal below. I gaze through the wide arch at the frenzy of activities taking place there: cargo barges loading and unloading their wares, the dark-skinned spice merchants in their strange, foreign dress, market traders loudly negotiating their business from the rows of gondolas, and on land errand-boys running here and there, fetching and carrying for their masters. Chickens, dogs and cats run freely, picking at scraps and scavenging from stalls, and maid-servants haggle for a fish here, a pot there, to take back to their kitchens. Their shouts carry from one bank to the opposite; they go about their daily business as though there were no canal dividing them and they were simply in the market square of any town.

There is noise here such as I never knew in Bologna – oh, and the smell! On a warm day the odour of rotting produce and fish and the stench of the water itself is so at odds with the beauty of the place that it is quite impossible to fathom how they can coexist. I adore my new home, this vast city which seems to rise as though by some divine force from the sea. As we approached in our vessel only two months earlier, I could not comprehend how man alone could have created such a miracle, such is its beauty. And I am so contented here with my love, Tito, and my constant companion and friend, Clara; I no longer need to earn a living for myself, and I have everything provided for my luxury and comfort. But that odour – I am sure I will never grow used to it, despite everything!

Tito enters the room and Clara vanishes as though she were never here, leaving the air barely disturbed by her fleeing presence. He takes me gently in his arms as though I were a precious casket of jewels, kisses me softly and stands back to admire me. He places his hands gently at the nape of my neck and lifts my hair high into the air, gazing in wonder as it tumbles around my shoulders in a flaxen cascade, catching the light in golden rivulets, and inhaling its sweet perfume.

'I must paint you now,' he says. 'This light today is so vivid and you, my darling, ever more beautiful. The Venetian climate seems to suit your countenance, my dear. Thanks be to God that we came here together.'

As he poses me for his work, I consider how his last statement is not entirely truthful. We cannot wholly be together, for he has a wife and family, already installed in Venice, with whom I am forced to share him. I knew nothing of their existence until I had already been plucked from Rosetta's care, although I consider that I would still have come here, had I known.

So it would appear that in some ways I am still plying my trade as I was in Bologna, the difference being that I now have just the one client, and my payment is my keep, my sumptuous surroundings, and of course his boundless love. He truly does love me, of that I have no doubt, but a man of his standing cannot be divorced from his wife and be seen to abandon his family. If a gentleman's heart is engaged outside of the marital home, it is far more decorous simply to keep a mistress in such circumstances. It must be so, until such time as the Fates decree that we can be together, wholly and utterly.

'Lift your head, my love,' he instructs, 'turn just a little towards the window.' As I position myself better to suit him, I cast my eye over the many works of his which already cover these walls. My surroundings are sumptuous and luxurious, but they also double as his studio; in this way we can be together for a greater part of the time. Even when I am not the subject of his paintings, (which for the moment is rare) then I can at least be near him whilst he works, attend to his needs and enjoy his attentions.

One thing that pains me deeply is that I cannot be seen with Tito in society here in Venice. He is a man of the world, and influential with powerful people in this city. His circle of acquaintance embraces ambassadors, politicians, writers, artists, such great and important people of the Venetian world, and on the grounds of common decency, I cannot be the one to accompany him. That being the case, he has promised to take me with him whenever he is required to travel, and during these times we shall live as man and wife. But I have little to be sorry for; I am happy here and I consider myself a very fortunate young woman indeed. To be loved is the most wondrous thing in the world, I know that now. That emotion which I had never before felt is now at the very core of my life, and I can no longer imagine a loveless existence.

'Carissima Maria,' *he calls softly, trying to wake me without startling me and destroying the pose in which he has set me, as I feel myself slipping into slumber. How hard it is for me to sit still for hour upon hour as he puts brush to canvas; I find myself day-dreaming and quite often even falling into a deep sleep. This time I am fortunate to be comfortably reclined, and it is all too easy for me to close my eyes for a few small moments and slip away…*

'Carissima Maria,' *he calls again, and this time he is laughing. 'My precious Maria cannot stay awake today. Have I tired you so?' As I open my eyes and focus once more on the room, he comes towards me and sits down beside me, stroking my face and teasing at the ends of my hair with his fingertips. 'How wonderful it is to have you here in Venice, by my side. After these weeks together, still I cannot believe my good fortune! We have all the time in the world to paint you, my dear. Let us not rush to do so this day if you are feeling indisposed.'*

Of that I am glad. On occasions I feel I am a distraction to him, and that I keep him from his work, but this time as I reach to pull him into my arms, it is with little heed for the furtherance of his work that he drops his tools onto the floor beside me and reclines into my embrace.

It's pretty rare for me to be able to look at the Venus painting without falling asleep, but there she is, projected on the whiteboard in front of me, in all her glory. And here I am, wide awake, looking at her, being able to study all the detail for once, and not feeling even remotely like I might have to take a bit of a nap. But then I have just had one – I woke up from it barely twenty minutes earlier. I didn't need my alarm in the end; I seemed to 'receive' today's little instalment by room twenty-eight satellite transmission into my brain, then when enough information had been imparted, I was wide awake again.

Two dreams in one day would really be something – I haven't yet put to the test if that's a possibility. My head is usually buzzing so much when I leave the gallery that I wouldn't dare go back for more. It's as though there is far too much information to process in one go and my awakened brain is way too busy trying to make sense of it all, so I've never revisited room twenty-eight on the same day to try for a second instalment.

The other fairly crucial factor in the whole scenario is that I have only ever fallen asleep in room twenty-eight; nowhere else in the gallery, nor anywhere else around Florence when I've seen images of the painting (and let's face it, Florence is inundated with shops selling prints and postcards). So I am hopeful for today that I will make it through the lecture in a state of wide-awake consciousness. How rude Signore Di Girolamo would think I was, if he were to spot me snoring during one of his lectures! This lecture theatre isn't exactly huge, and I would stand out like a sore thumb as the one who wasn't paying attention. I can't afford to have black marks like that against my name.

Signore Di Girolamo really is a brilliant man. He has that special quality, surprisingly rare in the teaching and lecturing professions, of being able to completely hook his audience in right from the start. And it's not simply because the topic itself it is really interesting in its own right, and for me, one in which I have a vested interest. He just is an incredibly captivating man, simple as that, and he delivers his lectures with all the charm and composure of a TV personality, in spite of his odd appearance, which places him at completely the opposite end of the glamour scale. The poor man definitely has a face for radio, but look past the shabby façade and you have a speaker of the finest calibre. I would happily challenge anyone, even a complete art-virgin, not to be engaged in this or any one of his lectures from the very first minute.

'…and the dog sleeping at the foot of her bed has of course been interpreted in several ways by many of my learned friends over the years,' Signore Di Girolamo continues. 'My own view on this small creature is quite firmly that he is a symbol of fidelity. Whilst the model for Venus is captured looking wantonly at whomever her audience may be, the dog slumbers on, indifferent to the commotion in the background, and sensible only to his mistress's relaxed pose on the day-bed.' To me, it looks like the dog isn't actually asleep, but curled up with his eyes half-open, like dogs do, ready to pounce should his mistress require him to. Why would she need to have a dog, even a small one, on guard at the foot of her bed? She doesn't exactly look like she's got anything to worry about. Maybe he's right and the dog is actually fast asleep. It's hard to tell. He's the expert after all and has probably seen the painting – and been able to look at it – a lot more than I have. Even with my being a frequent-flyer to room twenty-eight.

This woman strikes me as perfectly relaxed and at ease with her nudity, lying there oddly clutching that posy of roses as though she doesn't care that she might be crushing the blooms. Whoever the model was, she must have been quite happy to pose like that for hours on end. I'm not sure I'd fancy it, although as I consider the state of mind you'd have to be in to do it I have a real sense of déjà vu from my dreams. I've dreamt about being painted, after all, and somehow it didn't seem at all wrong in the dreams, or uncomfortable, or sleazy. I can't help paying a cursory thought to Vincenzo and the scores of student models that have traipsed through his studio and a shiver runs down my spine. I suppose it all depends on exactly who you're taking your clothes off for…

It's as though she's looking directly at you, this Venus, but the expression on her face is one of serene devotion – did she love the artist, or perhaps her lover was standing nearby whilst Titian painted her? Was that why she found it so easy to pose, with the man who loved her gazing on?

'…the hair tightly braided around the face as was the custom of the day but then tumbling down around her shoulders…' Signore Di Girolamo goes on. Hang on a minute, I've seen that hair somewhere before, and I don't just mean in other Renaissance paintings. Didn't 'my' maid carefully un-braid a style for me which was not dissimilar to this one? I have a recollection of being seated at an ornate dressing table of sorts, gazing into a gilded mirror, whilst she painstakingly disentangled a head dress and a tight plait from around my face, combing out my flaxen hair with an old-fashioned comb which seemed to catch the light – something smooth and opaque, mother-of-pearl maybe?

After the lecture is over, Eduardo and my new friends from the course make a bee-line for me again, begging me to join them for another coffee. They've all been so kind and I feel a bit guilty as I fib my way through an excuse about having to be somewhere, but I just want to get back to the apartment and get on with documenting these dreams. Now that there have been so many of them, I really do need to crack on, otherwise I'm going to lose the finer detail, a bit like you do during the course of a day, when you've had – and remembered – a really good dream the previous night.

It's now starting to stare me in the face that there's something momentously important about these dreams, even if I still have no idea what that is. Nor do I know why it should be me having them, but I know that if I don't get something down on paper soon, start cataloguing them, then they are going to beguile me for a long time yet. I really want to, and need to, make some sense of them all. I just hope that the missing bits come back to me as at the moment my memories are about as robust as a very holey patchwork quilt.

As I'm dashing through the side streets around the Duomo, my phone rings. It's Leonora. 'Can you make coffee?' she asks. She sounds a bit down in the dumps, and as I make an excuse for the second time in minutes I feel a bit guilty for side-lining my lovely friend. When she informs me that she's on the other side of town from me, then my resolve to get on with my own task strengthens and somehow my little white lies don't seem so bad. I couldn't really get over there in time anyway. Whatever it is she wants to talk to me about, I'm afraid it will have to wait until tonight, back at the apartment.

Maria. I'm pretty convinced now that in the dreams 'I'm' called Maria.

I've dragged my huge oak desk across the room so that it's in front of the window. The panes are open and the shutters thrown back to allow in maximum light and warmth. And aroma. Those climbing roses out there are still going for it like it's mid-summer in a stately home garden. Don't they know it's a fully-fledged autumn back in the UK, and by rights they should be sporting lovely ripe and round rosehips by now? I'm no gardener, and I confess to knowing absolutely nothing about plants, but there's just something about the smell of those roses that takes me right back to childhood summers, when Mum would help me pick the fragile flowers and press them in my little wooden flower press. I'd then forget about them for months, open the press one day, and out would tumble the beautifully fragmented wisps of paper-thin tissue that were once rose petals. I used to plaster them all over my exercise books for school, covered in sticky-back plastic, or make little collages with them. Funny how smells can take you straight back to a place and time, almost as though you never left it behind.

Maria. There it is again. Has the man in the dreams actually called me Maria, or is it just a feeling I have that Maria is my name? Either way, it seems right somehow. When I'm not being twenty-first century Lydia, I am Renaissance Maria. I'm quite sure now that my dreams are in the Renaissance period. Signore Di Girolamo's lecture this afternoon helped me to confirm that. Actually, I think it was the thing about the hair that finally validated it.

I grab the brand-new notebook that I've labelled simply 'Dreams' and write down 'Maria' with a big question mark next to it. Then I cross out the question mark. Yes, I am Maria, I'm pretty sure of that, if nothing else.

10

The librarian dumps another pile of books on my table and scuttles off in her very noiseless, very librarian-ish sort of way. How odd that even Italian librarians, with heaps more flair in the fashion stakes than their English counterparts – silk shirt and well-cut pencil skirt replacing twinset and tweed – still have that authoritarian air about them which whole-heartedly conveys the message: 'Make a noise, and I will ram the largest and most unwieldy volume down your throat and you will be barred from this institution for life.' I've yet to meet a librarian who doesn't instil the fear of death in me.

Anyway that aside, here I am, in the Biblioteca Nazionale Centrale di Firenze. Or in other words, the biggest, grandest library Italy has to offer. And big and grand it certainly is; awe-inspiring really, just like the rest of this city. It's another one of those buildings, two-a-penny in Florence, which don't actually need a *raison d'être*; they are historical and architecturally significant enough just to exist as a work of art in their own right. But the fact that this one is crammed with books and other articles of reference makes it all the more inspirational.

When I'd sat down yesterday to document my dreams and attempt to derive some significance from them, I expected to feel a sense of clarification about the whole thing, just by virtue of the fact that I was actually doing something. Instead the process has left me more baffled than ever. Where I'd thought there were images and memories that would pull everything together, vast gaps now yawn and I find I have even less of an idea where the dreams are supposed to be taking me, if indeed anywhere. Yet again I wonder if I have been reading too much into them. Is it just coincidence that I always fall asleep in front of that particular painting, or is someone, or something, a higher power of sorts, really trying to get a message to me, tell me a story? Despite my muddled brain, I still have this odd, underlying feeling that so much of this is 'beyond my control.'

As well as trying to catalogue the dreams, I've also taken Vincenzo's advice and attempted to sketch 'Maria' from memory. When we'd gone out for dinner that night he was far more sceptical than I'd expected about the whole thing, so for a 'non-believer' to come up with an idea like this was surprisingly pragmatic. No doubt he will be amazed (as I was initially) that the image I've produced actually bears a striking resemblance to the woman in the Venus of Urbino painting. Looking for some affirmation for this train of thought, I'd decided immediately to back-track across town to the University, sketch-book in hand, to pay him a visit.

'Well, you do spend hours in there, so is it any wonder your picture turns out like her?' he'd commented tartly, his attitude once again dismissive as he returned with a shrug to rearranging the books on his shelf, his back towards me, mind clearly made up.

'But that's what she looks like, or rather, how I look in these dreams,' I'd said to him. Why was I bothering? He is no more convinced that I'm not totally bonkers than he was on our night out together. 'Don't you see, I've even dreamt about having my hair done like her,' I'd continued.

I don't know why I so desperately want him to believe me; his opinion shouldn't really matter, but for some bizarre reason, it does. He'd turned to look at me with one of those half-pitying, half-mocking smiles of his, made to say something but then stopped mid-breath. Instead it was as though a light-bulb had come on in his head, and rather than uttering a small flippancy in an attempt to get rid of me, he'd climbed the library ladder propped against his vast bookshelf, reaching upwards to the top rack. What he pulled down and presented to me was a book about Titian – written by none other than our great Signore Di Girolamo.

'Take this,' he said. 'It'll get you started. And go to the library, too, there's a ton of stuff on Tiziano Vecellio in there, as you'd expect. I don't think you're mad, Lydia, I just think you need to be careful. You don't know what it is you're getting dragged into here – but try and keep a check on reality, won't you?' Finally a sign that he was taking me seriously, but more than that, some show of concern!

I'd left Vincenzo's office feeling confused. After giving off signals initially that he thought I was nuts, then coming over all supportive and worried about me, I didn't really know what to make of him. But once again I surprised myself just how much I wanted him to believe me. Finally I did feel I had him more on-side than off, and it shored me up a bit against the barrage of confusion that was – and still is – blasting around inside my head.

I'd gone directly over to the library as Vincenzo recommended, the walk along the north bank of the Arno soothing me a little and providing some time to ruminate on my situation. I pushed on through what was easily the most bustling part of Florence, that patch around the Ponte Vecchio which never seems to be free of tourists, shopping and taking photos, whatever the time of day. Onwards I walked, past the southern end of the Uffizi, gazing upwards at the exquisite renaissance and gothic architecture as an escape from the hubbub of the sightseers' enthusiastic meanderings around me.

Approaching the entrance to the library, there was none of the flurry of the rest of Florence and with a huge sigh of disappointment I spotted the reason why: *'Mercoledì – chiuso'*. Damn. I just wanted to get on with my research, now I knew that research was what I needed to do. Trust the Italians, closing a huge institution like this on a busy weekday, with no regard for the fact that students like me might be in desperate need of something important which just couldn't wait. I suppose we Brits have become an impatient race, getting too used to everything being open twenty-four-seven, always available on demand. Which isn't necessarily a good thing for the culture of a nation, I suppose. I just hoped all those library workers were off somewhere exciting, enjoying the sunshine, to justify the frustration I was suffering that they weren't here when I needed them. Oh well, it looked like I'd be back the following day then. At least I had Signore Di Girolamo's volume to be going on with.

As for today, my visit is a more fruitful one, and after three hours of library time my head is reeling. For an artist who is quite poorly documented compared to some of the other great masters of the Renaissance age, there is a veritable mountain of stuff about Titian in this place. The trouble is that the majority of books in here look to be mostly about his work and the purely historical facts about him, which is inevitable, I suppose. There's precious little surrounding his private life, other than the bare-bones details about when he got married, to whom, where he worked, which commissions he undertook, all that sort of stuff, and even then some of the facts are pretty sketchy.

Could the Tito in my dreams actually be Tiziano Vecellio? If Maria is the girl in the painting, then is he the artist, the man she is in love with? If that's the case – and there's a growing feeling inside me that it is – then these books aren't going to bring me any closer to the real man behind the paintbrush. But then history books don't do that, do they? Especially since many of these ones were written sixty or seventy years ago, a separate historical era in its own right. They are factual record books, and nothing more.

Thinking back to my own history lessons at school, there was a lot of parrot-fashion learning, memorising kings' and queens' names and dates, and I clearly remember reciting the dates of Henry VIII's wives and their fates as though my life depended on it. My Maria and Tito seem so far removed from that text-book memory of an era, when in fact is their very same era. At school, the 'realness' of history was never brought to life for me, but these two characters in my dreams are making it jump off the page and into 3D. I question what use I really have for these books, when I can get to know Maria and Titian more intimately from my dreams than from a dusty old tome, written by a long since deceased academic.

History books just don't tell you what sort of person someone was, what their likes and dislikes were, what idiosyncrasies they possessed. I can imagine having been heaps more engaged with Henry VIII if he'd been sold to me as an athletically handsome womaniser who, despite his great physical attributes, had some major insecurities about his own personal worth and just wanted to be loved. Instead he is portrayed as a war-mongering monster with a habit of despatching his wives in one form or another when he became bored with them.

So maybe I am wasting my time trawling through all these books, particularly as the main issue for me is that although I suspect dear old 'Tito' to be Titian, under the pet-name which Maria has given him, and therefore a valid historical figure, I know absolutely nothing about Maria, and is she a significant enough person to have an entry on record? Somehow I doubt it. I have no idea who she was, other than the snippets I have gleaned from my dreams. I don't even have a surname for her – maybe I will dream that later?

I know she was a prostitute, albeit a high-class one with a very selective clientele, in Bologna; I think I remember that city being mentioned in one of the dreams… But apart from that I know very little about her. Being a low-class citizen of her day, she was probably pretty invisible and there might not even be a record of her birth and death. One thing in all this is certain: the history books aren't going to reveal any links between a world-class painter and a lowly whore, are they? I'm sure I could keep delving into the life and times of Titian himself until I'm blue in the face, but in doing so I may never learn another single fact about Maria. How frustrating it all is. However, being a glass-half-full sort of person and therefore not inclined to give up at the first hurdle, if there's any chance of there being just one teensy weensy little snippet of something about her for me to discover, then I will stick at it. Hence the three fascinating but fairly fruitless hours I've spent here already.

A beep from my phone brings me out of Maria and Tito's world and back into my own. I see that glamorous-but-scary librarian scowling at me from across the room and smile my humble apology to her. I thought I'd switched it to silent, but never mind…

It's Leonora: 'Need to see you, come to Café Strozzi asap?' I feel a moment's guilt that I still haven't managed to catch up with Leonora after turning her down yesterday. She didn't come back in till late last night, and I was already catching up on my beauty sleep by then. This time I can't let my friend down so I send back by return of text-post: 'In library, can be there in 20mins. Lxx.'

I hope she's OK. Leonora is one of those eternally good-natured people for whom life's ups and downs don't generally seem to cause too many hurdles. She's had a pretty privileged upbringing from what I can gather, but it hasn't spoiled her, and she's just a gorgeous, kind and caring sort of girl. I feel bad about not being there for her yesterday and hope to goodness that there's nothing too major troubling her. In the few months I've been over here, she has been my rock, and I owe an awful lot to her. Let's just hope it's a case of man-trouble, or something simple that can be ironed out over a coffee and a pastry. She keeps her love-life pretty close to her chest, so I don't actually know if she's seeing anyone, seriously or casually, at the moment.

As I walk into the café, Sophia and Leonora are huddled in the depths of the smoky gloom – no chance of smoking being banned in public places over here, just imagine the outcry! – and its pungency hits me full in the face as I cross the room towards them. Leonora looks dreadful, her face pallid even through the olive glow of her complexion, her hair unbrushed, and she looks as though she hasn't slept in days. What have I been missing here? I've been so caught up in my own dramas that I've failed to pick up on the fact that one of my friends is in trouble.

'Lydia, so glad you're here,' Sophia starts breathlessly. 'Leonora's pregnant.' Whoa, there's nothing like coming straight out with it. I haven't yet sat down but feel the need to very quickly as Sophia delivers this pretty major bombshell, and I pull out the one remaining chair at their table and park my bottom quickly before my legs buckle. I don't know what to say. That was the last thing I was expecting and the ability to speak seems to have been knocked from me. As I look at Leonora properly, I realise that it was probably the last thing she expected too. Fear, worry, shame and horror all pass across her face in turn. I reach out towards her and pull her close, and she starts to sob gently into my shoulder.

'I can't believe I was so stupid,' she says. 'God knows, we're always telling each other to be careful, aren't we, and there you are, I go and do it myself. I can't believe this is happening to me. What am I going to do? What's my Dad going to say?' Her concerns all start tumbling out, one after another.

'Don't worry, we're here for you,' I say, realising how insipid and patronising that statement sounds, but all we can really do in times of trouble is resort to such platitudes.

Once Leonora has had a few moments to get over the initial shock of having to tell me, she expands on the details a bit more. Apparently the father is one of her tutors. What is it with these oversexed tutors in this place? Can't they just get on with the job they're meant to be doing instead of trying to get into their students' underwear the entire time? I am furious with a system that allows this sort of behaviour to happen as much as it does, but then how difficult it must be to enforce a policy of 'No student/teacher relationships' when all the parties involved are consenting adults.

Poor Leonora, I think, vowing that there is no way I am ever getting myself into that situation. Life's great plan for Leonora has just been rocked on its axis in one fell swoop.

11

Bad idea *numero uno*, this was. Here we all are, the 'gang' in its entirety, in one of Florence's loudest, trendiest, and bizarrely, gayest, nightclubs. The room is dark and noisy, the music – to give it its due – incredibly good, the drinks extortionately expensive, and the clientele, well, interesting. How we ended up here I really don't know, but apparently it's a variation on a theme cooked up by Dante, Lanzo and Stefano, with all the best intentions they could muster between them, called 'Getting Leonora Out of the Apartment and Cheering Her Up a Bit'. Hmmmm, jury's still out on that one, as Leonora is not currently up and dancing in some lurid, barely-there outfit, nor is she drinking herself into oblivion (the poor girl is pregnant, after all), nor does she appear to be having a particularly good time and partying hard.

At the moment she's hemmed in between what look like a couple of rejects from one of those once flamboyant, now middle-aged, eighties' pop groups who have all been making a comeback recently. These two young and very colourful individuals appear to be having a bit of a lovers tiff and Leonora, for some bizarre reason only known to her, is acting as mediator. Returning from a trip to the *bagno* I decide she needs rescuing and park myself on the other side of 'Blond-spiky-hair-lots-of-eyeliner'. Leonora quickly introduces him as Matteo, who, it turns out, is a fellow law student, although you wouldn't recognise him if you saw him in his 'day' clothes apparently. The other guy, 'Dark-asymmetrical-haircut-and-red-lips', real name Alberto, is a 'true' Florentine, a local, and works in some administrative role or other at the arts faculty. Well at least she knows them both; it's not as though a couple of complete – and slightly unconventional – strangers have foisted themselves upon her in the hope that she will sort out their tangled love lives.

There seems to be a bit of a truce in this 'Handbags at Dawn' scenario as soon as I arrive on the scene, with both parties settling back into their seats and calming down a little. I suppose it's one thing airing your dirty laundry in front of someone you know, but when a complete stranger – me – pulls up then it's easier to put it all into perspective and come to the conclusion that the argument wasn't worth having in the first place. Within minutes of my arrival, Alberto has wiggled his pert, leather-clad bottom round next to Matteo, arms have stopped being waved around windmill-style, and they sit together, legs crossed neatly and holding hands as marital bliss reigns once more.

I consider that maybe Leonora is having more fun than I'd first suspected, as she leans in to have a bit of a giggle and a gossip about this curiously surreal situation we find ourselves in. 'You lot couldn't have picked a better place to take my mind off things,' she laughs.

'What a distraction! Although I can't believe what some of these guys are wearing in here. I thought all that went out with the turn of the millennium. I'd never have recognised Matteo if he hadn't spotted me first.'

A week or so on from her life-altering announcement, Leonora looks much better. She's had time to digest the news, I suppose, work out what to do and get her head round everything. She's been amazingly strong; she has decided to keep the baby – she's in her third year after all so will have just about left the university by the time it's born – and the father has said he will stand by her. That's half-decent of him, I suppose, when it's his career on the line too… More than some would do. Although as far as I know, at the moment he is still in his lecturing position and barely an eyelid has been batted by the academic powers that be. Obviously that's just the way it happens around here.

'Fancy moving off somewhere a bit quieter soon?' Leonora suggests, much to my relief as it's nigh on impossible to have a conversation without some sort of semi-permanent damage to your vocal chords and a voice like a forty-a-day smoker for the rest of the weekend. However did I get to be so sensible and grown up?

'Fine by me,' I reply and set off to round up the others. None of them looks too engrossed in their current activity; they don't take much coercing to down what's left of their current tipple, or prise themselves from the dance floor, and within minutes we are heading off. As we move through the darkened streets in search of somewhere slightly more sedate to end our evening, Leonora is at the centre of our little group, as though to shield her vulnerability from the big, bad world outside.

'Thank you, you lot,' Leonora says, throwing an arm around the two friends closest in proximity – me and Lanzo. 'I really appreciate this, all of you trying to cheer me up.' We amble along in companionable silence for a few minutes before we spot a bar that is (a) still open at this unearthly time of the morning and (b) displaying no sign of fights, drunken youths or dodgy old men hanging around the doorway. That probably has something to do with the fact that it's the Savoy Hotel's very upmarket L'Incontro Bar on the Piazza della Repubblica, open for as long as it needs to be for any residents who care to carry on drinking and socialising to this hour. They seem happy enough to admit entrance to a group of sensible, respectable-looking students (is that really us?) who are willing to open their wallets wide enough to let the vast sums of money which are required in a drinking establishment such as this float skywards.

'We'll just stay for the one,' Stefano suggests sensibly, 'or we'll all be getting phone calls from the bank on Monday morning.'

The bar is atmospherically lit, with some amazing artwork on the walls and waiters who look far too fresh-faced to have worked the entire evening shift (and night and a substantial part of the morning). We find a corner to park ourselves in and one of these elegantly attired *baristas* is by our side almost immediately, proffering the cocktail menu. Think we'll give those a miss, just waters and beers and fruit juices all round on our budgets, thank you very much.

Across the bar from us an extremely attractive but slightly over-dressed young woman is seated alone, alternately twiddling her hair and checking her mobile phone. She can't be unaccompanied as there are two glasses in front of her, one a lavish-looking cocktail. Not sure I could stomach one of those at this time of night… I'm caught up in my contemplations when her companion reappears from the direction of the toilets. It's none other than Vincenzo. Well it would be, wouldn't it? And he's working on his next conquest, by the look of things, taking her to flash bars and plying her with expensive cocktails before luring her back to his den. In fact, given the time of night, I'm surprised they're not already in his den, in which case he's not quite the fast worker I though he was. I wonder if she's another student, perhaps his next model and muse-in-waiting? I can't help the outwardly imperceptible but strong jolt that runs up my spine when I realise it's him, and I see what he's up to – again. But I can't deduce if it's envy, relief that it's not me sitting there, or just plain curiosity running through my veins as I watch this mating ritual unfold before my eyes.

'…what do you think, Lydia?' I catch the tail end of Stefano's question and realise that I have been completely ignoring the conversation I should be following whilst fixating on Vincenzo and his latest love interest. Stefano follows my gaze and as he realises who I've been watching, I see a brief but dark cloud pass across his animated face. I'd not given much thought to what Sophia had said about him liking me as more than just a friend, but if it's true, then he has done very well to keep his feelings in check till now. Quite understandably he won't care too much for Vincenzo, or any other man I might happen to give the once-over to. But that's not really what I'm doing; it's purely interest, or should I say concern, that history doesn't repeat itself and another young student's heart gets broken. It's that oddly morbid fascination we all seem to have with people who constantly screw others' lives up.

As we leave the bar, I pull back towards the rear of the group and fall in alongside Stefano. I decide not to say anything about the Vincenzo thing; I don't want him to see that it bothered me, or that I'd noticed his reaction to it. There's no reason why I should need to justify anything; Vincenzo is my tutor and nothing more. I know Stefano has heard about his reputation and doesn't much care for him, but that doesn't have to matter.

The aforementioned flirty tutor had departed with his new conquest pretty soon after we'd spotted him – probably feeling as though his safe territory had been infiltrated – following a cursory pause by our table for a quick exchange of pleasantries, and introducing the girl as Stéphanie, who was clearly French and, up close, a lot younger than she'd first looked. Not my place to comment, of course…

As Stefano and I fall into easy conversation I can't help thinking what a lovely guy he is. And who could ask for more in the looks department? At home this man would be fighting off the girls; a lone tall, dark stranger in a sea of pasty-faced Brits. I for one would have been at the front of the queue. It just shows how spoilt for choice the ladies of this country are – lucky things – and I count myself amongst these favoured few now that I live here too. I should have been born Italian; after almost three months in Italy I can fully appreciate just how beautiful their men are, but not be rattled by it.

Not only is Stefano gorgeous, he's also really kind, and a very special friend. I have been so impressed by how all three of these close male friends of ours have handled Leonora's news, and just how supportive and non-judgemental they've been.

So at that moment I have a bit of an epiphany where he's concerned and bravely decide to go for it; if Stefano does like me and wants more from our friendship, then what exactly is holding me back? I don't have to marry the guy, after all. We could have some fun, he would be a distraction from the confusion of my dreams – and stop me thinking about Vincenzo. There, I said it. I don't think about Vincenzo a lot – honestly – but I do have to be true to myself and admit that there's something about the man that fascinates me, despite my better judgement and my sure and certain knowledge that I don't want to become another of the many notches on his bed-post. How fair it is to use one man to take your mind off another, I really don't know, but hey, it happens, and I think I could be missing out on something lovely with Stefano if I don't at least try. But I'd hate him to think I was using him, so I have to go into this whole-heartedly or not at all.

'So, do you fancy meeting up for a drink or a coffee or something sometime, you know, just the two of us?' I begin nervously.

Stefano's face lights up as though with a thousand neon lights and he looks as if he has just won the lottery; it dawns on me at that moment just *how* much he likes me. 'Or we could catch an exhibition or something, anything you like, really?' Shut up girl, stop gabbling at him and give the poor guy a chance to reply.

'I'd be honoured to,' is all he says.

'Shall I call you tomorrow?' I ask, to which he replies with a nod and a huge smile. We're now a few yards back from the rest of the group, and he looks across at me, then down at my hand, then cautiously takes it in his own, and squeezes.

'Is this OK?' he asks tentatively as he keeps hold of my hand, his fingers finding the gaps between mine and interlacing with them.

'It's very OK,' I reply, and I am surprised at the warm, comfortable feeling that shoots through my body, as well as the sudden pang of lust that springs from nowhere. So I do fancy him after all, I tell myself. There is a spark of chemistry there. I'm glad, post-Ed and the trauma surrounding that little episode in my life, that I'm not entirely immune to the charms of a beautiful Italian man.

'Come on you two, keep up!' yells Lanzo, spotting that we have fallen back quite significantly. Then: 'Hey, where did that come from?' he asks, pointing towards our joined hands, voice rising into something of a surprised squeak. Sophia gives him a huge, very unsubtle comedy nudge whilst she smiles at me over her shoulder, and he shuts up, giving us both a wide, approval-laden grin. Clearly Sophia isn't the only member of our group to have picked up that there was a spot of unrequited love going on.

I'm relieved when I wake up and find it really is the weekend, and I haven't accidentally stayed up this late on a week night – something I always regret. But I'm not so delighted to find that someone has stolen my entire night-time and my precious eight hours sleep. Oh yes, I remember now, that was my reckless alter ego, out on the town till the small hours. One quick glance in the mirror is enough to prove that the very same thief has also made off with my youthful glow, glossy straightened hair and taut, bag-free eyes. Oh well, at least not too much is expected of me today, thank goodness. I can sit around with a complexion like a bowl of congealed custard without scaring anyone or committing offences to personal grooming standards.

It was a great night out though, and on seeing the impact it has had on my looks I feel I need to quantify it as such to make the after-effects seem bearable. Leonora had a great time and said she felt much better, even at 5.45am when we got back to the apartment, so our goal had been achieved, at least. Plus I have secured myself a date with Stefano so I have that to look forward to sometime this week…

We'd picked up freshly baked pastries from a little *panetteria* tucked away in the backstreets near the Duomo and rushed back the rest of the way to devour them whilst they were still warm. Catching bakers opening up in the early morning has to be the perk of an almost-all-nighter, I reckon. After munching my way through a *pandoro* and best part of a *bombolone* I'd actually gone to bed feeling like a human being, albeit a very well-stuffed one, so it was odd that now, with a few hours' sleep under my belt, I felt like something recently dug up from a graveyard. Oh well, such is the life of a party animal…

Eyes still half-closed, I struggle to the kitchen in search of coffee, stopping in my tracks as I'm confronted by the remains of that bag of pastries, doing its calorie-laden best to stare me down into submission. No, I can't go there again. I will turn into a pastry at this rate. But a small peep inside the paper bag reveals, amongst other things, a solitary *pandoro*, it's festive, icing-sugar-coated peaks one of the few indications that it's actually nearly Christmas.

How differently they do Christmas here compared to at home, where the shops are madly festooned with all things seasonal from September, and we all feel like we might decapitate a few plastic Santas if we're subjected to the strains of 'Merry Christmas Everyone!' one more time. It's so much subtler here; the Italians do love their Christmas, there's no doubting that, but they don't let it take over their entire calendar, and it's so much less commercial than in the UK. Unlike us, they seem to have clung on to some vestige of remembrance of what Christmas is actually all about.

I'm sitting at the kitchen table, contemplating how I can reasonably avoid having to go home and make the obligatory parental visit for the festive season, *pandoro* filling my cheeks like a half-starved hamster and coffee in hand, when Leonora surfaces.

'Ciao Lydia, come stai?' she asks way too perkily, looking like she has just surfaced from twelve hours of pure, uninterrupted sleep. How does she manage to do that, and be pregnant too? Not that I'd wish it on her, but shouldn't she be throwing up for Italy in the mornings by now? Knowing nothing whatsoever about pregnancy and childbirth and all that goes with it, I can't profess to even have a clue what ought to be coming her way at this stage, but I can't help the momentary, and very uncharitable, twang of envy that fate can deliver her to the kitchen looking like this, when I look like Lady Gaga after a fight with a bulldozer.

One extremely large sugar- and caffeine-hit later, and I am feeling a little less unfriendly. Leonora helps me polish off another pastry, and the two of us sit there together companionably, alternating comfortable silences with the odd observation or snippet of gossip from the night before.

'So, you and Stefano,' she begins, inevitably, a huge smile lighting up her face. 'Finally! I'm so pleased for you.'

'Well, nothing has happened yet, but I'm going to call him today, see if we can meet up in the week or something,' I reply.

'That's great, you'll make a gorgeous couple, the pair of you,' she goes on. 'And thanks again for last night. I know I keep saying it but you are all so lovely. Where would I be without you. . .!'

'We all know you'd do just the same for us. Although maybe not the gay club!' I joke.

'It was funny thought, wasn't it?' she giggles. 'Couldn't believe Matteo and his friend, what are they like!'

When Sophia eventually emerges, around an hour later, I have knocked back enough coffee to keep an entire city awake for a week, and Leonora, as a sensible concession to her pregnancy, has moved onto the decaffeinated version. Stuffed to the eyebrows with carbs, we vow never to touch another pastry as long as we live. Well, at least for the next week anyway.

Sophia is full of ideas for the day – she's another one with far too much energy after a late night. How do these girls do it? Maybe the warm Mediterranean climate gives them a bit more get-up-and-go than we Brits, but whatever it is, I haven't managed to absorb it by osmosis, and I am simply planning a lazy day here, with Signore Di Girolamo's Titian book that Vincenzo lent me. I haven't yet had much of a chance to read it, so that is me sorted for today, plus I have some real work I need to catch up on too. Oh, and I will definitely give Stefano a call sooner rather than later; I don't want to leave the poor man hanging on for too long, after giving him so much hope last night.

I've managed to convince myself, without actually having to try too hard, that the whole me-and-Stefano thing no longer feels like just a plan to rid myself of any inappropriate thoughts I might have been having about Vincenzo. Lying in bed last night in those few lucid moments before slipping into an alcoholic stupor, I realised just how much I really do like Stefano, and I can't wait for our first date, just for its own sake, not with some ulterior motive bubbling away underneath.

I will wait until a little later, when I can string two coherent words together and give him a call…

12

Stefano holds tightly onto my hand, as though he can't quite believe his luck that we are there together, terrified that I might at any time make a run for it. We stroll from room to room in the Galleria dell'Accademia, our 'first date' going really well so far. It's funny how the dynamics of a friendship can morph so suddenly into something more substantial, and away from the rest of our group of friends we are completely different with one another; totally at ease as we are well past those early days of unfamiliarity, but also highly flirtatious and – a surprise to me – just a little bit naughty.

I have to say, I haven't really taken in much around the gallery as we've strolled from room to room, but then I have been here countless times before, so it's serving its purpose as a neutral place for a date, without me feeling I'm actually missing out on the whole Art Experience. We've chatted incessantly, about anything and everything, each of us keen to know more about the other's background, likes and dislikes, families, all the stuff that makes us tick. Things you just don't talk about when you're merely a couple of friends in a big group.

I love this place, although it's never held the same fascination as the Uffizi for me, for obvious reasons, I suppose. I didn't want to take Stefano there on our first date though, again for obvious reasons. I have decided I'm going to tell him all about the dreams when we go for lunch later; not because I'm giving him the chance to get out of this relationship quickly if he decides I'm a total fruit-cake, but because the dreams are beginning to crystallise more and more in my head and I feel I need someone else that I know well to share them with and to help me rationalise everything. I have no doubt he will be as understanding as I'm expecting him to be.

As we stand in front of David – the real Michelangelo one – he makes a joke about David's physique as compared to his own, but then the jokey atmosphere changes instantly as he pulls me to him and suddenly we are in the centre-point of one of those corny scenes when it feels as though the milling crowds around us have simply disappeared off the planet. Were we in a film, all those extras would fade into the background in soft focus whilst we were propelled to the foreground in sharp relief, camera zooming in from afar to capture 'the moment' between the hero and heroine, music rising to a predictable crescendo to coincide with the instant our lips first meet.

Corny films aside, our first kiss is a very sweet one indeed, full of the promise of passion to come, and I am surprised at how, when we do eventually come up for air, my knees are undeniably weak and my heart is pounding. So, Stefano can do that to me, that's encouraging! I'd been so worried, after Ed, that I just wouldn't be able to feel anything for another man and that my ex had totally killed off any desire I might have had. So, Ha to you, Ed, you haven't, there is life for this girl beyond you and your betrayal.

I'm not usually one for such grand displays of affection in public places, but I'm not embarrassed in the slightest when I see onlookers regarding us with that 'Get a room' expression on their faces. They're just jealous…

Our first taste of passion produces an immediate hunger for lunch and two angrily growling stomachs, so we head off in search of a little *trattoria* Stefano knows, tucked insignificantly into a quiet back lane off the busy shopping street Via dei Calzaiuoli. Despite being situated just behind of one of the big Florentine department stores, remarkably there are very few tourists in here, and the overall impression is of Italian being spoken, not English, German, Japanese and whatever else all mixed into one discordant cacophony.

We devour huge bowls of *spaghetti con le polpette*, slurping as the rich tomatoey sauce runs down our chins and laughing as we share a single strand, both sucking until our lips meet in the middle. We exchange a little kiss before biting through the perfect *al dente* pasta. As we are waiting for our desserts to arrive, I decide to tell Stefano about my dreams – with some trepidation as I remember only too well the reaction I received from Vincenzo when I imparted the same news to him across a dinner table.

There have been further dreams, some more significant than others, and I am more convinced than ever that Maria is trying to tell me something. She has become like an imaginary friend to me; always there and seldom far from my thoughts as I go about my twenty-first century life. I sometimes feel as though I live part in the now, and part in the then, as there is no doubt that during the dreams I am Maria and I become her wholeheartedly. Experiencing her in the first person makes the love between her and Tito something I can feel almost as a tangible object, even after I've woken up.

Most of the time the dreams don't contain anything of earth-shattering importance – at least as far as I know, but I suppose they are all important in some way for what they teach me. Generally they seem to be little snapshots of the comfortable Venetian life of a rich man's mistress and some only last a few brief moments: Maria being painted by Tito – frequently; circulating in society – when propriety allows; and idly chatting with her maid, who seems to be developing her own strong character in my head and is a massive mainstay to her mistress. No history book could ever give me such a clear insight into the life and mind of Renaissance Woman.

When I look through the textbooks at how life was then, what women wore, how they did their hair, what cosmetics and perfumes they used, I feel a real sense of familiarity, almost like flicking through a fashion magazine in the twenty-first century, getting ideas and choosing what would suit me. But my recently acquired insider knowledge allows me to quickly spot when a detail isn't quite right, when a historian has seized on something which is actually of very little importance but has skimmed over the more significant details. I reckon I could rewrite some of these books quite easily, removing the erroneous data and inserting my own first-hand knowledge of how it all was. Just imagine what use I could be as a real historian, although I'm more likely to be written off as a dreamer and a loony than be taken seriously by the likes of modern-day historians such as David Starkey and Martin Kemp, with their apparently expert knowledge of the sixteenth century.

'I've not read much of Signore Di Girolamo's book as yet,' I tell Stefano, 'but already he talks about this woman Titian brought to Venice. I'm wondering if that's her, if she's my Maria.' He has been listening intently, trying to take in all this confusing stuff about his new girlfriend (which I have to assume I now am!)

'Finally I've found a mention of her,' I continue. 'Or at least I hope it's her. She's just not in any of the major history books, you see. Why would one of those important historians write about some prostitute that Titian fell in love with? She's a nobody as far as they're concerned, but she has got a story to tell, you see, and it looks like she's chosen me to tell it for her. God knows why though? Why me and why now? And what am I supposed to do with all this information? I really don't know what she expects of me.'

Stefano sits there looking pretty confused. He takes hold of my hand and tells me simply that he'll support me in whatever I decide to do. He admits to being surprised to hear all this, but it's fine, he says, and part of what makes me an interesting person to know.

'So you're not going to dump me on the first date, then?' I ask nervously. 'It's not too late to get out now, you know, if you think I'm completely nuts.' I try to smile normally as though to convince him I am normal, hoping against hope that he isn't just going to walk away from me now.

'I don't think you're mad,' he replies. 'But I do think you have to be careful.' Uh-oh, another one advising me to tread carefully. But short of avoiding the Uffizi (which is unlikely as I need my regular fix of Maria and there is still so much I need to know) the dreams are going to keep coming and I will carry on finding out more and more about her until – hopefully – there is some kind of resolution to her story and her reasons for choosing me become clear.

But until such a time comes, I intend to keep 'visiting' her.

13

A week or so later I wake in a blind panic to the sound of someone screaming. It takes a few moments for my addled brain to click into gear and for me to realise that the sound is coming from within the apartment; I quickly dash from my room, fearful of what I might find. It sounds like someone being attacked, and there I am, in my skimpy pyjamas, with no form of defence available to me beyond my bare hands, but determined nonetheless to save whichever flatmate is in distress from whatever the threat might be. Burglar, rapist, axe murderer, you name it, I am ready to show them what I'm made of.

Fully on the defensive and prepared for the worst, I burst into Leonora's room, the source of the screaming. She is sitting up on the bed, Sophia cradling her, as she rocks to and fro, alternately keening in anguish and screaming with pain. I notice the blood on the sheets and think I know what's happening.

'Have you called for an ambulance?' I ask Sophia, sounding a lot calmer than I feel. Somehow she manages to hear me above Leonora's screams and shakes her head, motioning that I should go and do it, and be quick about it. As I pick up the phone and start to dial '999' I realise that I don't know what the emergency services number is over here. How foolish I feel, but then I never expected to be dialling it in the middle of the night whilst my gorgeous friend is having a miscarriage…

I have to presume it is a miscarriage – all that blood. I don't think I've ever seen so much. Leonora needs to be in hospital as quickly as possible, there isn't a moment to lose, so I rush back into her bedroom, discover from Sophia that I should be dialling 118, and get through to the operator within a couple of rings. I am so relieved that my Italian is good enough now for anyone to understand me, even with my panic-ridden voice squawking down the line. The calm, quietly-spoken lady on the other end of the phone reassures me that help will be with us in the shortest possible time. She instructs me to unlock the doors to the apartment block (I would never have thought of that in my current state) and then wait downstairs to show the *paramedici* where to come. She sounds so kind, I wish she was coming too. Why can't she come over and put her reassuring arm round us all, tell us Leonora is going to be OK and there is nothing to worry about…

I nip back into the bedroom to check on the girls and update them on progress. Leonora has stopped screaming now; she's lying on her side, facing away from me, knees pulled up and her arms wrapped around them, sobbing violently into her pillow. Sophia looks on helplessly, rubbing her back and making soothing noises; neither of us knows what to say or do as we wait in silence for the experts to arrive.

As Leonora is carried from the apartment, the strong Sophia finally crumbles and I cradle her in my arms as she sobs for her friend and her lost baby.

'I think one of us should go with her in the ambulance, don't you?' I ask, 'And one of us should probably call her parents too.'

'That's going to be tricky – I don't think she's told them about the baby yet. And now, well, now there isn't even any baby to tell them about, is there, just a load of blood. Oh, please God, don't let anything happen to her.' At this point she dissolves into floods of tears again. We follow the medics down the stairs and I propel her into the waiting ambulance before the doors close quickly and it zooms away.

I decide to wait until we know more about Leonora's condition before I call anyone, and hopefully she will be well enough soon to make the decision for herself about who she does or doesn't want to see. I just hope to goodness I'm making the right decision. God forbid that anything should happen to her in the meantime and we haven't even summoned her family to her bedside. I shudder and try to push the looming image of the grim reaper to the back of my mind, get dressed quickly and run to the nearest taxi rank. I need to get to the hospital as soon as I can and find out what's happening to my friend.

'I know I never really wanted a baby, not right now at least, but it was like, once it was there, it was a part of me, you know.' Leonora is sitting up in her hospital bed, surrounded by friends and flowers, and, thankfully, looking heaps better than she did in the early hours of this morning. She looks as white as a ghost, but then she did lose loads of blood, and very thin and drawn, almost unrecognisable as the Leonora we know and love. But at least she is still here, alive and well and with us, thankfully. I did wonder at one point last night if she really would make it.

'I did want it, you all know that, don't you?' she asks. It's as though, now the baby is gone, she needs to explain that she would have loved it and looked after it, even if it had come at a time in her life when she wasn't ready for it. 'It was a part of me…' she says again, as tears roll silently down her cheeks once more.

'We know,' I say, perching on the side of her bed and holding her hand, 'You were so brave about the whole thing.' For some reason, which I can't even begin to fully comprehend as I've never been in this situation, she feels guilty for losing the baby, almost as though the miscarriage was all her fault, which couldn't be further from the truth. But secretly, deep down inside and as something I would never voice, I can't help the feeling that this outcome is actually for the best; she doesn't need a baby at this time in her life, and now she will be free again to take up the fantastic career in Law which is so rightfully hers. She'll have plenty of time later in life to have babies with a man she loves, not with some casual fling who didn't really mean much to her and is unlikely to be around to be a real father to the child. No, it's definitely for the best, and I suspect that similar thoughts are spinning round in her head too and causing these feelings of guilt. Relief doing battle with guilt doing battle with common sense. Poor thing.

There is a knock at the door to Leonora's little private room and a tall, dark man sheepishly wanders in. From what Leonora has said, I suspect he is the father of the baby, her lecturer friend, Federico. He looks somewhat ill at ease to find so many of us crowded around Leonora's bed, and a glance flies between Sophia and me, both of us quick to judge the situation, as if to say, 'We need to get these boys out of here before there's trouble.'

'Come on, you lot, let's go and grab a coffee,' Sophia suggests, as Stefano, Lanzo and Dante all start doing that alpha male posturing thing, shoulders back, pulling themselves up to their full height and squaring up to Federico as though they'd like to take him outside and collectively put their fists in touch with his face. Poor bloke, I do feel for him a bit, but I can see that no such empathy is emanating from the boys; as far as they are concerned, he is simply the person who is responsible for putting their precious friend through all this and therefore should be dealt with accordingly. Sophia and I practically drag the three of them from the room by the scruffs of their necks and head for the furthest flung hospital café we can find; we need to give Federico a chance to talk to Leonora and then get himself well clear of the hospital before these three raging bulls are unleashed again.

Sophia and I sip our coffees with excruciating slowness, then feign interest in the pastries and snacks, and then order another coffee. All in all we manage to give Leonora a clear forty-five minutes to talk to her ex-lover. When the boys look like they are fit to burst with wrathful testosterone and the impatience to reassure themselves of their friend's safety, I send her a quick text just to check the coast is clear before we head back to her room.

After succeeding in convincing them that she is OK, that Federico has been reasonable and treated her fairly (all of which he has, the poor man isn't a monster and was also devastated at the loss of the baby, despite the circumstances in which it had been conceived) Sophia and I manage to persuade Stefano, Dante and Lanzo that crowding out Leonora's tiny room with this many visitors might just be a bit too much right now. She needs some serious rest after everything she's been through, and maybe a teensy bit of 'girl time', with Sophia and me sitting quietly beside her bed whilst she sleeps.

Reluctantly they say their goodbyes, but not before trying to inveigle out of Leonora which direction Federico is heading in, so they can go after him and give him a bit of a 'talking to'. Seeing straight through the transparency of their plan, Leonora isn't forthcoming with that information and, whilst thanking the boys for their concern, she makes it quite clear that she doesn't want to hear of them causing any trouble:

'Thank you guys, I know you're concerned, but really, it was as much my doing as his, wasn't it? It takes two and all that! Having a go at him now might make you lot feel a bit better, but please don't. I really don't want you to, much as I appreciate you all being so protective of me,' she says. 'Come in and see me again later, will you? And behave, promise me that!'

So finally this feral trio shuffles from the room, metaphorical tails between their legs (I know they will heed Leonora's advice) and Sophia and I settle into the comfy armchairs on either side of the bed. Leonora definitely needs the rest, and fortunately for us the chic little dark-haired nurse who'd just come on shift had popped her head around the door a moment ago and reiterated just that, helping us immensely in our mission to eject the boys. Given that Sophia and I have been up half the night too, we're also quite glad of the calm that now descends and I think there's a pretty strong chance that we might grab a few zzzz's ourselves whilst we're sitting here.

'Those are lovely flowers, did Federico bring you those?' I ask Leonora, pointing to the unusual dusky pink roses in a vase on her bedside cabinet. 'They smell gorgeous.' I'm no rose expert, but I can't help thinking I've seen that variety somewhere before. The petals are so delicate and paper thin they look almost as though they've been dried.

Leonora drifts quickly off to sleep, leaving the two of us reading our magazines in companionable silence…

'Maria, turn your head to the side just a little, my love. That's it, yes, perfect.'

Tito is sketching me – again. I simply adore being the subject of his work, and I love that he wants to commit my image to canvas so frequently but sometimes I feel I would like to be a little more active during the time we spend together, instead of constantly pinned into one, not always terribly comfortable, position; it makes expression of any sort so difficult. How refreshing it would be if we could take a turn together outside and promenade around this beautiful city. I've seen it a-plenty with Clara at my side, but not with my love… But I know that such a thing is a rare event indeed whilst we dwell so close to his family home.

This morning he brought a beautiful little gift with him when he arrived at my casa*: a small dog, so pretty and delicate, with her silky gold and silver coat, light brown ears and dusky, dark patch over one eye. As soon as Tito handed her to me, her tiny pink tongue began covering my face in her warm and wet kisses. How I love her so dearly already!*

'To be always by your side when I cannot, my dear,' Tito had announced. 'If only I could sit in your lap and be petted quite as much as she can! What shall you call her?'

'I think 'Bella',' I reply, 'as that is what she is, a great beauty.'

'Her beauty is nothing compared to yours, although she is indeed a very sweet-natured creature. I do hope you will enjoy her and keep her with you always,' he says. And then he betrayed the real reason for such a generous gift: 'I have to go away for a few days, my love. She will keep you company in my absence.'

So there it is, the dog is not simply a token of his love for me, but a sweetener to lessen the pain of our separation. 'But you promised me I would always accompany you on your travels,' I protest, knowing that being away from Venice would be our one chance to live properly together, far from the prying eyes of this city, as though we were man and wife.

'Not on this occasion, my love, and for that I am deeply sorry. It will pain me so to be apart from you, but it shall only be for a week, two at most. I am not to travel alone this time, you see, and the company I am to keep is of high ranking within the city and also well acquainted with my wife and eldest son. Such impropriety would only serve to cause trouble for the both of us. Next time you shall come too, I promise you that.'

I cannot hide my disappointment at his news and bury my crestfallen expression in the soft fur of my new pet. But beautiful as she is, she can be no substitute for the love of my man. Two weeks! How am I to manage without him for so long? I do fear I shall go mad with unrequited love and the sheer anguish of not being near him.

Thinking again of our separation makes me restless and I find can no longer remain in repose. I rise from my daybed and begin to pace the room, much to his frustration as he has not yet completed his sketch. I pass from object to object, rearranging, tidying, fiddling, moving trinkets and small possessions to a more favourable position, in an attempt to calm my disquiet. Only it does not calm me, it simply serves to make it more evident just how much his news grieves me. Passing by a vast bowl of roses, I pluck one roughly from the receptacle and begin tearing the poor undeserving thing apart, petal by petal, casting them to the floor.

Oh, wretched man, how he vexes me and yet how I love him so…

So that's it. That's where I've seen the roses before, in the dreams.

I don't nod straight off in the chair beside Leonora's bed as I'd expected, but instead sit there, lazily flicking through my magazine and feeling quite grateful for a few moments of peace and quiet. Those roses that Federico brought are baffling me with their familiarity, and I desperately start to trawl back through the dreams, wondering if they're haunting me because that's where I've seen them before, in my subconscious state.

I turn the page in the magazine, something along the lines of Italy's answer to 'Beautiful Homes' – the kind of reading matter my mum normally likes, not me – and am faced with the gardening section, which ordinarily I would flick straight over. But my eye is caught by an article on, yes, you've guessed it, roses. And back it all comes. I recall the roses that Maria had decimated when

Tito announced he was going away, and if not identical to the ones on the page in front of me, then they are pretty damn similar. It's my first and only link between the two centuries, but how amazing that a particular species can remain largely unchanged for nearly five hundred years – today's roses triggering the memory of yesteryear's.

I sit there, staring into space as if under hypnosis, whilst I try to work back through the dream in its entirety. Fortunately at this stage Leonora has gone to sleep, and is quietly snoring away, curled on one side, her face pale and ghostly. One glance across at Sophia confirms that she too is no longer in the waking world. She looks almost as washed out as Leonora; poor girl, the two of them had been close for ages before I came on the scene, friends since school apparently. She has had to see her friend go through such a lot in the past twenty-four hours, more than anyone should have to.

I remove my 'Dreams' notebook from my bag and add a quick update before I forget any of the detail, copying down, too, the name of the rose species from the magazine. Another little piece in the jigsaw, although what the final picture is going to be, is still anyone's guess.

14

'Yes, Mum, they do have turkeys over here but I think we will be having lamb actually… Yes, lamb. Yes I know it's not the same, but I'm in Italy, Mum, not Sussex, I have to go with the flow, and anyway it will be nice for a change… No, not sure about crackers… Jokes in the crackers? Well, yes, if they do have them then they'll be in Italian, of course, won't they… Yes, Mum, my Italian's really good now, it won't spoil my enjoyment of the day I promise you.'

Finally, with a week to go until the big day, I am making the dreaded call home to my parents to reinforce my reasons for not coming home for Christmas. I'd taken the coward's way out and emailed them first; I thought I could break the news gently and in a more ordered fashion if I wrote it down, instead of it coming out in a garbled mess over the phone and Mum getting all upset. This way she has had time to digest the news; she'll have done the tears, then the anger, then the disappointment, all with me a thousand miles away. Now she's made it past that stage and is just worried that I won't be getting a 'Proper Christmas' as 'They all do things so differently over there.' Bless her, I appreciate her concern and I do realise that it will be hard for both my parents, as I've never missed an Irvine Family Christmas before. It will be hard for me too and I'm sure I will feel more than a little homesick on the day, despite my resolve to stay here.

'Proper Christmas' or not, I'd been looking for a reason not to go home for the festive season, and Leonora's miscarriage has given me the perfect excuse. Not that I'd want to profit from her misfortune or anything – I really genuinely don't want to leave her in her still fairly fragile emotional state. But this is the only chance I will have to experience a 'Proper Italian Christmas'. I'll be back in the UK again before I know it and won't get another opportunity like this. And, of course, there are the dreams. I've always been a bit worried that they might desert me if I don't keep up my visits to the Uffizi. I still have so much to discover about Maria. I couldn't possibly leave her behind, with her story only partially told; Mum would spot instantly that I was distracted by something, and I don't really need her curiosity right now. Besides which, I'm not in any danger from what's going on, I still have my head screwed on pretty firmly and I'm able to put it into perspective perfectly well. But I do need to keep following it through, on my own – with the support of my friends, of course.

'Wow, Sophia, that looks amazing.' We all gasp in unison as she places the huge, steaming dish containing the roast lamb joint, encircled with tiny, roasted baby vegetables, on the table. Heavenly aromas of rosemary, garlic, thyme and lemon juice fill the apartment. A huge, steaming bowl of *lenticchie*, lentils flavoured with herbs, follows this, enough to feed about four times the number gathered here. Stefano picks up the knife and deftly begins to carve the lamb, carefully laying the meltingly tender slices onto warmed plates.

The six of us are here together for Christmas day, and that's just perfect. We'd all eaten out last night, along with a few other friends who weren't decamping to the family abode for the festive season, a relaxed – but incredibly long – Christmas Eve supper at a fantastic fish restaurant south of the river, and I don't think I've ever experienced a meal quite like it. I know the Italians are passionate about their food, and despite the fact that we kicked off early, around seven, with the antipasti, several more courses had to be devoured before the fish course deigned to put in an appearance. Even then we were still going at around two in the morning. Finally there came a point in time at which we all decided it was physically impossible to eat, or drink, another thing – at least until we had to start all over again the next day. As we wended our way home across town, more than slightly drunkenly, we all gave a passing thought to whether we would get any presents like the good boys and girls of Florence, already tucked up in their beds, or would *Il Babbo Natale* spot us still out and about at this late hour as he shot overhead in his sleigh, and keep on flying?

Leonora is slightly subdued today. Not surprising really, as it has only been just over a week since the miscarriage. She decided not to tell her parents in the end; as she is now fine and there is no baby to make an issue of, she thought it was best to leave it unsaid.

Apparently her parents are deeply religious, and she feels it would simply be too much for them to handle, that they would take the news of their precious eldest daughter falling off the straight and narrow really badly. Ordinarily she would have gone home to them for Christmas, and so like me, she has had to make an excuse not to be there for the first time. It must be hard for her in so many respects; she seems to be having a reasonably good day and is putting a brave face on things, but it's very soon after the event and she is still going through the healing process, both physically and mentally. At least she now has the Christmas holidays to relax before her course starts back in January and it's full steam ahead for her final few months before exams.

'Lanzo, your turn,' shouts Stefano. After stuffing our faces until further movement was barely an option, we repaired to the comfy chairs and sofas to nurse our swollen stomachs, which sit atop our bodies like vast, obscene declarations of overindulgence. We abandoned the decimated dining table without a care, volunteering the boys to tackle it later, which we all know won't happen without some serious henpecking on the part of the female contingent.

Currently, and surprisingly energetically with stomachs like these, we are in the middle of a game which bears a strong resemblance to charades, only it's people we have to portray, rather than the usual film, book, song or TV show. So far Dante has plucked Marilyn Monroe out of the hat, who he manages to carry off with little more than a pout and a very sexy wiggle. Amazingly we all guess it straight away, which, we can tell, doesn't make him feel overly manly, but he takes it on the chin, bless him, hoping for a male character on his next turn and only sulking for a few moments before returning to his usual gregarious self.

Leonora has just picked Sylvio Berlusconi, whom she portrays absolutely brilliantly, by jumping excitedly on Sophia and me in turn, pretending to make mad, passionate love to us, and then proceeding to chase us round the room, rubbing her hands together in full dirty-old-man mode. This has us all roaring with laughter, and as Leonora collapses back onto the sofa afterwards in a fit of giggles, I can't help thinking just how much better she is starting to look this afternoon. Unlike the rest of us, she hasn't touched a drop of alcohol all day as she is still on some serious antibiotics, but it's heart-warming to see my friend with a smile on her face again, and this time I know full well it isn't just for show.

There is no doubting that I do miss my family and our normal Christmas routine to some extent, and I have a bit of an emotional, wobbly moment when I call home to wish them all 'Merry Christmas' and can hear the festivities going ahead in the background, same as ever, without me. But what I don't miss is Mum's strict adherence to what she calls 'Christmas Day Etiquette'; she always insists we sit down to dinner at two, watch the Queen at three and open presents at four. Here it's entirely different, so much more relaxed, and we have made up our own day as we've gone along, ripping open our presents before breakfast, and downing several glasses of *spumante* before anything solid even contemplated passing our lips. I am enjoying the freedom of today so much, and with the alcohol making me more than a little emotional, I realise how lucky I am to have fallen in with such a fabulous group of friends. If I hadn't met them, I'm sure I wouldn't have pulled myself out of my post-Ed torpor and settled into the Italian way of life quite so well. I owe them all such a lot.

And then there is the added bonus of having Stefano here with me. I've never before spent an actual Christmas day with a boyfriend, and so waking up here with him beside me, warm and sleepy and still just a little bit woozy from the night before, was perfect. He was still asleep when I threw open my shutters to let the Christmas sunshine flood in. I stood there for a few moments, inhaling the fragrances of the garden and feeling very pleased with myself for managing to be here, enjoying the final moments of solitude that a still-sleeping household offers. Eventually I coaxed him awake and we took our time opening our gifts to each other, snugly tucked under the duvet, flutes of fizz on the bedside cabinet. Stefano bought me a gorgeous little silver heart necklace, just perfect, and I gave him a friendship bracelet he'd seen in a shop window a few weeks earlier and admired. We'd cuddled together under the duvet until we heard the others stirring, (Dante and Lanzo had stayed over too, but it was sofas for them) then it had been a mad frenzy of present opening and further popping of corks. I don't think the excitement levels have diminished all day; I am being carried along on a whirlwind of euphoria and I don't want to get off.

Boxing Day, or Santo Stefano, finds the Uffizi open to visitors once more, and I decide I need some fresh air, a brisk walk across town and a visit to my favourite sixteenth century friend. I'm sure she will be there waiting for me, desperate to impart some more of her story after a bit of a prolonged break due to both the festive period and all the drama just before that with Leonora.

I am bursting with excited anticipation as I wonder what she has in store for me today. Most of the time I find the dreams don't contain anything earthshattering, although each is amazing in its own right purely for its added insight into what life was like in the sixteenth century, and more importantly, what the implications of that life were for Maria and Titian. I'd left a sleepy Stefano at the apartment with him warning me to 'Go carefully', and I know his concern is more for my mental state in the gallery than any risk I might face from being mown down by a mad Italian driver or passing tour party bus.

As I stroll across the Piazza della Signoria, it's almost as though the all too brief Christmas shutdown never happened. Hordes of tourists, who must have found somewhere to hibernate yesterday to celebrate their Christmases, eat their lunch and open presents, are today back on the streets in full force, as though there is no time to waste, queuing for the Palazzo Vecchio again, crowding round the statues with their cameras and, despite the slight nip in the air, drinking and dining al fresco at the cafés and bars which, although the majority of the shops remain closed for business, are mostly open as usual. The only exception to the rule, in this Piazza at least, seems to be Rivoire, which remains resolutely closed, its shutters uninvitingly bolted down and chairs and tables on the terrace stacked up under awnings, a lone declaration of independence in a sea of mass market conformity. And who can blame them; at least their staff will be enjoying another day of festivities, at home with *la famiglia* instead of hoofing it straight back to work the minute the Christmas spirit has been drunk dry.

I reach the steps of the Uffizi and pause for a few moments to take stock before heading in. Does the sun never stop shining here? It's a chilly day and I'm wrapped up in lots of layers, including my thermals, but the sky is just as blue as when I first arrived back in September, and barely a day has gone by which hasn't been just so. My sunglasses have been a permanent appendage on my head, through the autumn and on into winter. The rain which beleaguers us at home seems so fleeting here; it comes and goes, serving its purpose, refilling reservoirs and watering plants, and the transitory grey skies which follow don't linger like they do in the UK. It's uplifting for the soul to see so much sunshine, and glancing upwards at the azure marvel above me I take a deep breath of the clear, frosty air before I skip up the steps and into the building which I have come to know so well.

Maria is waiting for me in her usual place – well, where else would she be? – but the surprise is that I arrive to find room twenty-eight uncharacteristically quiet. Despite the milling crowds outside, not many have yet made it this far.

There seems to be just one guard for this set of rooms; she is sharing herself between the Titian room and Parmigianino next door, so hopefully she will park herself down on the comfier of the two guards' chairs in that room and leave me to it in here. I've seen her before and she knows I'm no art vandal. She nods in acknowledgement as I take up my place on the usual bench. I'm genuinely surprised that no one has ever bothered me on the multiple occasions when I've snoozed away in the gallery; no official has ever questioned what I do here so frequently and why I always fall asleep. So I have to presume it's not uncommon for people to pay their fee just to come in and seek respite from either cold or heat, spending a few quiet moments catching up with a bit of rest in a tranquil spot. I suppose that when the crowds are milling around I'm less conspicuous, although that might be different today when there are fewer visitors passing through…

15

'Carissima Maria, sono ritornato!' Tito whispers softly in my ear. It can only be another dream; since he went from me I find I dream of him nightly. It is of such comfort and for those few brief moments I can imagine he is by my side again. Only when day breaks does my heart break too as the reality dawns once more that he is still far from me…

I turn drowsily towards the voice to find that I am not dreaming: my lover has indeed returned to me! He is here in the flesh, already divested of his clothing, and in the bed beside me. Despite my drowsiness I am surprised and delighted to have him with me once again, where he belongs.

'Oh, I have missed you so,' I say, waking a little more and shuffling across the wide expanse of starched linen to be closer to him. He pulls me into his arms and our bodies desperately cleave together in their longing for one another. Our parting was so distressing, but now those depths of despair are forgotten as we are together once more.

We lie there silently, our bodies joined; no words are needed to communicate as we rediscover our love and our passion for one another. When we are both sated at last, he props himself up on one elbow, looking down at me as he plays with a loose strand of my hair, twisting it around his fingers, then letting it go and watching it spring back like a piece of coiled twine. Only then, when he has absorbed my face entirely, as though a forgotten image which he needs to imprint in his mind once more, does he speak:

'My family do not anticipate my return for another two days; I travelled with the advance party and many of the others are still on the road. So I am a free man for the moment, which means I may remain here with you, my dear. We can go into hiding, lock ourselves away from the world and catch up on all the time we have missed.'

I pull him back into my arms and our re-acquaintance begins once more. Bella, who's furry form had hitherto had been curled up in a tight ball at the foot of the bed, as she does nightly, suddenly finds her sleeping quarters too unsteady. With a little grunt of dissatisfaction she jumps down, yawns and stretches first her front legs, then hind, and trots off to the fireplace where she resettles herself in front of the still smouldering embers and is soon asleep once more.

'We can go to the Carnevale!' I shriek, with the realisation that Tito is in fact invisible for the next few days. And how invisible he really will be, both of us shall be, behind our masks! 'We can go to the Carnevale!' I shout again, and seeing the look of acceptance and approval of my plan slowly dawning on his face, I leap from the bed and begin dancing around the room, humming a little tune of pure joy to myself, holding my nightgown as I sway from side to side. Bella, whose patience is wearing thin with this uncharacteristic nocturnal behaviour, looks up at me and growls gently before resuming her slumber.

Tito roars with laughter. 'We shall go to the Carnevale, my dear one, of course we shall! We shall have the finest masks Venice has to offer, and parade and dance, be seen by society, and no one will know who we are!'

Finally, a means for us to go out into this city together! And with no risk of us being seen by a family member or some important acquaintance of Tito's. Not a soul will expect him to be here, least of all his own flesh and blood, so no one will be looking for him.

Why did we not think of it sooner? But then I had expected my dear Tito to be away from me for much longer, and by that time the opportunity for making merry at the Carnevale would be past. Besides which, were he officially known to be here, society would dictate that he attend with his wife, not with me. I would have been able to enjoy certain parts of the festivities with Clara, but two women out on their own are likely to attract a good deal more attention than a man and a woman together, even with their faces hidden from view as they would be. She and I could not risk being mistaken for a pair of courtesans and falling into bad society.

'I will send for my mascheraro *first thing in the morning. He is the maker of the finest masks in all of Venice and will no doubt have a workshop full of the most splendid masks from which we can choose. What shall you be? A beautiful swan, a dazzling princess, a mysterious mythical creature?'*

There is no chance of further sleep as we excitedly discuss our plans for the morrow. I pull Tito from the bed and he joins me as we cavort around the chamber like a pair of marionettes. I cannot believe it; finally I am to go outside with my love! At long last, even if I am masked from view, I will be able to promenade with him at my side! This means so much to me, and the excitement is overwhelming. And then of course, after the day's festivities, we will be able to return together to my casa *and be together for the entire night, such as we have not been since we came together to this city. My delight is so intense, I can barely contain myself!*

I do not recognise myself as I stand before the mirror, and that is the desired effect, seeing as Tito has procured the finest, most expensive robes and masks for us both. My new gown is made from golden taffeta, embroidered with the most delicate beads and gems, and my mask appears to have been hewn from the same fabric, although in fact it is crafted from gilded glass, made by one of the much-fêted glassmakers of Murano, its colour exactly replicating the tones of my robe.

The mask covers my entire face, and I have to confess it is far from comfortable, tied firmly behind my head as it is and only allowing two small pairs of holes by means of which I am able to see and to breathe. To speak or to eat will no doubt prove problematic, but I do not care, as I look beautiful – not in my usual natural and unfettered way, but as though I am a statue carved from a piece of the finest and most priceless golden marble.

Huge swirls of fabric cascade around my head, interleafed with golden flowers, covering my hair entirely and giving me great height beyond my normal stature. I am like a giant, golden, goddess, and I clasp my hands together with delight, my whoops of joy muffled by the enclosure of the mask. My hands too are encased in golden filigree gloves, with painted golden glassy nails where my own nails should be.

'Tito, you are so clever to find these costumes so quickly!' I gasp. 'And such a perfect fit, too! As though it were made just for me.' Not even my voice sounds like my own; that too is in disguise. Not a soul in this city shall know who I am.

Tito's costume is very similar to my own, only masculine where mine is very, very feminine. How he was able to obtain such magnificent outfits at such speed I do not know, but my lover is a man of great means and of fortunate acquaintance, used to procuring what he wants, and for that I am grateful. This mask is my entry point into Venetian society, albeit incognito, so I do not intend to trouble myself too much with the finer details of its source. My intention today is simply to enjoy myself.

Venice is alive! I cannot believe the sights and sounds before me. In the end, it is early evening when we finally leave my casa, *such is our joy to be together again, and our desire to make the most of Tito's snatched hours. The sun is starting to set, the waters across the lagoon as still as a mirror crafted by the maestros of Murano themselves.*

A gondola awaits us at the dock in the Piazza San Marco, and Tito holds tightly to me as I climb aboard, the waters of the lagoon slapping gently against the quayside. Today the gondolas are bedecked to reflect the mood of the city, the ferri, *the high, curved and carved bows of the vessels, decorated with bright garlands, ribbons and flowers, so very contrasting to their usual sombre blackness as they slice through the water. The canal is a sea of colour and light from these barques and their occupants, and the whiteness of the vast Palazzo Ducale and its brilliant, carved stonework is thrown into stark contrast by the vibrant hues which mill around it.*

As we begin our journey and glide past the Piazza San Marco I see the swarms of costumed revellers filling the lighted square, parading in their finery, and I gasp again at the spectrum of colours and shapes before me. I have never before seen such a sight. They look almost other-worldly, no longer human, with their carved, smooth and gilded faces, outwardly expressionless whilst beneath the masks great excitement must surely bubble forth, just as it does for me.

'Facciamo una passeggiata?' *Tito asks, after we have travelled only a short distance in the gondola. He explains how much more exciting it will be for us to walk amongst the crowds, instead of gliding past them, and beckons to the gondolier to pull alongside at the next* fondamenta *so that we might alight. He is right. Holding tightly onto his arm, we tiptoe through two or three darkened* calles, *the narrow, identical-looking alleys and passageways that network through the city, away from the Canal Grande, to emerge in a piazza just in front of the Campo Santo Stefano. Here we are overwhelmed with vibrancy and opulence once more. Huge sconces light the piazza as brightly as if the sun itself were high overhead. Music and dance, theatre and comedy are taking place in abundance around us, antithetical to the unadorned serenity of the church before us. Small crowds gather to watch as these masked artists perform their trickery. Beguiled by the mastery of a juggler I have spied, I wish Tito could see the delight on my face, but it is enough to be here with him, and I only hope his joy at this day is as great as my own; I cannot believe it could be otherwise. As darkness falls completely, there is a tremendous crash and a flash of bright lights as* fuochi d'artificio *shoot up into the sky and fall to earth like a thousand shooting stars. We pause to gaze up at them in sheer wonder. I have never before seen fireworks.*

We promenade a little further along, past the fire eaters and stilt walkers, taking in the sights and sounds around us when suddenly a man steps out of nowhere and places his hands over my masked eyes…

'Stefano! What are you doing here?' The shock of being woken abruptly from my dream leaves me disorientated, gasping for air as though I am having a panic attack, and when I realise I'm safe and not actually being assaulted, mugged, or whatever fate Maria thought awaited her, certainly less than pleased. Stefano had obviously hoped to surprise me, and he's certainly done that, but it's far from the sort of surprise I like.

I've never been woken unnaturally from a Maria dream before, and I'm not sure I like the feeling of total bewilderment that being dragged from the sixteenth to the twenty-first century within the space of a millisecond has produced. I feel like I've been whisked forwards through some sort of time-travelling vortex, and my head is spinning. Usually I wake up in my own good time and the transition is a gentle one, leaving me to sort my memories and catalogue the dream in my brain before having to go back and face the real world. Right now I feel like I've been thrown into the deep end of a swimming pool whilst asleep, fully clothed, and with bricks strapped to my ankles; shocked, scared and pretty traumatised.

What had Tito and Maria been about to do at the Carnevale? Was Maria really about to be attacked, or was it simply Stefano's invasion that entered my dream state? I might never find out now. No dream ever seems to pick up exactly where the last one left off; they are all snippets, snapshots of a moment in time, and like a child woken from a fantastical dream of being a prince or princess, a dragon or a magical fairy, only to find they are a mere mortal with no super-powers, my disappointment is overwhelming. I might now never find out if something momentous was going to happen to my sixteenth century friends, or whether this was just a scene-setting moment from their lives.

I get up from my bench, hurriedly gather my things and leave the room, Stefano trailing behind me with protestations, but still no apology. I'm not sure he quite realises what he has done.

'You shouldn't have woken me,' I shout at him over my shoulder as I stomp angrily along the corridor towards the *terrazzo* café. Right now I need a large cappuccino to sort me out, and today I don't care that it's the typical

Brits-on-tour beverage, I just need the reassurance of its milky frothiness and the hit of the underlying espresso to sort me out.

'Lydia, I'm sorry,' Stefano says, finally apologising as he pulls on my arm and tries to turn me towards him. I stand resolute in the queue, still giving him the cold shoulder and turning my back on him as I place my order with the barista. But I'm no good at keeping up a temper and soften just a little as I glance behind me, catch his eye and clock his crestfallen expression. 'I was worried about you and these dreams, that's all. I wanted to come over here and see you, make sure you were OK, take you for coffee… Tell you what a lovely Christmas night I had…' This last sentence he whispers in my ear, scooping my hair from the nape of my neck and placing the most fleeting of kisses there as he tries to make me recall the night we had just spent together.

How could I forget; it had been gorgeous. We'd rolled drunkenly into bed sometime around two in the morning – again – and made soft and gentle love for what seemed like hours. Then whilst we lay there entwined he had told me he loved me. It wasn't just drunken ramblings or the effect of the endorphins from our love-making; he'd said it with the utmost sincerity. The trouble was, I didn't, or couldn't at that particular moment, say it back to him. But he was very sweet and didn't push me to return the endearment; he just looked me in the eye and said simply, 'Soon?'

I suppose I do love him in my own little way, but I don't know what it is, maybe after Ed I'm just not ready to proclaim this as a serious relationship just yet. Maybe I still nurture that fear of trusting someone too much and then being hurt again.

Stefano is a good man, and I know I'd feel pretty silly if things had been the other way round last night. I realise I have to tread carefully here, so I decide to stop my sulking, forgive Stefano for disturbing me, and get on and enjoy the rest of the day. Finally I turn round to face him, give him a huge smile which melts his worried frown, his eyes lighting up once more, and plant a massive kiss on his lips. The barista coughs politely as she tries to draw my attention back to the two coffees steaming on the counter, and the fact that they are as yet unpaid-for. I prize myself off him and do what I need to do.

'I'm sorry, Stefano,' I say as we park ourselves at a table by the window in today's near-deserted café. 'I suppose I overreacted, but it was all a bit of a shock being woken up so suddenly. I felt like I was abandoning Maria and I was worried I might not be able to get back to her again. You understand that, don't you?'

Stefano nods and enquires: 'So what was today's instalment?'

As I talk him through the Carnevale and all its glory I realise that I have remembered quite a lot of the dream, despite being snatched back to the current day so quickly. I'm glad at least that my time spent snoozing wasn't lost, even if it would have been nice to stay in the sixteenth century just a little longer.

I can still recall so vividly the sheer splendour of that Carnevale; all I've seen before now are pictures of it from recent years. I can't help thinking that in its basic format it probably hasn't changed too much over the centuries;

it's one of these major historical happenings which have weathered the passing of time.

Venice is somewhere I've never been to even on an ordinary day, and my experience in that dream is enough to make me realise that the tourist brochures don't do justice to the splendour of it all. And I don't mean just to the Carnevale in all its colour and glory, but to the fabric of Venice itself, all those unbelievably beautiful buildings, rising from the lagoon as though dropped into the blue waters by the hand of God. And I have been fortunate enough to vicariously experience Venice in its prime through Maria, not visit it in its twenty-first century state as it crumbles into the waters, shrouded in graffiti and shored up with vast buttresses. How privileged I am to have witnessed so much that in theory no one of our day should ever have seen.

'So, what next?' I ask Stefano, once we're back on solid ground and he knows he has been fully forgiven. For a split second he looks confused, presumably thinking I am referring to the next development in our relationship, not our plans for the rest of the day.

'How about a bit more culture? Shops are shut, so that's a no-go, or there's always back to your place… plenty to do there…' he proposes, with more than a little twinkle in his eye, his eyebrows whizzing up and down suggestively.

'Culture first, I think,' I reply. 'Give a girl a chance to recover, won't you?' I joke, although actually I can't think of anything nicer than holing up with him in my room for the rest of the day, only emerging for refreshments. But I know the others will all be there, so it wouldn't afford us a huge amount of privacy, and I would actually like to stay out and about for a bit longer first. It's my place or nothing for later though, as Stefano flat-shares with three other lads, so the chances of finding his house empty are even less likely; in fact it's just not worth even bothering to try.

We leave the gallery hand in hand, back out into the winter sunshine, and although there is decidedly more of a nip in the air now, I am as warm as toast, safe in the knowledge that I have a man who adores me and would do anything for me. As I gaze up at him I know there is something I want to say to him.

'I love you too,' I reply finally. It's several hours late, but now I think I mean it.

16

'So how many are coming?' I ask Sophia. She and Leonora have decided we need a New Year's Eve party. Our apartment is probably the largest out of all the friends', and the most central, so, with one day to go, bravely we decide to go ahead with it, contacting everyone via the networking sites we all use, and texting those we know are still out of town to see if they can get back in time to join us. Thank heavens for technology – within half an hour it's confirmed that we have enough would-be partygoers to make it worth the effort.

'Last count, forty-two,' Sophia replies. 'Plus us lot, of course. More than enough to make a party, and there are bound to be loads more that just show up. Everyone is going to bring food and booze – we said we were happy to provide the venue if they could do that, so there you go, looks like we are having a party!'

Leonora, who has been head-down, quietly doing the sums, suddenly shrieks: 'Let's make it fancy dress, a masked party! Like the Venetians, all those mysterious masks and painted faces! Everyone can get their hands on a mask, can't they, it's not like they need to get a whole costume or anything? I'll send another message round again now – No Mask, No Admittance!' She's off on a roll now, in full-on party-planner mode. She is doing so well, she has really come through this miscarriage episode brilliantly, and having a project like this to focus on is perfect for someone who, when in good health, is the world's biggest party animal.

It's weird seeing all these people in their masks, right here in our flat, so soon after dreaming about the Carnevale. I almost feel as though the dream has come to revisit me in my twenty-first century life. Of course, not everyone has a fabulous glass (or even fake plastic) Venetian mask to hand which they can produce in time for a party with just a day's notice, but there are a fair few nonetheless, dragged out from the backs of cupboards, or brought back from the family home in time to wear tonight.

Some people are wearing those little half-face black eye masks – my Gran used to wear something similar when she had her daytime naps – only with holes for their eyes, obviously, but most have gone in for the full-face version, so it is actually quite difficult to work out who's who. And I don't know all of them, which adds to the air of mystery and general excitement for me.

The party is just about in full swing when Leonora emerges from her room, quite unintentionally making a very dramatic entrance. She was so busy getting everything ready earlier that she simply didn't have time to change, instead disappearing into her room as soon as the first guests arrived, to make her transformation.

Wow, I cannot imagine where she pulled a costume like that from at such short notice. As she stands in the doorway to her bedroom, back-lit in a golden ball-gown of epic proportions, I do a double-take as I realise how similar she looks to Maria in my Carnevale dream. I'm glad no one can see my face under my own mask as I'm sure I must have turned bright white. Her long, dark hair has vanished, swept up into the twisted organza back of the golden mask, and her face is completely hidden behind the gold-painted façade of the frontispiece. I only know for sure that it's her from her body language and the fact that I recognise the shoes she's wearing.

I wander over to her to compliment her on her costume. 'No wonder you wanted to have a masked party,' I joke, trying to calm myself down after the shock of seeing her. 'If I had a costume like that stashed away I might have come up with that idea too!'

'I went to the Carnevale with my parents a couple of years ago, and for some reason the dress ended up here, in a box at the back of my wardrobe,' she explains. 'Truthfully I'd forgotten about it – I knew I had the mask here but finding the dress was an added bonus.'

'You look fabulous,' I say. 'Amazing.' I still feel a bit like I've been transported back five centuries, and also wish just a little bit that I had a costume like that to wear too, instead of just a cheap mask from a costume shop. But the jeans and casual clothes sported by the bottom halves of most of the other partygoers prove that she's in a minority, dressed like she is; it's just a bizarre coincidence that she chose this theme and looks so like Maria. I'm not caught up in some kind of strange cross-century conspiracy after all.

Stefano hasn't arrived yet and I'm starting to wonder where he has got to; I need him here to get me into the party spirit. I've never been a great one for New Year's parties. I can appreciate that they are the perfect distraction from either the fact that another year is over, during which time we may or may not have achieved what we set out to do – with all the resulting emotions stemming from that – and a new one, full of hopes and dreams and as yet unfulfilled ambitions, is about to begin. But for me the festive season has always been about Christmas and nothing else, so New Year might just as well be any other day. I'm glad we are having a party, but if the girls hadn't suggested it first, then I wouldn't have gone out of my way to propose it. As New Year's parties go though, it looks like it has all the promise of being a good one, as the atmosphere is buzzing already – but I need my man in tow before I can really start to enjoy myself.

Over in a corner of the room, one of the guests has taken control of the iPod, and the music has increased both in volume and liveliness. We've borrowed Lanzo's docking station for the night – he has one of those enormous testosterone-fuelled ones with boomers and bashers and woofers and tweeters and whatever other technical terms might be needed to produce an industrial strength sound for a residential party. We've invited our neighbours from upstairs, downstairs and side-ways, and I think they are all here already, so hopefully we have covered our backs and no one will feel the need to put in a complaint about the noise pollution levels on Via de Ginori.

Finally Stefano arrives, looking gorgeous in his trademark tight black jeans. I would recognise that bottom anywhere, which is just as well as his face is completely hidden by a black, slightly scary mask, changing his appearance quite dramatically from the lovely, kind and smiley man I know into something from one of those teen-horror novels. I make my way across the room to him and pinch him hard on the bum.

'Owww, you! Hello gorgeous!' he shrieks, squeezing me affectionately around the waist, seeing as he can't get near my face to kiss me. I think both our masks might be coming off later – I can't survive a whole party without kissing him.

'You look scary,' I say, and he growls at me in full teen-horror spirit.

'You look gorgeous,' he replies, slightly muffled under that monstrous mask. 'Or at least I have to assume you do. Can't see your lovely face, can I? But you look gorgeous from the neck down so I have to assume the rest is up to the usual standard!'

'Cheeky!' I say. 'Actually I've got no makeup on, I've got a massive spot on the end of my nose and my eyebrows need plucking – joke!'

'Well I might just have to drag you off to your room later to check,' he says. 'Actually, no one's looking, let's go now.' He casts a conspiratorial eye around the room before leading me by the elbow in the direction of my boudoir.

'Stefano, you are incorrigible,' I protest, very lamely, as I am more than happy to be dragged off to my room for a while and don't feel in the slightest like a party pooper; the night is yet young, with all these masks no one will notice we're gone, and we will be back soon. Better lock the door though…

Several hours in, the music is more subdued in deference to the lateness (or earliness) of the hour, the old year has been well and truly sent on its way, and the new one welcomed in, toasted and drunk to profusely. The pace has slowed significantly when a pair of new arrivals comes through the door. No masks for these two, and given the hour we will let them off, as they've clearly been elsewhere first, our party obviously not at the top of their agenda for the evening. Probably half-way down a list of several, given the time they've arrived here…

'Nice of them to show their faces,' I chuckle, pleased with my masked-party pun, as Vincenzo and Stéphanie join us.

'Sorry we're so late,' Vincenzo mutters, slurring his words a little as he uses the unbelievably pert Stéphanie to prop him up. She looks as sober as the day she was born (which, let's face it, wasn't that many years ago), and I feel for her with Vincenzo draped across her shoulders – although with that inane grin on her face you'd quickly jump to the conclusion that actually she doesn't mind too much.

I hadn't realised anyone had invited Vincenzo, but clearly they have and that's fine by me. He must know so many of the people that have passed through here tonight, so it's no wonder that word got round, even if it wasn't a direct invitation. I'm fine with him being here, anyway. I'm secure in my relationship with Stefano now; seeing Vincenzo out and about with his latest flame doesn't bother me, why should it? Stéphanie is doing very well – she seems to have managed to hold onto him for quite a few weeks now, which has to be something of a record. I haven't seen him with anyone else recently or heard any rumours about the next girl on the list, so presumably they are monogamous, or at least to the extent that Vincenzo ever is monogamous. Good luck to her...

For an old bloke – well, old in comparison to the rest of us, I still have no idea what age he actually is – Vincenzo can certainly party hard. Within moments of arriving, he has commandeered the sound system and rejuvenated the music, dragged Stéphanie up off the sofa to dance, and the two of them are currently gyrating around like a couple of teenagers. Well, she still is a teenager, but it must be a fair while since Vincenzo sported spots, a bum-fluff moustache, and raging hormones. Oh I forgot, he still has the hormones, but at least his complexion and hirsuteness have caught up with his age.

In the name of goodhearted, New Year's forgiveness and all things nice, Stefano appears to have buried the hatchet when it comes to his feelings about Vincenzo. I suppose it's largely due to the fact that he and I are now an item, and secure in the knowledge of that, he is no longer threatened by the presence of his perceived rival – if Vincenzo ever could be classed as a rival, which I'm not sure he could. He sits amusedly observing Vincenzo in action, without the usual peeved expression the sight of my tutor seems to put on his face.

'Bella Lydia, Buon Anno!' Vincenzo squeaks drunkenly, as he drags me from my comfy spot on the sofa, where I've been quite happily watching events unfold before me, snuggled sleepily into Stefano's arms. As he pulls me up onto the dance floor, abandoning the sober Stéphanie to the crazy dance antics of a couple of male students much closer in age to her than he is, he plants a big, wet kiss on each of my cheeks.

'So, how was your Christmas, dear Lydia?' Vincenzo asks, as he holds me unnecessarily close for a fast dance, alternately gripping me firmly by the waist and spinning me round with some force. I can tell he's not really interested in my reply – he is just using it as an excuse to get close to me. Stefano is trying so hard to pretend he isn't watching us, let alone feeling jealous, so when I see him look my way I pull one of those 'get me out of here' faces just to show him I'd much rather be back on the sofa with him. Just then Sober Stéphanie pulls Stefano to his feet and he too is up with us, a reluctant dancer who's already done all this several hours earlier and is actually looking forward to the party wrapping up, so that he can spend the night alone with his girlfriend.

The music switches to a slowie, and I decide it's time to make my exit and reclaim my man from Stéphanie. But before I can release myself from his clutches, Vincenzo whips me tightly to him, his hands roving up and down my back as he makes small grunting noises in my ear. With the closeness of him I detect a presence in his trousers that really should be reserved only for his girlfriend, not for me, so I give him the biggest shove I can muster without completely unbalancing him, and plead needing the loo as my reason for escape. As I dash off I send eye-signals and a nod to Stefano to follow me, and we reconvene in the sanctity of the kitchen.

'What is that man like!' I say to Stefano, although I don't go into detail on just how much Vincenzo was enjoying our little dance, for fear of Stefano going back in there and giving him a piece of his mind – or fist. He might be doing a good impersonation of someone who has his feelings under control, but for how long that control might last, I wouldn't like to speculate.

'*È viscido, Lydia*,' he replies. 'I thought you'd shaken him off now he knows we're together, but he just has to keep on trying, doesn't he? I wish to God he wasn't your tutor, I really do.'

And then, quite bizarrely, I find myself leaping to Vincenzo's defence. 'But he's a great tutor, and, you know, he's never tried anything funny with me.' Apart from tonight of course, but then he is very drunk and it is New Year.

'Come on, let's leave them to it and call it a night,' Stefano suggests, leading me quickly to the safety of my room and away from Vincenzo's lasciviousness. He can stay and party until there's no one left to party with if he really wants to, but we've had enough, we're off.

'Ow, my head hurts,' Stefano moans as I throw open the shutters the following morning. 'Whatever did I do to deserve a girlfriend who likes to get up soooo damned early.' He pulls the duvet back over his head and disappears with a sleepy groan.

I leave him to snooze and park myself at my desk, window open and chill, new January air streaming in, with Signore Di Girolamo's tome on Titian. Up until now I haven't got very far with reading it, and I need to, and want to; there are still so many things I need to find out about Titian and Maria, so many gaps to fill in the jigsaw puzzle of their lives.

'Wow, this man writes like he almost knew Titian,' I mutter, more to myself than to Mr Sleepyhead in the bed over there, who grunts in reply, aware probably that I said something vaguely stimulating, but not so interested in hearing what it was to bother waking up.

Di Girolamo has a fantastic style to his writing, but then he would have, given how riveting his lectures are. He writes more as though he wants to convey the personal side of the artist to the reader, instead of all the factual stuff, which is already well-known and well-documented and we can read in any old history book. So there are surprisingly few references to dates and conventional historical facts in Titian's life, and it reads more as a story book – and a gripping one at that – than a work of non-fiction. And it's huge; at over fifteen hundred pages, it's going to take me ages to get through it, but that's fine, as every tiny morsel is as riveting as the next and I am thoroughly enjoying it. Aside from the knowledge of that era that my dreams have given me up until now, I don't think I've ever learnt so much about an artist and his way of life.

One factor that I find really interesting is the detail Di Girolamo goes into about the patrons that Titian worked for. I knew he was well-connected and that these people were wealthy aristocratic types – they would have to be to afford a commission – but what is outstanding is the way Di Girolamo manages to convey the working relationship between master and artist as though he were actually there. Reading this book feels more like watching a film on the life and times of Titian, and short of documenting conversations between them – which of course would have been ridiculously impossible – he manages to show

how their friendships grew, in particular with Federico Gonzaga, for whom he painted loads of pictures, and who, along with his brother-in-law Francesco Maria della Rovere, became a very close friend and confidant. Until now, those names to me were synonymous with the ugly mugs flanking Venus in the gallery, but Di Girolamo's writing brings these characters to life, and makes their scowling expressions excusable when I discover how kind and supportive they were to Titian.

I know that many of the paintings Titian produced for Gonzaga have not survived to the present day, so I am amazed when he goes on to describe some of them in great detail. They seem to float off the page and into my head as fully formed images, and I can almost see the brush strokes and nuances of shading. He mentions a painting called 'The Virgin and Child with Saint Marguerite' which sounds like a particularly intriguing one, infused with radiance and using a lighter technique than some of his earlier paintings, so Di Girolamo says. I've never heard of it before, and even with an extensive internet search I still can't track down any mention of it. There's one with Saint Catherine, quite a well-known painting, and Saints Anthony and John too, but no mention of this Saint Marguerite as far as I can see. Di Girolamo hasn't reproduced the picture in his book – how could he if it no longer exists? But presumably his references must be genuine, or they wouldn't have survived the scrutiny of all those other historians out there who also write about Titian, would they? I'm baffled.

I flick to the bibliography at the back of the book and am surprised to find that there are very few references to other works. So where does Di Girolamo get his information from? To me it almost feels as though he has taken the bare bones of recorded history, padded them out with a multitude of fascinating facts, and turned this book into a work of fiction. But he can't have done, surely? He's a respected, published historian, one of the most revered in the art world.

I am so engrossed in my reading that I almost jump out of my skin when Stefano comes up behind me and puts his hands gently on my shoulders, planting a kiss on the top of my head.

'Breakfast,' he mumbles. 'Need breakfast.'

'Good morning to you, too,' I reply. 'Feeling any better now?'

'Fine. Nothing some good strong coffee and carbs won't fix. How's your research going?' he asks.

'Good thanks,' I say. 'This book is amazing, it's almost like he was there. I don't know where he gets half his stuff from. Might have to go and talk to him about it, I think.'

'Great,' says Stefano, still too sleepy to share in my enthusiasm. He saunters off, yawning, stretching and scratching his armpits in true bloke fashion, in the direction of the kitchen, and I hear him greet Sophia. A few moments later a more livened up version of him pops its head round the door. 'Grab a quick shower, Lydia,' he says. 'We're all off to Epoca for breakfast.'

Given the choice I think I'd rather stay here with my head in my book and grab a quick coffee and a bowl of muesli from the kitchen, but I am made to feel like that isn't an option which is open to me. It is New Year's Day, and therefore still officially part of the festive season, which means I have to be sociable. Apparently, for the Italians, the whole shenanigan carries on until Epiphany on the sixth of January, so it looks like we could still have a few days of this enforced celebration left before everything returns to normal. Right now I could do with a bit of normality – I'm all partied out and I'd quite like to get back to my dreams, my research, and of course my studies, given that they're the reason I'm actually here. Maybe I'm just tired, but I can't help the Bah, Humbug feeling that's trying to take me over.

Each of us a couple of coffees up, and the crumbled remains of a plate of pastries before us, we are all starting to feel slightly more human. We compare stories from the party, and there are plenty. Over all we must have had about a hundred people passing through the apartment during the course of the evening, and there are some interesting snippets of gossip to exchange. The general consensus amongst us is that the party was a huge hit, and everyone had a great time. The downside of such a huge party is that now we are saddled with the mess to clear up – no wonder everyone wanted to go out for breakfast, as the kitchen has disappeared under enough bottles and rubbish to warrant its own personal recycling plant.

We stroll back at a leisurely pace across the Piazza della Signoria as morning turns to afternoon, idly window shopping on the way. No one is in that much of a hurry to get back to the dishes and tidying up, but at least no one has shirked off with an excuse of somewhere else they need to be. At some point today it will all get done and our apartment will be our own once more.

Hands to the glass, I peer into the murky gloom of a closed gallery window as I wait for the others to catch up. It's one of the more upmarket shops on the square, still catering for tourists, but aimed at the upper echelons of this market, those with a few more Euros in their pockets, who want to take home with them something longer-lasting than the plastic models of the Ponte Vecchio or snow domes with tiny David statues inside. I spot a print I recognise: it's one of Vincenzo's, one of his modernist landscapes – not a nude, for a change – but it is quite unmistakeably a work by Tizzaro, that up-and-coming young artist and tutor of mine.

'Do you like that one?' Stefano asks, coming over to see what I'm looking at and throwing his arm around my shoulders. 'Why don't I get it for you, for your room, when they open up again? Call it an extra Christmas present,' he says.

'It's one of Vincenzo's. Good, isn't it?' I reply. But instead of waiting for my answer to his offer, he bluntly removes his arm, grunts something unintelligible and wanders off to join the rest of the group. So maybe I won't be getting it as an extra Christmas present after all; suddenly it's not such a great painting as far as he's concerned. His issue with Vincenzo is still ongoing then, by the looks of it.

I walk back the rest of the way with Sophia, whilst Stefano skulks at the back of the group. I'll cut him some slack and put it down to tiredness for now.

17

'*Hai letto questo?*'

I practically accost Vincenzo, brandishing the weighty 'Titian, A Life In Art' by Antonio Di Girolamo, as I arrive for my weekly tutorial. '*È IN-CRED-I-BIL-E!*' I gasp as he stands at his easel, twiddling his brush around like the stereotypical arty type, adding a few theatrical flourishes to his work before downing tools and gathering his notes together for our meeting. I have a feeling that display was purely for my benefit, and there probably isn't even any paint on his brush.

'Actually, I'm embarrassed to say I haven't read it,' he replies. 'He gave it to me a couple of years ago. But it was around the same time I was publishing one of my books, and I think I felt a bit threatened by the size of his compared to mine.' Here he pauses to raise his eyebrows, a double entendre twinkle playing in the corner of his eye. 'So I stuck it on that shelf up there and it's stayed there ever since.'

'You should read it, really you should. I've never read anything like it,' I go on, still pacing around the room in my excitement, unable yet to settle down and get my books out of my bag. 'I don't know what he's used as his sources, but there is stuff in there and I don't have a clue where he got it from. Unseen, unheard of stuff, you know? Almost as though he made it up, but he can't have done, can he?'

'Somehow I doubt it, Lydia,' Vincenzo goes on, seriously. 'He is one of the most respected historians we have in this country.' My thoughts entirely.

'Anyway, read it,' I implore, before planting myself excitedly in one of the comfy chairs to one side of Vincenzo's office. He joins me on the other chair, first tugging it a little closer so that our knees are almost touching.

Vincenzo places a hand confidently on my knee. I look down at it pointedly and then up at his face and he removes it, coughing slightly to hide his embarrassment at over-stepping the mark. When sober, he can behave honourably, see? He asks me if I've had any more dreams, and once again advises me to be careful. Yeah, yeah, yeah, blah, blah, blah. Unfortunately, such words of wisdom tend to fall on deaf ears these days.

Our tutorial goes on to be a good one, though. We get into a heated argument about the validity of the inspiration of Homer and Virgil on the work of Botticelli, with Vincenzo admitting at the end of the debate that he was purely playing devil's advocate for the sake of a good discussion and to push me to air my views fully – actually he agreed with everything I'd said. I am close to thumping him with frustration but I do appreciate that he has a certain way of bringing the best out of his students, even if slightly unorthodox in his methods, so I manage to restrain myself.

Once we've had our officially allotted time, I contrive to bring the subject back to Signore Di Girolamo and his book, as I'm convinced Vincenzo must know more about it than he does, and I offer to read him an excerpt from it. Fortunately he agrees, and for once drops his air of competitiveness and relaxes back into his chair to listen.

I read him the section about the prostitute Titian encountered on his travels in Bologna. Di Girolamo goes on to explain how she was the love of his life, and how he moved her to Venice, despite his family also living there and him having to live a double life and keep her secret for so many years. The depth of emotional detail he goes into is amazing, almost as if he knew this girl – presumably Maria – himself.

'She has to be my Maria,' I say to Vincenzo, imploring him to back me up and by doing so give my own personal story a stamp of validity 'But why, if Di Girolamo knows so much about Maria, doesn't he name her in the book? Surely someone with so much insight into Titian's life must know who she was and where she came from? How he possibly could know is beyond me, but with the level of detail he gives on other stuff it just feels like he should.'

This is the part which is really frustrating me. I know I haven't read even half the book yet, but if 'Maria', as I think she must be, is already a feature in the story, why would he wait until later in the book to name her? Maybe he doesn't name her at all; maybe he doesn't know her name? But she is so pivotal, so influential in Titian's life that she warrants a title, thank you very much Mr Big Historian Di Girolamo. He simply refers to her for the moment as 'The Girl from Bologna'. It's so frustrating to think I've found her at last, only to lack any definitive confirmation.

Vincenzo has very little to say on the passage I read to him, shrugging his shoulders and admitting that, whilst Di Girolamo writes with great insight, he needs to be able to provide his sources to give it any credibility. I suppose I shouldn't be surprised as it has been quite obvious since he loaned me the book that there is more than a hint of professional jealousy involved here.

I realise I'm getting nowhere with Vincenzo, and what I actually need as I leave his office is another 'fix' of Maria, another chapter in her life story, to convince myself that she is, or rather was, real. I pack up quickly and head straight for the Uffizi and room twenty-eight again.

'Calma, cara mia!' Tito exclaims as I fidget and twist on the lettuccio, trying to settle myself into a comfortable position. I may only be in the first few months of my pregnancy, but already my belly feels ripe and swollen, my body no longer entirely my own. And I am so pleased at that! How delighted Tito was to discover that we have made a new life between us, a child who is to be part of his body and soul, and part of mine, a new life to cherish and to love!

Tito approaches me and removes the shawl which until now has covered my nudity. He sits beside me and gently caresses my growing belly, bending to kiss it and softly saying, 'Mio figlio.' 'My son.' But I have no inkling that this is a boy-child within me. Never before have I experienced the joys of being with child and therefore I have no knowledge of how it should feel, but there is such a strong sense that the life within me is female. I could be mistaken of course, and we will both have to wait for the day of delivery to discover what the Lord has chosen to bless us with. But even so, I am gently preparing Tito for the fact that our child may well be a girl. In any case, he already has sons, and not being a legitimate provider of his heir, I do not feel any pressure at all to provide him with another. Whether male or female this child will be loved like no other.

My girl-child. She lives within me, growing every day, and how I love her so already! I run my hand once more over my smooth, firm stomach before readjusting myself into the position which Tito requires for this painting. I am to lie demurely on the bed, which is draped with a silk cotton sheet, crumpled as though I have just awoken from a dream. Bella is to be painted too, curled up at the foot of the bed, although for the moment she refuses to perform her artistic duties, and remains where she is, obdurately dozing in front of the fire. She has no calling to this artistic way of life, bless her! Occasionally she deigns to peep at me from one eye, as though she knows what is required of her but today has chosen not to participate. It does not matter, Tito can paint her in at a later date; there will be plenty more days like this, posing for this same painting. Tito has proclaimed that it will be one of his finest, and as ever he is approaching his work with the utmost dedication and perfectionism.

Tito comes to me and adjusts my pose so that I am in the position in which he sketched me yesterday. He flits to and from his canvas, comparing still life to real life, adjusting a hand here, a lock of hair there. He ruffles the soft, downy pillows behind my head and bends my elbow, which has the effect of turning my body towards him a little more. In my hand he places the posy which I am to hold, a small bunch of pale pink roses, so fragile that they look as though they should crumble to dust as I touch them. In fact they do crumble a little, and I exclaim as one bloom drops to the bed, believing I have ruined the impression.

'Never mind,' Tito says. 'We will leave them like that. In fact the effect is more natural. It looks as though you are crushing the roses, as though you do not want to hold them, and I like that. It sits well with the somewhat defiant expression on your face, my dear,' he adds, smiling.

Clara had braided my hair around my head this morning, provided me with my drop pearl earrings to wear and added a little rouge to my cheeks to give them a glow fit to complement the shade of the roses. With one final adjustment to my tresses, bringing some more soft curls to sit around my face and tumble over my shoulder, Tito declares he is ready to begin today's work on his masterpiece.

He has told me what the backdrop to the painting will be, but for now I am positioned in front of a plain black canvas so that there is no distraction, better to capture each small detail that he needs, so he says. Everything else will be added in later. My dear Clara is to be immortalised on canvas too; this will be a veritable portrait of our household! She will be to the rear with another maid, and they are to be pictured in their duties, preparing my trousseau, or some other such domestic chore. Clara is to be clothed in a fine, red velvet gown, the wearing of which she is utterly giddy with excitement about. The other maid, who will be a pure figment of Tito's imagination, is to be quite obviously of lesser standing within the casa, *her dress fashioned from simple calico, as she fumbles in a wedding chest, in search of some garment or other.*

The outlook through the window at the back of the room is to show a hint of the setting sun, with a myrtle plant silhouetted in the vast frame of the aperture. I cannot wait to see it! I know I have posed for countless paintings for my Tito, yet this one incites so much enthusiasm in him that I am expecting something very special indeed. He paints with a small smile playing at the corner of his lips, as though he can barely contain the excitement as the work takes shape; the knowledge that ultimately this is to become a great masterpiece.

'Who is this painting for, my love? Who has commissioned you this time?' I venture to ask.

'It is for a new client,' he replies mysteriously, although he does not look me in the eye, and once again I suspect that it is purely for his own whim. All this effort, and such perfectionism, when it will more than likely be seen by none other than our immediate household. He earns a very handsome living from his work, but on occasion he cannot bring himself to part with a certain painting, especially if it is of me and therefore very dear to him. I envisage this one will soon be hanging on the walls of my casa, *along with the multitude of other such works…*

I laugh as my contrary little Bella rises from her position at the fireside, stretches languidly and comes towards us, pausing to yawn and have a little scratch of her ears as she makes her short journey across the room. She jumps onto my bed, circles around a few times in search of the comfiest position, first in one direction and then the other, finally choosing her spot just beyond reach of my feet, and settling down into the most perfect pose for the painting.

'Well, would you ever believe it,' Tito shrieks in mirth. 'I swear that dog must be related to you, for all she is stubborn and single-minded. If we ask her to come, she will not come. No, this little creature must decide for herself and then she will deign to bestow her presence on us. She is such a funny little thing, just like you, my dear.'

I wake up with a jolt and a sudden realisation. I have to write this down, and quickly. I do believe I have just dreamed my way into the very moment in time when Maria sat for the Venus painting! I can't quite believe my luck. Have I really just experienced first-hand Titian painting 'me' as Venus?

All that stuff with the black canvas was interesting; that sumptuous background, the embossed fabric wallpaper, those cloths, those ladies-in-waiting – all added in later... And I can't believe I've never noticed before that the chief maid is in fact Clara! How could that have slipped through the net, when now it seems so blatantly obvious? OK, so she doesn't normally wear such sumptuous costumes in the dreams when she's going about her daily business, but that face, that poise – it's most definitely her. I really do feel like I have just been the most privileged and fortunate onlooker into the making of a piece of history. I gasp at the enormity of it all. Surely no fantasy alone could conjure up something which seemed so lifelike – this really is pure insight into someone else's life, five centuries ago. What a shame that the snapshot ended so suddenly, but at least I have had that much.

I scribble down as much as I can in my notebook and leave the gallery, calling Stefano as I run down the steps into the piazza. 'Can you meet me?' I ask breathlessly. 'Just had the most amazing dream.'

I know he isn't all that keen on me pursuing the dreams, and I know he worries about me and what I might find out and what it might be doing to me and all that sort of concerned boyfriend stuff. But this is momentous; I have to share it with him, whatever he thinks. I need to bounce it all off someone before I burst with excitement.

Stefano has just finished a lecture, so we meet up not long afterwards for coffee in a side-street bar off the Piazza della Signoria.

'So, tell me,' he says, a wary 'what's-she-done-this-time' expression fleetingly crossing his face before he covers it up with a more welcoming smile.

'You'll never believe it,' I begin. 'It was only Titian painting me, or rather Maria, as the Venus of Urbino! I was there, on the couch, naked,' I look at him for a reaction but he's fairly deadpan, 'roses in my hand, hair braided, dog at my feet – well, eventually,' I add, 'but that's another story. The WHOLE package. JUST like in the painting. UNBELIEVABLE!'

'Lydia, don't you think this has all gone too far?' he begins. 'Can't you see it's just all wishful thinking on your part? It has to be all in your head. OK so for some reason you do fall asleep in front of this painting, maybe there's a logical explanation for that, maybe not, but don't you think it's just your imagination running wild with you? You've gone and developed a fixation on this painting, and every time you go and visit it you drift off, have some lovely dream or other, but it must only be because you're obsessed with it. Your brain's working overtime to conjure up all these stories, and when you wake up you think they're real, because you've dreamt you're the woman in the painting. Don't you think it's all starting to sound a bit mad? Time to give it a rest now, I think. Don't you?'

Well, I'd never expected a tirade like that. Last call, Stefano was on my side with the whole dreams thing. I thought he supported me, that he understood that it really was some kind of weird insight into real history, not just his totally bonkers girlfriend and her hyperactive imagination. I hadn't even got as far as telling him the momentous news that Maria was pregnant…

I'm so shocked I don't know what to say, so I don't say anything. I just grab my things quickly and leave the café without a backwards glance, humiliation burning on my cheeks.

18

'Stefano is really worried about you, Lydia,' Sophia says as we sit across the kitchen table from one another on Friday morning, each nursing a cappuccino. Both of us have lectures to get to, but neither is showing much inclination to actually head for the door. I have the feeling she's been leading up to this; clearly nominated by the group as official spokesperson, she just needed the courage and a shot of caffeine to launch in and come out with it.

'Huh, well he would be, wouldn't he?' I reply with sudden vehemence. 'Bet you all just think I'm mad, don't you? Go on, tell me you think I should stop, why don't you? It's all in my head, blah, blah, blah. That strange English girl and her crazy dreams.'

I am still fuming with Stefano, and haven't seen him or spoken to him since storming out on him earlier in the week. He's been trying to text me, and there have been a multitude of messages in several different veins: the worried ones, the angry ones, the sad and sorry ones, the begging-you-to-contact-me ones, but I have just ignored them all, hard-nosed, stubborn person that I am. Only

I'm not hard-nosed and stubborn; I know it's a sorry state of affairs to be in, and aside from the fact that I really, really desperately miss him, I'm worried more than anything that I might have completely blown the status quo of our little group of six fabulous friends. I remember when I first arrived here and met them all, I was adamant that I wouldn't get involved with any one of them for fear of spoiling the friendships we all have. But there you are, it looks like I have done just that.

I don't know if Stefano and I will survive this as a couple or not – somehow I doubt it – but either way it's going to be hard for us to go back to being 'just good friends' without some serious baggage clogging up the space between us.

'Don't be silly, Lydia, of course we don't think you're mad,' Sophia says softly, as I realise just how viciously – and unjustifiably – I'd snapped back at her. 'We've always supported you, you know that. And yes, you are slightly, well, unusual, aren't you? But we're your friends and we're behind you and we love you and… Do I need to say any more?' She gives me a huge smile which proves just how much she cares, but serves to make me feel even more of an undeserving grump.

'Do you think Stefano hates me?' I ask, deflated again, knowing full well that he could never hate me, but wanting to hear it from someone else's lips.

'Of course he doesn't hate you. He's just worried about you. And he wants you back. I probably shouldn't be telling you this but he called a meeting with us all last night to talk about you.'

'No, you shouldn't have told me,' I say, back on the defensive once more, jumping up from my seat and furiously pacing the room. Sophia is out of her chair in a flash and grabs me by both arms to still me.

'Don't be angry, Lydia, he just wants us to keep an eye on you, that's all. You have to admit, this whole thing is taking over your life a bit, so it's no wonder he's concerned. Don't be cross with him, and don't hold it against us either, will you, we just want to help you through this, really we do.'

I slump back into my chair with a sigh. 'Where do we go from here?' I ask.

'Where do you want to go?' she replies. 'Do you want Stefano back? I have to warn you I got the impression from what he was saying last night, that it's either the dreams or him. He's not prepared to share you with 'some sixteenth century bloke', as he puts it.'

'Well you really did have a good old chat about me,' I say in a sarcastic tone, anger rising in the back of my throat again as I take my seat and strap myself in for the next choppy ride on this emotional roller coaster. 'Funny how I get to hear about all of this from you – he hasn't even spoken to me.' Rage subsides again and hurt takes over as I crumble once more, my head slumping into my folded arms on the table. 'But he was so supportive at the start, when I first told him about the dreams.'

'He hasn't had the chance to speak; you've been avoiding him, Lydia. He's tried so hard to get hold of you, and short of turning up here and forcing you to see him, which he didn't want to do, he hasn't had a lot of choice. Talk to him. Talk it through, explain how you feel and see what happens. Go from there.'

She's right, I know. I can't avoid him forever. 'I'll call him after my lecture,' I say. Sophia looks deeply into my eyes to make sure I really mean it.

'Do,' she says.

'I promise,' I reply, pulling myself up to head off and face the day.

Eduardo greets me with big kisses on each cheek as I take up what has become my regular spot beside him for Signore Di Girolamo's lecture, which today isn't on Titian, thank God. After all the hoo-hah surrounding my own personal adventures in – purportedly – the life and times of Titian, I'm giving room twenty-eight a wide berth for today; I'm not sure I could cope with another instalment of Maria's history, the way I feel right now. The topic today is completely unrelated, totally different period, style, everything, which is quite a relief for the time being. Not even a whiff of anything Renaissance for the next hour.

'Come stai, Lydia?' Eduardo asks me.

He's so lovely, I can't possibly tell him that actually everything isn't entirely *'Bene, grazie'* at the moment. It's good to have a friend who represents neutral territory in what at the moment feels to me like a war zone, who doesn't know about my dreams, and to whom I don't feel obliged to recount the latest development or reassure them that I'm not in danger of emotional meltdown. With Eduardo and this little posse of friends from my course, things are simple and uncomplicated. We meet for regular coffees, have a straightforward chat about life and the world in general or our course work, moan or gossip about the tutors, all the usual sort of studenty stuff, and don't stray down the route of the deep and meaningful too often. It's so refreshing, and I want to keep it that way.

'You look tired,' he comments. 'Everything is OK?' Bless him for caring, but I shrug it off with a flippant comment about too many late nights, give him a big, reassuring smile, and we settle down for the lecture, poised to be impressed by another gem of knowledge from the great man himself.

Afterwards, despite my earlier resolve to leave Titian alone for today, I find myself wandering up to Signore Di Girolamo, with the intention of talking to him about his book. As far as I'm aware, and unless Vincenzo has told him he lent his copy to me, he doesn't know I'm reading it. Nor would he be aware that I have such an avid interest in Titian, above and beyond the requirements for the coursework.

'Can I talk to you for a moment?' I ask the great man, who as usual is fighting his way through the student groupies and their reams of questions. He is one tutor who is continually mobbed by students, all desperate to get at a bit more of his great brain.

'Could I talk to you about your Titian book?' I ask again when the coast is clearer and I finally have his attention.

'Yes – Lydia, isn't it? Our English visitor?' he replies, smiling, and suddenly his attention is focused on me alone. He dispatches the remainder of his groupies with a quick nod and a promise to talk to them later, and hones in solely on me and my query. 'Ask away. What would you like to know?'

'Well, I'm really enjoying your book,' I begin tentatively, 'but I'm baffled as to where you get some of your information from. I don't want to seem rude or anything, but I can't reference some of this stuff anywhere else,' I tap the volume I've placed on his lectern as I speak. To start with he looks a little taken aback that I should dare say such a thing, his already grey pock-marked face paling further, and I wonder if I have gone a step too far. But then he seems to brighten, pulls himself together with a slight shudder, and gives me another of his rusty park-railings smiles (no lady-killer, this one) as I go on to say: 'How do you get inside Titian's head like that – it's almost as though you knew him. How could anyone know those things about him?'

'Sit down, Lydia,' he says, leading me to the front row of the lecture theatre and taking a seat beside me. 'You're the first person ever to ask me that, you know.' Actually he looks very pleased to have been asked. 'But that could be largely due to the fact that I didn't actually print many copies of this book. I only produced fifty and I still have half of those myself. I didn't think it would be too much appreciated in the world of, well, proper historians, of which I am, of course, supposed to be a member.' His smile becomes more enigmatic and I am confused even further.

'I don't follow you,' I say, intrigued. 'Are you saying it's fictional then?' I am mystified as to why a historian of such renown wouldn't make his book available to the wider public – isn't that how they justify the research grants and make the serious money?

But instead of answering my question he says: 'Can you come to my office later? Let's talk about it when we have a bit of time and space.' He glances towards the small crowd of students who are still lingering hopefully at the door. 'I take it Vincenzo lent you that copy?' I nod. 'Yes, I thought so. Not that he'll ever have read it himself, of course,' he chuckles. 'I wouldn't mind betting he uses it as a door stop and kicks it about his office.' How close to the truth he is.

Signore Di Girolamo packs away his notes and folders and gives me a time at which I am to come to his office – half hour from now – then quickly leaves the lecture theatre.

My mobile rings as I'm crossing the Piazza. It's Stefano and this time, after what Sophia had said earlier – and what I'd promised her – I don't really feel I can ignore it.

'*Pronto,*' I say, my voice sounding a little flat as I bravely hit the green button, despite an overwhelming urge to hit the red.

'*Lydia, ciao, come stai?*' His voice, the same as ever, has the effect on me, the same as ever, of turning my legs to jelly. Only this time that feeling makes me want to cry, as I remember how I'd walked out on him, and how I've cruelly managed to ignore him all week. What an awful person I am – he doesn't deserve this.

'*Mi manchi tanto, cara.*'

I miss you too, Stefano, only I don't say it out loud; it stays in my head, along with all the confusion of emotions. I can't say it out loud, it's physically impossible as I'm too choked up and trying hard to pretend I'm not. I'm trying to put on a brave face, only Stefano can't see that, he can only hear my muffled sobs.

'Can we meet up?' he asks, ever so tentatively, as though I might hang up on him at any minute.

'I have to see Signore Di Girolamo now but shall I text you when I'm free? Are you around all afternoon?' I manage to get my voice back sufficiently to ask him.

'Yes – please,' he says with an audible sigh, sounding relieved. 'Thank you Lydia. See you later.'

Signore Di Girolamo is waiting for me as planned. His office is wildly different to Vincenzo's smart pad, every inch the abode of the mad professor. As far as I know he's a single man (well, you'd have to get past those teeth, and although he's a wonderful person, it would take a very brave woman…) and his room only serves to reinforce the impression that he totally and utterly married to the job, or rather the vocation.

I don't think I've ever seen so many valuable-looking books in one place, other than in some of those palatial libraries you get in stately homes. The difference here being that these ones look like they are picked up and read on a frequent basis, not just catalogued for the sake of having a beautiful library to show off.

'Thank you for seeing me,' I say, as he guides me to a rather threadbare chair, first relocating discarded piles of papers and books so that I might use this piece of furniture for its intended purpose.

'I didn't realise you had such an interest in Titian,' he says. 'Have you always been interested in him?'

'Not really, no,' I reply. 'Only since I… um… came to Florence. It must be the effect of this place, I reckon. There's so much of his work here after all, and as an artist he just seemed to hook me in. Right from the start really.'

I can't tell him about the dreams, can I? Just imagine the conversation: 'Oh well, actually, Signore Di Girolamo, I have regular excursions to the sixteenth century in the guise of Titian's lover. He paints me naked and I've even posed for the Venus of Urbino painting in my dreams. Beat that.' No, I'm not sure he's the sort of person I should be telling all that stuff to. Not yet, anyway – if ever; I hardly know the guy and I don't want him to write me off as a complete fruitcake right from the start. I want to find out more, not scare him off.

An hour or so later – in fact I have no idea exactly how long I spent with him – I leave Di Girolamo's office with my head in a whirlwind and just keep walking. Suddenly caffeine makes its way to the top of my must-have list and this achieved, I sit in an absolute trance, at a table outside Rivoire in the Piazza della Signoria, not caring that I have just paid seven Euros for the world's smallest beverage, just needing somewhere for a few still moments to try and get my head back in gear. I am not people-watching and taking advantage of the perfect positioning of my table as I normally would, soaking up the wonderfully colourful Florentine comings-and-goings. I may as well be anywhere; this landscape is wasted on me today. The waiter passes by and asks if I'd like another espresso, and the second shot hits my veins as quickly as the first.

Against my better judgement I had told Di Girolamo about the dreams – it all just kind of slipped out somehow, and his reaction had surprised me.

'Please call me Antonio,' he had ventured as I started my story, but somehow with him first names just seem too informal – I am still in awe of the man and not ready to bring him down from his pedestal just yet. As I nervously began the tale of my first trip back to the sixteenth century he turned as white as a sheet and began to cough ferociously. He staggered over to the other shabby armchair, clutching his neck, and to start with I thought he was having some kind of attack, and that I was going to be called upon to provide first aid or ring for an ambulance. Then he took a sip of water, seemed to regain his composure and within seconds the colour returned to his cheeks. He nodded cursorily to confirm his restoration to health and that I should continue, and from then on he sat riveted whilst I recounted the story of how I came to know so much about the man I believe to be Titian, and of course, Maria. It was as though the attack had never happened.

'You talk about a girl a lot in your book, Signore Di Girolamo,' I asked when I'd finished recounting my tales, 'but you never actually name her. She sounds so like my Maria, it has to be her, but what I don't get is that if you know so much about Titian and his personal life, all these details which no one else seems to mention, then why don't you give her a name? Surely you must know who she is?'

'She is indeed your Maria,' he replied. 'You need to read on, my dear, and then you will see that I do in fact give her a name. When I started the book I didn't know her name, I only discovered it later on, and, well, as this wasn't the sort of book to be edited and re-edited before going to print, I just never got around to going back and adding in her name whenever she gets a mention. But yes, she is your Maria.' Here he sat back in his chair and smiled, as if my recognition of Maria was the best acknowledgement he could have of the accuracy of his own research.

'Have you been writing all this down?' he asked. 'These dreams of yours? You really should. You might not think so now, you probably think you're going mad or seeing things, or… I don't know what, but what you're experiencing is of truly historical importance. You must keep a record of it all. The human mind is a very forgetful instrument, and it is so easy to distort the facts over time or indeed lose them completely.'

A light-bulb of recognition suddenly came on in my head and I found myself asking: 'Is that what you did? Did you have dreams about Titian, like I do with Maria? Is that how you know so much?' I don't know why I hadn't recognised a fellow dreamer sooner. It all seems so obvious now.

At this question there was a complete sea-change in his attitude towards me. Gone was the helpful professor; shutters up, discussion closed down, he escorted me from his office as quickly as he could, inventing, I'm pretty sure of it, some excuse about needing to get to his next lecture. Manners not entirely departed though, he closed the door on me with a perplexing smile and: 'Fascinating to speak to you, Lydia, please excuse my having to rush off like this.'

But he hadn't convinced me; there was something going on and I don't know why it hadn't occurred to me sooner, what with all the hours I have spent poring over his book and trying, and failing, to find references to the facts elsewhere. Di Girolamo had to have had a similar experience to me in order to know so much about Titian – the man must have had dreams just like mine. I can't fathom how anything but first-hand experience could have enabled him to write such things.

But if he did, for whatever reason and despite sharing my own experience with him, he wasn't about to divulge his sources to me.

I am brought back into reality with a beep from my phone. Damn, it's Stefano, and with a pang of guilt I beat myself up for having completely forgotten about him. After the way I'd felt when he called this morning, I really am desperate to see him and try to work things out, but you'd be forgiven for thinking he was the furthest thing from my thoughts at the moment. Well, he has been for the past few hours, but it's not like I haven't just had yet another major distraction to throw me sideways. I got caught up in the Di Girolamo thing and the afternoon slipped by without me realising.

I call him straight back, apologising furiously and feeling like the meanest person in the world.

'Are you still in the *centro*?' I enquire. I wouldn't have been surprised if he'd just given up on me and gone. In my dreamlike state I'd ambled through the streets unseeingly and I realise I have almost made it back to the apartment, so we agree to meet in a bar off the Via De Martelli, not too far from either of our homes.

The Stefano I spy as I walk into the bar is a shadow of the man I know. He looks dreadful, like he hasn't slept for a week, and his body language as he waits for me in the booth is of a broken man, shoulders hunched, head drooping down. Oh God, have I really done that to him?

But other than ignore him for the past few days, which, yes, I know was mean, what am I guilty of exactly here? He doesn't like me getting mixed up in all the dream stuff, but I did the honourable thing and was honest with him right from the start and still he chose to get into a relationship with me, didn't he? He could have opted out early on and then we wouldn't be in this mess. And more importantly, I wouldn't have lost a friend – the aspect of all this which saddens me most. If our romance is to fail, which at the moment seems highly likely, I can't bear the thought that we won't go back to being like we were before.

'How are you Lydia?' he asks as I slide onto the bench opposite him, He leans over to kiss me – on both cheeks, not the lips. He hadn't seen me observing him from the door, but as he greets me he seems to visibly brighten; he pulls himself upright and his eyes light up just a little bit, so that the familiar twinkle in them almost returns.

'I'm so sorry, Stefano,' I say, referring more to my lateness and forgetfulness than to my recent behaviour. 'I was with Signore Di Girolamo for ages and time just seemed to run away with me.'

'Something important, no doubt,' he says, and the bright expression he is trying so hard to maintain is at odds with the underlying hint of sarcasm in his voice. 'I've been trying to get hold of you all week. Why didn't you return my calls?'

I don't know why I didn't. I suppose I was just too stubbornly upset by the fact that I seemed to have lost his support, and for no apparent reason. Until Sophia told me this morning about the conversation they'd all had with him, I hadn't realised that the dream thing was such a big issue to him. I make a lame excuse about needing some time to think. Actually I'm still pretty cross with him about what he said to me when we last met, but I decide against bringing that up right now; the atmosphere is brittle enough as it is.

I don't interrupt as he goes on to explain why he is so concerned about me, why he feels I am not really 'his' when I have the dreams, how he thinks it's dangerous for me to 'time travel' as he calls it. Gone is the empathy and the understanding for my situation, and in its place is what I can only describe as a kind of jealousy. Bizarrely, he says he almost feels as though I am cheating on him with Titian! I am so energized when I come round from the dreams, he says, that he feels I have more enthusiasm for the relationship that's playing itself out in my head than for the one we have together, or rather had, in the here and now.

I suppose I can see to a point where he is coming from, but at no time have I ever felt like the dreams are overtaking my life, overshadowing reality. I've always tried to treat them for what they are – dreams and nothing more – and I've always involved him in what's been happening with them. I know it's hard for him to fathom; there's no way he could ever fully understand the depth and reality of the emotions I experience in the dreams when he hasn't been through it himself. But any attempt at understanding has gone, and for reasons I fail to comprehend.

'I can't compete,' he says sadly. 'Until these dreams have stopped, or you put a stop to them, or whatever it takes, I don't think there's much point us carrying on, is there?' He speaks with his eyes downcast, and as he looks up to me a small tear escapes from the corner of each eye. I reach for his hands across the table, but he pulls them away, and goes to stand up, ready to leave. He can't bear for me to touch him.

'Don't go Stefano,' I plead. 'We still have so much to talk about.' Despite his views, I still feel I want to tell him about today's events, but then what's the point? It would only bang yet another nail into the coffin that was once our relationship.

He sits back down, I imagine with the expectation that I will launch into an apology, or admit that the dreams are a bad idea and I won't visit the gallery any more. But I can't do that. I didn't choose to have these dreams, they chose me, and I'd always thought he liked me – loved me – enough to understand that and to cope with it. Obviously not.

'What about our friends?' I say instead. 'I don't want this to spoil our little group of friends. You all mean so much to me.'

'Huh,' he snorts derisively. 'So I suppose you're going to throw that 'let's go back to being friends' line at me are you? Pretend nothing's happened and slip back into our cosy little ways, just like before? What do you think?' he concludes and storms out of the café, calling 'Goodbye Lydia,' from the doorway.

Looks like that's it then.

19

This book is so good. I have been drowning my sorrows this weekend, post break-up, not just with more than a teensy bit of alcohol, which always helps, but with Signore Di Girolamo's book. Honestly, I get so engrossed in the thing that I forget to eat, be sad, be sad a bit more, get dressed and visit the bathroom. I think Sophia and Leonora believe I am slipping into a slough of despondency, and that my failure to shower, feed myself and perform other basic human functions is a sign that I am in dangerous need of cheering up before some kind of text-book depression takes over. I really appreciate their efforts, but actually, even though I'm missing Stefano and I'm really sad we broke up, I'm fine. Really I am.

I couldn't stop them from insisting on dragging me out tonight, though. Girls only, of course. It would be too weird to include Lanzo and Dante and not Stefano, but it is way too soon for us to have to try to pretend to be friends in a big happy group again. No, they're not that unsubtle. But I do hope we can get back to that one day. It breaks my heart to think we might not, and I feel awful for Sophia and Leonora that they can't see the boys in the relaxed atmosphere we've all been used to. Still, I'll be out of their hair in a few more months. My time here is whizzing by so fast; I can't quite get my head round the fact that I won't be here forever, and that in the not too distant future I'll be required to return to the green and pleasant lands of home. It all seems so far away, another world, and sometimes it takes a conversation with someone back in the UK to jolt me into remembering that England is my home, and I am expected to go back there. Mum keeps nagging at me to pop home for a weekend, but at the moment I'm just not sure I could fit it in. Or cope with leaving Maria behind.

I've gone native, I suppose. I even dream in Italian now. And I don't just mean the Maria dreams; as far as I remember they've always been in Italian. But my normal night-time reveries are mostly in Italian now too, which to me is a real sign that I have well and truly mastered the language. I even talk to animals in Italian, for goodness sake. I found myself petting a friend's cat the other day and cooing at it in Italian, calling it a '*Bellissima gattina*'. I'm sure the aloof creature wouldn't have cared if I'd spoken to it in Swahili as long as I tweaked its ears and rubbed its tummy, but I had to pinch myself afterwards at how weird the whole thing was.

The girls have brought me to a party at the home of a friend of Alessandra's. They'd made earlier reassurances that connections are too far removed from our circle of friends to bump into anyone we know, and that there is no way Stefano will be there. (Leonora had a discreet word with Dante to ensure Stefano is being taken out to the opposite side of town tonight, just to be on the safe side.) I'm not really in the mood – to be honest I'd have quite liked to stay in and read some more of the book – but I appreciate their efforts and feel obliged to go along with the plan.

Actually it has been a good night so far. Amongst a few others I do know, Francesca is here – she is a close friend of Alessandra's so it would have been surprising if she wasn't invited. (She is the one I'd suspected of having a bit of a fling with Vincenzo at some point, although she's never admitted as much.) Like some cruel twist of fate, we are having a good old natter when who should appear but the man himself. Honestly, is there no one that man doesn't know, no party in the whole of Florence he doesn't get invited to? Alessandra's friend must know of Francesca's history, so I'm sure she wouldn't have invited him directly, so maybe it's just that he has tagged along with someone else.

I have to say I am a bit surprised to see him, but not half as much as Francesca, who splutters on her drink, blanches to the colour of a boiled potato and quickly makes an excuse to move on somewhere else. Poor girl. Still, it confirms my suspicions that she is the 'friend' she'd talked about.

'*Ciao Vincenzo*,' I say as he breezes into the room, full of the usual brash confidence and arrogance I've become used to handling with more like a large ladle, than a mere pinch, of salt. He's definitely a man who's comfortable in his own trousers; completely at ease in any situation, happy in the knowledge that wherever he goes, there will be someone who either knows him, recognises him, or has admired him or his work from afar and therefore relishes the opportunity to be introduced to him. How great it must be to hold oneself in such high regard.

'Are you on your own tonight?' I enquire. He made his grand entrance with a couple of male friends – no sign of his adolescent arm-candy. 'Where's the lovely Stéphanie this evening? Having a night in playing with her dolls, is she?' I ask, immediately regretting the vitriolic twang to my question.

'Actually, Stéphanie and I broke up. I'm much older than her, in case you hadn't noticed.' Really, I never would have guessed. 'We both wanted different things from the relationship, so, there you go, I am a free man again,' he replies. 'Anyway, where's the lovely Stefano, tonight? Not deserted you as well, has he?'

'Yep, we broke up too,' I say in a matter-of-fact tone, managing to sound as though I am on top of it all.

'We're a right pair, aren't we? Look at us, two of the most gorgeous people in the room,' and he says this without the slightest hint of self-mockery – he really means it – 'and both of us single. Alone at a party. Well, we're not alone any more, we've found each other.'

God, that man is so cheesy, but I have to say his breezy air does help to cheer me up. I detect few signs of broken-heartedness at the loss of the gorgeous Stéphanie as we slip easily into an animated conversation, but then finding something to talk about has never been a problem with us. Despite that, the thought is running through my head as we enjoy light-hearted banter: 'Make any attempt to crack on to me tonight and I will knee you in the balls.' I'm not in the mood for being chatted up, and in my situation, and with Leonora and Sophia here, it would be wholly inappropriate. But actually he is great company and we get along just fine, without any innuendo or sense that he is encroaching on forbidden territory.

I make eye contact with Sophia, who is talking to someone just across the room and she mouths at me: 'You OK?' clearly poised to pounce and rush to my rescue should I need it. But I am OK; actually I'm enjoying Vincenzo's company more than I have done in a while, and aside from his corny opener, it doesn't feel wrong at all. And don't misunderstand me; it's not some kind of lame rebound thing, a need to feel attractive to the opposite sex after a break-up, or anything like that. We're just chatting – and enjoying it – and pleasantly passing the time at this party until I'm allowed to go home.

Vincenzo is interested to hear about my latest instalments in the Maria saga, and I also tell him about my conversation with Signore Di Girolamo. I don't mention the fact that I suspect him of having dreams too. No, I need to have that confirmed by the man himself before I go around casting such wild aspersions. I would hate to be the one to ruin his reputation as a respected historian, for the sake of justifying my own situation. Believing Di Girolamo has had a similar experience to me gives mine some credence, but if he doesn't want to tell me about it, then I have no right to voice my suspicions to others.

At breakfast the following morning, I expect to be on the receiving end of a deluge of warnings from Sophia and Leonora about Vincenzo. He and I had chatted for the rest of the evening, and we had a thoroughly pleasant time to boot. I can imagine to the casual onlooker we'd seemed pretty cosy, but it hadn't been necessary for my knee to make contact with his groin after all. Actually he'd saved me from the boredom of a party at which I didn't know too many people, at a time when I lacked the inclination to make an effort to get to know any more.

But surprisingly the girls remain mute on the topic, I imagine assuming that, so close to breaking up with Stefano, I wouldn't dream of contemplating hooking up with someone else. And they're right, I'm not. Vincenzo was extremely good company, I have to admit, but he is my tutor.

Today I have cleared the decks for a spot of work, and then some reading – hopefully finishing Di Girolamo's book. After last night, I think I've managed to convince the girls that I'm not bordering on a breakdown, and it's perfectly safe for them to leave me in the apartment on my own, without the presence of a responsible adult. They are off to some lunch or other in town, and I am glad for the time to myself.

Coursework done, I relocate to my bed, prop myself up with a few squidgy bolsters, and settle down for an afternoon of reading. I'm now beyond the stage in the book when Di Girolamo gives Maria her name. Still no surname for her, though, which is frustrating as I've never dreamt it either. But the revelation that really hits me full-square in the face today is this: Maria had a daughter with Titian.

I feel my head swim as I make the connection between my pregnant Maria and the woman in this book who bore Titian a child. So I am not mad or imagining things! Just as Di Girolamo admitting that he dreamt all this would add substance to my own dreams, mine also serve the purpose of backing up his story. He HAS to confess to me that he dreamt this; I need to see him again and put him on the spot, force him admit to it. This is so exciting! My dreams are true, I'm not insane, not imagining things, and it's all here in this book!

The child was called Emilia, and she was born some time around 1541. Her birth takes place quite near to the end of the book, and I am dreading it finishing, as I just want the story to carry on forever. Di Girolamo mentions very little about the child – but then maybe his dreams ended at this point for some reason, and with it, his writing. That must be the case, it has to be. I've never actually heard any dates mentioned in my dreams – there is no reason why I should – but the impression I get is of mid-sixteenth century, so the period would appear to be right for Emilia being the same child that Maria was carrying when she sat for Venus of Urbino.

Di Girolamo's Maria would seem to be about the same age as my Maria. I've never dreamt that she had any children prior to this, so all the connections ring very true. So when 'I' sat for the painting in my last dream, 'I' was carrying Emilia. A shiver runs up my spine as the sudden reality of this hits home. This is no longer just a series of dreams, but a collection of real snippets of sixteenth century life, containing real personalities. Although Maria has been more than real to me since the very first time I dreamt about her, today I feel that reality confirmed once and for all.

As the book ends shortly after Emilia's birth, the trail effectively goes cold. I don't know what happens to Emilia – or to Maria, come to that – and I won't do unless that's something that I'll later experience in one of my dreams. Presumably Di Girolamo doesn't know either, or he'd have written about it.

I wonder what happened to Emilia; where did she end up, what kind of life did she lead? I can't help feeling a kind of personal attachment to her, and hope for her sake that she was born healthy, flourished in the love of both of her parents, lived a long and happy life and died at a ripe old age surrounded by a throng of grandchildren…

20

'*È per te,*' Sophia says, brandishing the phone as I lounge on the sofa on Monday morning. '*È Signore Di Girolamo.*'

He sounds a bit frantic and preoccupied with something.

'Can you meet me for coffee this morning?' he asks hurriedly. 'I have something I need to tell you.'

Is this it? Is the big confession coming? *Actually, Lydia, I had dreams just like yours. I understand exactly what you're going through…* I sincerely hope so, and this hope makes the excitement bubble up inside me. After finishing his book yesterday I've been left hanging; I need to know more. Not just how he knows what he does, but what happens next. Did he have any more dreams after finishing the book? Does he know what happened to Emilia? I have been unable to stop thinking about that child; there is so much more I want to know about her.

Today I have to go back to the gallery; I need another dream of my own. The trouble is, they don't always follow in sequential order. I could just as easily dream about Maria's early days with Titian than the next instalment in her story; something which might help to build up an overall image of how she lived and loved, but doesn't progress the storyline at all. It's all very well me trying to 'pre-order' a dream about a specific event, but that doesn't tend to be the way it works.

We meet in a little bar just round the back of the Duomo. Di Girolamo is there before me, seemingly agitated and nervously fiddling with the catch on his bag as he waits for me, a cooling espresso congealing on the table in front of him. A gentleman of his generation, he stands to greet me and waits until I have sat down before taking his own seat again. He clicks his fingers and gives the barista a nod; she scuttles away to fetch two more coffees.

'I needed to see you. To explain,' he begins, a nervous cough playing at the back of his throat.

'What is it, are you OK?' I ask, wanting him to get straight to the point and tell me everything.

'I'm so sorry, but I wasn't entirely honest with you the other day. Will you please forgive me for pushing you out the door like that; it was very rude of me.' He takes a short pause and a deep breath for courage, before continuing:

'You see, I've never told anyone about my dreams before, and when you told me about yours, I couldn't quite believe it could be possible for someone else to have them too. I was overwhelmed with the discovery, I suppose. In shock, you could say.'

YES!! Finally. What a relief to hear him admit it. I was right.

'It's OK, Signore Di Girolamo,' I begin, 'you don't have to apologise to me. You know I'd suspected all along that you'd had dreams too, and I'm so glad you feel you can tell me about it now.' Here he looks relieved, the nervous tension caused by the build-up to telling me starting to lift a little from his shoulders. 'I just couldn't see how you could know so much – after all, none of this stuff is in the history books, is it?'

'You and I, we are very fortunate creatures,' he goes on, more calmly now. 'We have been given a rare insight into what happened in these people's lives. But you can understand now why I didn't make the book widely available, can't you? It would have caused a scandal. I'd have been forced to confess I had dreamt it all, and, well, how many respected historians do you know of who write their books based on dreams? It could have finished me. They'd have put it down as a work of fiction and that would be my reputation in tatters. I'm a historian, not a historical novelist.'

He continues: 'Finding you has been like a dream come true, if you'll pardon the pun. All these years I've been thinking that maybe I just made this all up, that the dreams were my fantasies, but now I know you have them too, and bizarrely with such a similar subject matter, it corroborates our stories, doesn't it? Quite marvellous,' he says with a huge smile, clapping his hands together. 'Whoever would have thought it!'

Di Girolamo (I still struggle to call him Antonio, despite his insistence) goes on to tell me about his dreams. Apparently they started when he was in his thirties, at which time he was a visiting tutor on a year's fellowship at the Sorbonne in Paris. He'd not long moved there and had barely settled in to his new job when he found himself being drawn daily to Titian's *Concert Champêtre,* 'The Pastoral Concert' painting in the

Louvre. Pretty soon he was visiting it regularly, just like I do with Venus, desperately hoping for another instalment in the story which seemed to be unfolding in his head. He, of course, took on the persona of Titian in his dreams; who else could he possibly have been?

He became totally obsessed with it, he says, so much so that it started to detract from his work in the university. So after his academic obligations there were over, he decided to stay on for a further year, on an unpaid career break, putting together all the notes he'd taken at the time to make into a book.

'Despite my initial confidence in it all, when it came down to publishing I lost my nerve,' he admits. 'In the end I paid a publisher quite a substantial amount of money to produce just a couple of copies for me, one to keep and a spare one just in case the first one became lost or damaged. Those were all my precious remembrances in there; I pretty much kept them under lock and key for fear of losing them, and with them losing the valuable insight I'd had into the sixteenth century.'

'So why did you publish the second edition again recently, and why not make it more widely available? Couldn't you have changed your name or something, used a *nom de plume*?' I ask.

'I don't know what compelled me to do it. I suppose part of me wanted some recognition for what I knew, yet the other part was still holding back for fear of exposure as a fraud. Historical novels seem to be all the rage these days, don't they, but I didn't want my book being classified as one of those, even if it sold well and made me lots of money. I suppose it's just a point of principle. So once again, I published – a few more copies this time

– but I still didn't distribute it widely. Only to a few select people who I thought might enjoy it, or even just like to have one on their bookshelves, unread, like Vincenzo.'

'You're no fraud,' I say. 'Your story backs up mine and vice versa. But I don't know how we'd ever convince the art world that all this stuff really happened, do you? And now with media coverage the way it is, I do understand your motives for keeping quiet; they'd have ripped you to shreds, wouldn't they?'

He doesn't answer my question, but instead goes on: 'Lydia, I have to tell you this. That painting, the *Champêtre*, they say – these so-called experts – that it was painted circa 1510. But I know for a fact that Titian didn't meet Maria until some time around 1537…'

'…the Pope's visit to Bologna! You dreamt about that too. That's a well-documented historical event,' I interrupt.

'Yes, exactly. But my point is, the girl on the left-hand side of the painting is Maria. Just look at this.' He pulls a copy of the book from his bag and opens it at a marked page, tapping the picture with his index finger. 'Could there be any doubt in your mind that it's her?' he asks. 'I, or rather Titian, painted her in one of my dreams.

'You and I have both seen her face so many times in our heads to know well enough that Maria is that girl pouring water from the ewer,' he goes on. 'Not only is she Maria, but if you look very closely at this man here, playing the lute, he bears a striking resemblance to Titian as a much younger man. He was quite a lot older than that when he met her, of course. You can imagine that's how he'd want to look, for her sake, how he'd want her to see him, I suppose. She was young and beautiful and he was an old man in his late forties, after all. This painting proves he was conscious of that fact. I always felt in the dreams that he believed himself so lucky to have a woman as beautiful as Maria as his lover.'

'You're right,' I reply, awestruck by his revelation. 'I've never noticed that before. It's definitely Maria, though. I haven't dreamt about that particular painting, but he's forever painting me – or rather her – in my dreams. There are just so many paintings where she was the model in one form or another. But, you know, in the dreams, I'm oblivious to Tito's age; it doesn't matter that he's older than me – her. And you're right, she worships the ground he walks on, has done right from the start. There's such a strong feeling of love in the dreams. Did you feel that too?'

'I did,' he replies. 'I think that's what made the dreams so addictive for me really. It was at a time in my life when I was alone, and that bothered me, and so I lived my love-life vicariously, through Titian, I suppose. To all intents and purposes, Maria was my lover, even if that sounds a bit weird.'

'No, not at all,' I say, so glad to have someone to share these deepest emotions with. 'Well, my boyfriend ended our relationship because he couldn't cope with the so-called competition from my sixteenth century lover. So there you go; we're not so different.'

Di Girolamo offers his condolences with great empathy. As we discuss each aspect of our experiences, we are both amazed at the similarities emerging. We've each been given our very own exposés of Titian's and Maria's private lives, from two different angles but with a corroborating storyline. And the way it has happened is very similar too; both of us have or had the very same urge to fall asleep within minutes of setting eyes on our respective paintings, both of us feel or felt a pull, as though some invisible force was trying to reel us in.

'So why did your dreams stop?' I ask. 'I'm desperate to know what happened to Emilia – why don't you talk about her more?'

'The dreams simply stopped once she was born. I don't know why. I tried going back and I'd sit there and wait and nothing would happen. For whatever reason, Titian only wanted me to know so much, and I have to be grateful that he has shared that much with me, I suppose.'

'I can't ever imagine my dreams stopping,' I say, 'but I suppose they will one day. When I leave here, if not before. God, imagine if I have to go back to England and I'm still getting them. It's going to be really hard to leave if I don't feel like the story is complete.'

Di Girolamo can't comment on that, of course. Nor can he answer any of my questions about Emilia and her destiny. She is born in his book and that is that. End of story. And we both know there's nothing about her in the history books. Yet Titian lived such a very long time after Emilia's birth, and went on to paint so many more great works of art. I'd like to think that Maria – and Emilia – had been beside him through all that, but at the moment I don't know any more than what I've dreamt.

'Why do you think we've been chosen?' I ask the all-pervading question. 'What makes us so special – receptors for these dreams?'

'Now, I haven't yet revealed to you my theory on that,' he says, conspiratorially. 'After the dreams started, I too was looking for a reason for being 'chosen', as you call it. So I started to look into my own family history, not really knowing what I was looking for, but with an inkling of suspicion that there might be something tying us. And I found a link. I'm related to Titian. I managed to trace my roots, with great difficulty, I can tell you, back to the mid-sixteenth century, and it turns out that I am a descendant of Titian. Via his wife, Lavinia, so I am no relation to Maria or Emilia.'

I sit back in my seat in shock. Wow, that really is something of a revelation. Titian is one of Di Girolamo's ancestors! The implications of this are overwhelming. Could this mean that I too might somehow be related to one of these characters from my dreams as well?

I must have turned a deathly shade of pale as Di Girolamo asks:

'Lydia, are you OK? You've gone very white. Was that a shock to you?' He summons the barista again, who this time fetches me a glass of water.

'So, do you really think I might be related to them, too?' I ask.

'It has to be a strong possibility, but really there's only one way to find out,' he replies. 'And if you do decide to go down that route, then you have a lot of work ahead of you. It would, of course, be my pleasure to assist you, to the best of my abilities.'

Oh my God, this really is a lot to take in. I could have some kind of family tie to these people, and that is why they've chosen me – and chose Di Girolamo too – to tell their stories. But why have they chosen me again now, when he's already been through it, already lived out the story once before in his head. All I can think of is that there must be more, some aspect of the story they still need to tell, something Maria wants to reveal to me that didn't make it into Di Girolamo's book. Maybe even something Maria knew but Titian didn't. Baffling.

Even if I'm shocked at this discovery, it's reassuring from talking to Di Girolamo to discover that I'm not a freak, that there's a reason for these dreams and I'm not alone in my experiences. But even so, to be told there might be a verifiable reason why I've been 'chosen' is slightly unnerving.

I've never really been into family trees and all that stuff. I love the history side to my course, and history as a subject for its own sake, but I've never felt the urge to go digging into my own family's past; my present-day relatives have always been quite enough for me. Until now. How could this regular little suburban family from Sussex be related to one of the greatest artists the world has ever known? It's pretty mind-blowing stuff. It's scary, but it does make me feel quite special, reinforces that feeling of having been 'chosen'.

And what if I'd never come to Florence? If the idea of us being related turns out to be true, would Maria have had to wait until another distant relative came strolling by one day to sit in front of one of her portraits? Or was it always written in my destiny that I would be the one to come, that she would be able to reveal her story to me? I'm struck momentarily by that same sensation I get when I lie under the stars, gazing upwards and wondering at infinity, trying to grasp how small and insignificant we all are down here. Maybe 'The Fates' have more to answer for than we think, and this moment has been mapped out for me from the day I was born.

'So how did you do it? How did you trace your family history all the way back to Titian?' I ask.

'Well, that year, after I'd published the book and hidden it quickly away again, I started trawling the libraries and archives, looking for clues, anything I could, really. And it wasn't as easy in those days; we didn't have the internet to help us, like you will do now, if you decide to start investigating. All those wonderful ancestry websites that are out there, there was nothing like that. It was the old-fashioned way, searching for actual, physical documents, or looking at ream after ream of stuff on microfiche. It ruined my eyesight, I can tell you. I didn't need glasses until I started my research.

'I spent months tracing back through generation after generation. Fortunately, in the old days in the little villages like the one I grew up in, people didn't move around like they do now. Families grew up and stayed together, sons and daughters setting up homes in the same town or village as their parents and grandparents. And being so deeply religious, a lot of them kept family bibles, and in those they would document all the births and deaths as they happened, creating their own family tree as the years passed. Some of these bibles are a couple of hundred years old. Both my sets of grandparents had bibles dating back to the early eighteenth century, so that was a couple of centuries covered off for me almost instantly. I was really fortunate. And from there backwards it was hard slog, I'm afraid. A case of the long trawl round archives, finding out little snippets when and where I could.

'The trouble with trying to trace your family tree with a particular person in mind (and I suspected at the start that Titian was the one to whom I'd be related) is that you don't know which branch to follow, which side of the family will lead you to them. What with marriages, or trying to follow down the female line of a family, names change frequently, so you just have to pursue every branch as fully as you can, hoping that somewhere along the line you'll hit on something hopeful. And that's a huge amount of people. It took ages, but it was all very exciting to do, I have to say.

'Fortunately I hit upon the Vecellio surname before I'd investigated too many branches of the family. It made its first appearance some time back in the late seventeenth century, so of course from then on I knew which branch I had to follow. And thereafter it was comparatively plain sailing, really. Which was just as well, as finding records which are that old isn't easy. Records aren't complete either, as you'd like to hope they are now. A lot more people would slip through the net of authority, especially those of lowly or illegitimate birth. And few people were literate, either. That proves a bit of a barrier sometimes.'

'It looks like I have a big job on my hands, then,' I say, feeling a bit overwhelmed but also quite excited now at the prospect that I might be related to one of these characters. 'Just supposing I'm related to Maria, I don't even know her surname! It's a very long way back from the Irvine family of twenty-first century Britain to the Vecellio's and co of Renaissance Italy. There's a long way to go until I – hopefully – bump into one of them, so with any luck her name will have come to me in a dream by then.'

'Her name is Maria Rossi,' he says simply. 'I don't mention it in the book, and I don't know why really. It just never became relevant, but it is definitely Rossi. You must excuse me now, my dear. I have a lecture to get to. But before I do, this is for you.'

He reaches into his briefcase and pulls out a mint condition copy of 'A Life In Art'. 'Your own copy,' he says. 'Look inside.'

I open the cover gently, with reverent respect for a brand new (and quite rare) book, not wanting to break the spine, and flick through the first couple of blank pages to the title page.

'To Lydia, a fellow dreamer. Wishing you the very best of luck with your research. All good wishes, Antonio Di Girolamo.'

'Thank you, Antonio,' I say.

21

I leave the café and cross the Piazza del Duomo, heading down one of the backstreets behind the main shopping area, not wanting to get caught up in the ever-present tourist mêlée, but needing to get to the gallery as quickly as I can. Florence seems suddenly changed to me; sunnier, brighter, more picturesque. But then it dawns on me that this isn't just a frame of mind brought on by my meeting with Antonio – and I feel we know each other well enough now for me to call him that – but spring really has sprung in the past week, only I've been too wrapped up in the Stefano and Di Girolamo sagas to notice.

Like the blossoming trees, my sense of self-esteem is bursting forth, and with it the value of these dreams, now that my story has been corroborated and I have a 'fellow dreamer'. After talking to Antonio, I no longer feel I'm some kind of circus freak, and most importantly, I'm no longer alone in my experience. I feel normal again, I have an ally in my dreams, a companion for my research and, most importantly for my sanity, someone I can turn to who will fully appreciate what I'm going through.

I'm moseying through the city on a mission, head held high and nose up in the clouds when I turn a corner and almost bump into a man clutching a take-away coffee. How un-Italian, carrying your espresso around in a Styrofoam cup, I think, then do a double-take as I look up and realise that the man is Stefano. Just as well we don't quite collide; I don't much fancy having to wear his coffee down my shirt for the rest of the day. But at this particular moment, that's the least of my worries.

'Stefano, hi, how are you?' I ask.

'Good thanks. You?' he replies rather curtly, his expression blank and unreadable.

This is the first time we have come face to face since our break-up. I suppose it had to happen some time, and it's probably a blessing that, as it's unprompted, it is also unscripted and therefore neither of us has had to worry about rehearsing embarrassing openers to hide our discomfort. This is as natural as it's going to get between us for the time being, and now that we have met, the situation has lost some of its scariness.

He leans across to kiss me on both cheeks, smelling of himself, gorgeous as ever, and a pang of something shoots through me, I'm just not really quite sure what. He looks well and I comment on this, my voice managing to sound normal and not betray me as either a heartless man-eater who hasn't been affected by the break-up, or a bitter jilted lover – neither of which I am, of course. Just keep it all on an even keel and you'll get through this, I think to myself.

A petite, dark-haired woman emerges from the coffee shop and links arms with him, as though staking her territory in the face of competition. Don't worry, darling,

I've been there. You can have him now. An unexpectedly bitchy thought, I know, and I am surprised at the shot of jealousy which spears me like a real physical pain in my chest. How dare he move on so quickly; I thought he was heartbroken after we split, but clearly he has found a diversion in Adriana, by which name she is introduced.

'Adriana, hi, nice to meet you,' I manage to utter without any of the rancour which only moments earlier had hit me full frontal.

I don't want to be with Stefano, and I know that. Our relationship was lovely while it lasted, but it was way too complicated. Stefano couldn't get to grips at all with the way I have chosen to live my life, and that makes us completely incompatible. But seeing his gorgeous, smiling face glancing downwards as a replacement pretty face glances upwards, so adoringly, really hurts. That was me only a few weeks ago. How nice for him that he had a reserve girlfriend waiting in the wings, to call on in his hour of need, and that he can move on so quickly.

I make my excuses about needing to be somewhere and leave them to one another and their coffees.

Today I am to be presented to the Doge! What an honour for a girl such as I, whose background could not be humbler! I cannot quite believe it.

The reception is a meeting of the great minds in the worlds of art, literature and music. Tito is well respected and well known within the Palazzo Ducale; he has of course been commissioned several times to paint for Monsignor el Doxe, the Doge, and the great man himself has many paintings in his palace which bear my likeness. Of course, like the rest of Venetian society, he does not know that I am Tito's lover, merely that I am the beautiful woman who has become his muse, the inspiration for some of his greatest works. For the Doge is a connoisseur of fine things and likes to surround himself with the best this great city has to offer.

Tito and I are so rarely seen together in public; even on this occasion we cannot appear overly familiar with one another, and no one must guess our secret. Tito's wife is not expected to attend, of which I am glad. I have not yet had the honour of meeting her in the flesh – and indeed have no desire to. But there will be a multitude of people who know him well, and whose respect he commands in the art world. As one of the more famous painters in Venice, he cannot afford to have scandal brought upon his head. If they choose to look at us together and interpret more than simply artist and muse, then they have the free will to do so. But at no time must we offer up any indication that we are lovers; this must stay as mere speculation on their part. This is a spiritual place, and Tito is a married man, after all. There are certain values which need to be respected in public, even if they may be flouted in private…

Tito spends more and more time at my casa *these days. Much as he adores his children, they are now growing and becoming less needful of him, and his relationship with his wife does not fulfil him in the same way that ours does, so he informs me. It is not just our love-making, which is always immensely satisfying to both body and soul, but simply the time we spend together just talking, about everything and nothing, as though no subject were beyond our reach. He discusses art with me as though I were an expert, and my own ignorance and lack of education aside, I am coming to understand something of this strange little world he inhabits.*

We feel as though we belong together and that my rightful place is by his side. It is through no fault of our own that destiny was a little tardy in bringing us to one another, even if he should by then be espoused to another woman and have fathered children with her. In that he was simply doing what society expected of him; marrying well, into his own class and continuing the family line. Now there is a child growing in my belly, it is confirmation for both of us that our relationship, though unrecognised in the eyes of the Church, is in fact blessed by Our Lord.

Fortunately our child is still small within me, and well disguised by the folds of my gown, so it is with a great sense of righteousness and a feeling that I have nothing of which I should be ashamed that we glide together through the magnificent Porta della Carta, the grand entrance to the Palazzo Ducale, in anticipation of the great event before us. We are greeted by a guard, immaculately attired in colours so vibrant that it takes me back to that day in Bologna, when I observed those magnificent soldiers in the procession of Il Papa, from a small window at Rosetta's.

Oh, but how I have moved up in the world since then! Today I am to be introduced to some of the grandest people in society; in the past I had met such people, but my place was to serve them with my body. Today it is my beauty, grace and demeanour they will admire, I am sure, not what feelings of lust I can inspire in them. Today I come before them as a lady, not as a whore.

The guard leads us up a vast flight of stairs and through a corridor to the most magnificent room I have ever set eyes upon. Tito whispers in my ear to inform me that this is the Sala del Maggior Consiglio. I would not like to speculate how many important decisions of City and Republic have been made here, when the Great Council meets to discuss its business. Tito has been here on many an occasion, to participate in such meetings.

Today the room is not set out for a council, however. With great awe I see before me a huge throne, fit for a king. A long line of finely-dressed citizens forms a slow and stately procession from that throne to the door by which we have just entered. We join the back of this body as each waits patiently for their own moment of presentation to the Doge, before moving to the end of the room where the less formal aspect of the reception is taking place. Here, a number of servants, also dressed in bright colours, flit amongst the crowd like exotic birds, serving titbits and small morsels of delicacies, whilst others follow behind more sedately with wine, which flows from their ewers into elaborate golden goblets.

Tito turns to me to ensure that all is well, and sees my face lighted up in wonderment, as I gaze from painted ceiling to gold-embossed chair, from vast window with breathtaking views of the lagoon to the fine robes of the crowd before me. It is too much for a simple girl such as me to absorb, despite the relative opulence in which I now reside.

I too am attired in the finest robes money can buy, and therefore feel I can match these grand people, at least in appearance. My gown is of the most exquisite silk and lace, my hair dressed in the most fashionable style of the day, with small braids around my face, interlaced with delicate pearls and other precious stones. My darling Tito is so generous in providing them for me, and my dear Clara is indeed a skilled artist to create this masterpiece of a coiffure that I sport this day.

Slowly we make our way along the line, exchanging small snippets of conversation with the persons around us. Already I have been introduced to so many people of superior class, some of whom have such important roles to fulfil within this great city. I feel very honoured to be here, as finally we near the great throne.

I am not surprised to see that His Serenity, Pietro Lando, is dressed in the finest garments of all, as befs his status as our esteemed leader. He wears luxurious golden robes and slippers, but his headdress, the corno ducale, is the most striking aspect of all: a strange horn-like bonnet made of gemmed brocade, beneath which I can see peeping out a white linen cap. It is a camauro, Tito *informs me, not unlike the ones that the Sisters at the convent are required to wear to cover their hair. Its modesty contrasts vividly with the opulence of the rest of his outfit, and indeed the surroundings.*

As we draw nearer to him he notices me studying him carefully, and to my surprise, holds my gaze for a few seconds. Is it that he recognises my face from the images covering his walls? And then it is our turn:

'Serenissimo Principe, may I present to you Signore Tiziano Vecellio and Signorina Maria Rossi,' the guard announces. I sweep into a deep curtsey before him, only looking up at the great man once I have paid my compliments and he has requested that I rise.

I rub my eyes as I wake up in room twenty-eight, hastily gathering my things together and heading for the door. I never feel like I want to hang around after a dream; I need to get outside and back to reality, clear my head with some fresh air.

So Antonio was right; the woman I need to search for in my family history is Maria Rossi.

But where do I start?

22

Vincenzo is not in his room when I arrive. But then he wasn't expecting me; I have called by unannounced. Maybe he's taking a lecture, or off doing whatever else it is he does in the name of being a tutor – which probably involves drinking coffee and chatting up pretty students somewhere, knowing him.

I decide to wait and plonk myself in one of his armchairs. I pull out my 'Dreams' notebook; I might as well put the time to good use and update my journal for the dream I've just had. So, Maria is genuinely Maria Rossi, it would seem, although why I should ever have doubted Antonio is anyone's guess. I suppose it just feels good to have it confirmed, via my own dreams, before I launch off into what could be an absolute bottomless pit of a family tree hunt. Let's face it, I have no idea whatsoever in which direction I should be heading.

What am I doing here? Well, for some reason I felt a strong urge to tell Vincenzo all about my conversation with Di Girolamo. Antonio did say it would be fine for me to share what he'd told me with my tutor, provided I stipulate that this gem of information about his dreams isn't then to be beamed across the art world. He doesn't want to see it up in lights on any of the social network sites, or have anyone from the press contact him about it. Actually I'm amazed he trusts Vincenzo – I know there's always been an element of academic rivalry between them, and they are like chalk and cheese – but at the end of the day I suppose they're both professionals and each strongly respects the other's abilities, artistic and personality differences aside. I'm glad he did give me permission, as I think being able to confide in Vincenzo will make things a lot easier for me.

That last dream – the scene at the Doge's palace – was amazing. I really must plan in a trip to Venice one day soon – before I leave Italy, otherwise it could be years before I can afford to come back. I'd love to visit some of the places I've been to as Maria, see them as they are now but with the advantage of insight into how they were then and what took place within the walls of some of the most historically significant buildings in Venice. Structurally, they're probably not intrinsically different, I imagine, other than that they are now overflowing with tourists instead of lords, ladies and gentlemen – well, maybe still a few of those, or the modern-day moneyed equivalent thereof, staying at the pricier hotels.

I pull my phone out of my pocket and run a quick internet search on Pietro Lando. And there he is – there's even a picture of him – Doge from 1538 to 1545, it says, so that would fit in just right with the period. I have to say he doesn't look half as formidable on my nine-centimetre touch screen as he looked in the flesh.

And that look he gave me, or rather Maria. A look of recognition, I think. After all, his walls were heaving with images of her in one form or another. Maybe – just maybe – despite all those strong Catholic ethics kicking around, he was just giving Maria 'the eye'. Looking a pretty girl up and down. With looks like hers, she must have stood out like a rose in a bed of weeds amongst all those stuffy artists and academics. I'll bet he thoroughly enjoyed being introduced to her. What a shame the dream came to such an abrupt end; I would love to have eavesdropped on the conversations which took place after the formal introductions were over. Did it turn into 'another wild party' at the Doge's palace? Somehow I doubt it, but it seems they got up to a lot more in those days than we give them credit for. I know for a fact that behind those chaste façades they well and truly lived the high life, but none of that detail reaches the history books, does it?

'Ciao, Lydia, è un vero piacere vederti! Cosa fai qui? Isn't our tutorial on Thursday, or is this just a social call?'

I'm lost in contemplation and almost jump out of my skin as Vincenzo bursts through the door, quite within his rights to be there, of course, and quite obviously surprised to find me in residence. Fortunately he's on his own and, after the initial shock of seeing me, is very welcoming.

'*Ciao, Vincenzo*,' I reply, 'I just wanted to pop by for a chat, that's all. I hope that's OK and you're not too busy? I have something really important to tell you.'

'Well, I suspected something similar,' Vincenzo says, once I've finished filling him in on Antonio's news. 'I know I've always been slightly sceptical about you and your dreams, but I'd like to think I've always been supportive, haven't I?' He waits for me to nod in confirmation before going on, so I do. 'Your dreams came as a bit of a shock to me, but I never doubted your sanity, or that you were telling the truth.'

How magnanimous of you, Vincenzo, I think to myself. What about that disastrous meal out we had together in the early days, when you treated me like some kind of lunatic and couldn't get away from me quickly enough? Have you forgotten that, now you know me a little better? But I don't voice any of these thoughts; I just sit passively and give him the chance to explain how he feels.

'So, hearing that he's had a similar experience to you just backs up what you've been going through, doesn't it? It's quite amazing that there are two of you out there. How long ago did he have his dreams? His book is quite recent, isn't it?'

I explain the background to him a little more, and Vincenzo is hooked. I think any final traces of doubt are erased from his mind by the fact that it's all centred on a different painting, in a different city, albeit with the same underlying story and some very similar experiences to my own. He is also intrigued to hear that the copy of the book he has is the second edition (he's probably never even looked inside the cover to discover this) and even more so to hear how Antonio lost his nerve with it at the final hurdle, failing to make it available to the wider public yet again.

'I will have to read it now,' he says. 'No excuses! And you've read it all presumably, and found a lot of similarities between his story and yours?'

'Yes, loads. In fact, there's nothing in there at all that I'd disagree with. It's more a case of him having seen things, or experienced certain events, from a different perspective, and very often it's something completely new, that I haven't dreamt about, but which fits in perfectly with my own story. But the frustrating thing is, Antonio's book stops too soon. When Emilia – his illegitimate daughter – is born, the story stops dead. He can't explain why; he just didn't have any more dreams after that. I really hope my dreams go beyond that point; I need to find out what happened to her. It might be the only clue I get as to where I fit into all this, and if I might be related to one of them as well.'

Vincenzo perks up at this. He sits upright in his seat, his hand goes out instinctively and lands on my knee, and there is an expression of deep surprise on his face. I know the hand-on-knee business is just his tactile Italianate way of doing things, and I've got used to it. Usually I brush it off, but this time I don't; it feels quite comforting, so I leave it there. His eyes meet mine – I imagine to check for a reaction when I don't flick him away – and, pushing his luck a little further, he gives my knee a gentle squeeze. Again, I don't react.

'Yes, it turns out Antonio is a direct descendent of Titian. Through Titian's marriage to Lavinia, his second wife, so he's not related to Maria or Emilia. He suspects that was the reason he was chosen, and he reckons it might be the same for me. Just think, we could both be related to one of the greatest artists of the Renaissance!'

'Wow! So what are you going to do? Start researching your family tree? It's pretty exciting, isn't it? It's all quite amazing, this idea of you being 'chosen', and being a direct descendant and all that! What a lot to take in!'

I'm pleased that Vincenzo is so enthused about it all this time round. He seems to have lost the air of concern and scepticism that he had before.

'I'll help you, you know,' he offers, excitedly. I am deeply grateful – and relieved – as this conversation could have gone either way. It feels good to have him on my side, and I say simply:

'Thank you, Vincenzo.'

'So, how about dinner?' he asks, cheekily striking whilst the proverbial iron is hot. He'd retracted his hand from my knee in order to give vent to his excitement just now, but with this proposal it comes creeping back again. But as he says this I become conscious of his touch and move away slightly so he can no longer reach my leg.

'Isn't it nearly that time of day – look?' He turns the face of his watch towards me to answer his own question. If not yet quite time to eat, it's certainly *aperitivo* time, and after all the excitement of today, I could really do with a drink. Then it hits me that I've spent the whole day caught up in Maria et al, and what with meeting Antonio, going to the gallery and coming here, I've managed to completely shirk my academic commitments. And missed two lectures, I realise. Oh well, it's a bit late now, and it's not like I haven't had an enlightening day, even if it wasn't entirely scholarly. Highly educational, nonetheless.

'Dinner would be lovely.' I accept politely, surprising myself to find that I really would like to go out with him, despite the lingering memories of last time, and my resolve never to get involved with him. 'But let's go and grab a drink somewhere first, shall we? It's a bit early, and I'm gasping. No fancy restaurants, tonight, mind you,' I tease. 'You treated me last time so this is my shout, but you know what a student budget stretches to, or rather doesn't.'

'Don't be silly. I would really like to treat you, Lydia, so please let me. After all, it's not every day you get such exciting news. I will take you somewhere nice and you can tell me all about how you plan to dig up your ancestors. We will formulate a plan together.'

Forty-five minutes later, after a quick prosecco in a nearby bar, which we both needed and which barely touched the sides, we are in a taxi on the outskirts of Florence, joining the Siena *superstrada* at Certosa and heading out to the countryside. We are going 'somewhere special' – the only clue Vincenzo would give me, and that was imparted with a secretive grin and sparklingly mysterious eyes. Uh-oh, what am I letting myself in for here? If we've journeyed off to the middle of nowhere together, I can't exactly beat a hasty retreat if things get too much for me. There's no way I can afford the taxi fare back from the back-of-beyond.

I relax a little though and banish such thoughts when I catch sight of the view. Since arriving in Florence, I haven't ventured out of the city at all, and even though it's a beautiful place to live, with more than its share of lush, green areas to stroll around in and escape the inner-city hustle and bustle, to see some vast open spaces out of the window of the taxi is nothing short of uplifting. Urban dwelling can be claustrophobic, and it's not until you remove yourself from it for a while that you realise just how much so. I love the countryside, and although I was brought up in suburbia, the rolling fields of Sussex were never far away. As a family we would escape whenever we could, for a walk or a climb on the Downs.

The day is warm, and despite the efficient air conditioning (this isn't one of your run-of-the-mill beaten-up Florence mini-cabs) I put the window down to allow the breeze from outside to blow in my face. It might only still be motorway air, but it's the widest, most open space I've been to for months, and I close my eyes as the wind whips my hair back from my face.

Once we pick up speed and my hair starts to fly in too many directions all at once, I close the window again and turn to look at Vincenzo. He has clearly been unabashedly watching me enjoy the breeze, and now that my eyes are open again, it's a second or two before he snaps out of his trance and reaches for my hand, which is resting beside me on the seat.

I look down at his large, tanned hand covering my more delicate, paler one and say: 'I hope this isn't some plan to whisk me away and seduce me, Vincenzo.' I whisper this in English as I don't want to incite the non English-speaking driver to start eavesdropping on our conversation. I think, and hope, it comes across in a light-hearted way, as it's meant as a bit of a joke. The trouble is, I have to lean in very close to him to say it, and as my lips almost brush his ear, he looks like he's enjoying our brief moment of close contact just a little too much. I see a frisson of something – I don't know quite what – pass across his face as he listens to me.

Vincenzo knows I take all his attempts at seduction with a pinch of salt, and that I have no qualms about giving him a big shove if he gets a bit too full-on.

Recently our relationship, when we're not doing the serious, academic stuff, has become one of good-natured banter, and I have to say it's fun. There's a bit of a standing joke between us that he will always have a pop at chatting me up whenever he feels like it, which is fine just as long as he doesn't mind me knocking him back gently.

But there's something different about today. Oh yes, I know I'm always saying he's a terrible flirt, and a womaniser, and I would never go there, not if he were the last man on earth and all that sort of stuff. But today…I can't quite put my finger on it. There's something about the way he's been looking at me, and he was so lovely earlier when I told him all my news, so understanding and sincere.

Stop it, girl, this is Vincenzo we're talking about here, you know, the one you swore you'd never get involved with. He's bad news, you know he is. And he's your tutor for goodness sake! Get a grip girl!

The angel on my right shoulder is doing battle with the demon on my left again. Yes, I know, I know. How many times have I said I wouldn't… Yes, yes… But today he does look even more gorgeous than normal and somehow it doesn't feel sleazy, or wrong.

We whip down the narrow lanes of the motorway at a speed likely to induce car-sickness in even the hardiest of traveller. The driver seems to take great delight in zigzagging in and out of traffic as though he were performing stunts instead of ferrying passengers; he's not simply using the inside lane to overtake, but undertaking and ducking and diving as he pleases. The Mercedes badge pointing skywards from the bonnet weaves from left to right like a gun sight, searching for the next victim to overtake. Aim… fire… we're off again, and I hold on to the passenger handle above the door as we swing once more to the left.

So, when we do leave the dual carriageway, remarkably still alive and with the contents of our stomachs intact, it's with a huge sigh of relief on my part. Vincenzo looks unfazed, but then he's been raised on that sort of driving. Perhaps his Mamma used to ferry him and his siblings around in a similar fashion, so it is second nature to him. I'm just left with the thought that they should provide sick-bags in the back of taxis, like they do in planes.

Off the motorway, the driving doesn't improve much, and in fact becomes more dangerous as there is now only one lane for each direction of travel. This doesn't prevent our driver from spending pretty much an equal amount of time in each, despite the fact that the road curls round a steep incline like a helter-skelter as we navigate the rolling Tuscan hills, up one slope and down another. I try to focus on the breathtaking scenery around us; the rows of majestic cypress trees, the tightly packed vineyards and olive groves which seem to hang on the most inaccessible of hillsides, but in such regimented lines that they look as though they have been measured out with a geometry set. Somehow the farmer must manage to negotiate his tractor down these steep slopes to tend to his crops; that must be an even hairier ride than the one we're experiencing now. Maybe that's how they learn their motoring skills round here…

I'm distracted from my still-heaving stomach, when what must be our ultimate destination starts to come into view. Atop a distant hill there is a fortified construction, a high wall interspersed with towers which must encircle a town or village within. It's a breathtakingly surreal sight; so austere against the backdrop of all this lush verdure.

'Is that where we're going? What's it called?' I ask excitedly.

'It's Monteriggioni,' Vincenzo replies. 'The most perfect little walled town in Italy. It's a sleepy little place in the daytime, there are just a few shops and suchlike, but there is lovely hotel with a fantastic restaurant. That is where I am taking you tonight. The views across the Tuscan countryside are unsurpassable. We can dine outside and watch the sunset together.'

'That all sounds very romantic, Vincenzo,' I joke, grinning at him flippantly, but then notice that he looks a little hurt. He's not playing with me; he's actually being serious for once.

Vincenzo was right; Monteriggioni is an absolute gem of a place. It's tiny; there's just the one main square where the taxi deposits us, avoiding the requisite dusty climb from the car park, like the majority of visitors. Flanked with tourist shops and pizzerias, it's set off by a church pretty enough to merit a bigger, grander location than this. A couple of parallel cobbled streets lead away from the square, one of which houses the hotel we are heading for. It's all very quaint and picturesque, and in the absence of a camera to capture the scenery, I have a sudden urge to go and buy a few postcards to mark the moment. I don't really feel like I've been a tourist since I arrived in Italy, but today I want to behave like one.

'Well, if we're doing some shopping before we eat, you have to come and see this little shop down here,' Vincenzo says as we leave the *tabaccheria*, pulling me by the hand towards the left-hand side street. We pass a shop selling enticingly colourful shoes and bags – but he pulls me quickly past that – and stop outside a tiny jewellery shop with a glass front door. A quick peep in the window reveals an Aladdin's cave of tempting display cabinets, glinting with gemstones and silver. *Creazione Gioielli – Artemisia* says the sign on the door, along with another one reading *Attenzione al gatto* – beware of the cat.

'Can we go in?' I ask.

'Why else would I bring you here?' Vincenzo replies, rolling his eyes, and pushes open the door.

'*Ciao, Simonetta*,' says Vincenzo.

'*Vincenzo, come stai?*' The pretty, dark-haired girl at the counter starts with surprise, removes her magnifying eye-piece and puts down her tools. She comes round to the front of the counter and kisses him enthusiastically on both cheeks. Oh no, not another ex, surely?

They launch into a burst of fast-paced Italian before Vincenzo pauses to introduce me:

'Meet Simonetta, my cousin,' he says. Phew, not an ex, after all. Although I then launch into another very uncharitable set of thoughts involving other possible ex's that Vincenzo might have brought here to visit his cousin and her conveniently-located jewellery shop. I go to shake her hand, in my formal English style, but she pulls me forward instead, and I am subjected to the double-kiss strategy as well.

'*Piacere, Lydia*,' says Simonetta, seeming genuinely pleased to meet me, and not in any way giving me that 'So you're the latest love-interest in Vincenzo's life' look. I would like to think Vincenzo and I are exclusive to Monteriggioni, and that this hotel we are about to dine at isn't his usual location for seduction – assuming of course that is what he has planned for this evening. With the number of women he must have gone through even in the few months I've known him, I'm pretty sure it would cost a fortune if he'd brought them all here. We'll just have to see what reaction we get from the hotel staff later, whether they recognise him, coming for the first time with his new… er… partner. Which I'm not, of course, and have no intention of becoming.

Whilst Simonetta and Vincenzo are busy catching up in break-neck Italian, I decide to have a browse around the shop. It's only tiny, but there are enough cabinets crammed with jewellery to keep me busy for ages. It's all painstakingly handmade – by Simonetta herself – and is absolutely beautiful. I stoop to stroke the black cat curled up on a chair at the side of Simonetta's workbench – hardly the scary creature the sign on the door implies. He purrs whilst I tickle his tummy, before settling back into his slumber.

Jewellery shops back home either seem to be high-end ones which I can't stretch to on my budget or the cheap-and-cheerful bangles and baubles ones, full of the sort of stuff I wouldn't give houseroom to. This place is in a league of its own. Simonetta's jewellery is expensive but not crazily so (although there are one or two locked cabinets which I will steer clear of). The quality is first class; everything is supremely original in its design and expert use of gemstones, yet it has nothing of the homemade look to it. It's gorgeous; I could spend the rest of the evening happily browsing my way through it all, maybe try a few pieces on, just for fun…

I am particularly drawn to a beautiful silver chain with a pear-shaped pendant containing a dark blue, iridescent stone which I don't recognise. When Simonetta notices that I might actually be a serious customer, she breaks off from her conversation with Vincenzo to come and help me.

'This is a Labradorite,' she explains, opening the cabinet and handing the necklace to me. 'Beautiful, isn't it? If you hold it up to the light, look at all the colours you can see.' Before I can say, *It's lovely thank you but a little out of my price range*, she has popped it round my neck and fastened the clasp. I move across the room to the mirror, fingering it gingerly. It is beautiful, the chain long enough for it to sit low down on my neckline, which is now far from pale due to the recent warm weather, and so creating a perfectly bronzed back-drop for it.

'It's gorgeous,' I gasp. But I have just spotted the price tag lying on the counter – one hundred and eighteen Euros, heaps more than I can afford.

'It's yours,' Vincenzo says, and I start to protest. I didn't come here to be lavished with expensive presents; it's just not the way I operate. This being Vincenzo, I can't help feeling he'd expect something in return, even though I know that's an uncharitable thought in the face of such generosity.

'I couldn't, Vincenzo, don't be so silly,' I continue to protest.

But he already has his wallet out on the counter and is reaching inside for his credit card.

'It's your birthday soon, isn't it?' he says. How does he know that? 'Treat it as an early present from me. I really want you to have it, it looks so perfect on you. Besides which, I'm family, and Simonetta will do me a deal, won't you? Really, it's not as lavish a present as you think.'

He is very persuasive but I don't want Vincenzo to think I can be 'bought', and in any case why would he buy me a birthday present at all, especially one as precious as this? But it is a beautiful piece of jewellery, and I have so few lovely, quality things like this, so I surprise myself by changing tack. I stop trying to argue against it and say, 'Thank you Vincenzo, you are very generous and it's very kind of you.' I plant a kiss on his cheek and his grin of satisfaction is almost as huge as my own.

Deal done, goodbyes said to the talented Simonetta, and wearing my new necklace, whose silky smoothness I keep stroking to reassure myself it's still there, we move round the corner to the hotel where Vincenzo has reserved us a table.

I start to feel underdressed for the occasion when the impeccably attired waiter greets us with a tray of aperitifs as though we have just arrived at a wedding, and escorts us to our table. We are seated in a prime position on the arbour-covered terrace, at a discreet distance from a couple of larger, boisterous tables, with the most stunning view over some of the countryside we crossed on the way here.

The view from up here is amazing. The whole town itself doesn't feel especially high as you approach (although I might feel differently if I'd had to climb up from the car park I suppose), but because the landscape drops away dramatically into the distance, there is a huge feeling of space and altitude, breathtakingly so. I spend the first few moments as we sit, taking it all in and looking around me.

'Beautiful,' Vincenzo says, but when I turn to agree with him I find he is studying me, not the scenery. 'That necklace really suits you, you know,' he continues.

Oh, here we go. Next it will be: Your eyes are like pools, I'd like to dive into them. Your lips are like cherries, I'd like to nibble on them... Or some equally corny chat-up line, like something out of one of those cheesy Mills & Boon novels.

But instead he looks me squarely in the eyes and says: 'You are so different, Lydia, different from all the other girls.' Yes, and there have been plenty of those to compare to, haven't there Vincenzo? 'I'm not trying to chat you up, believe me, it's just that I really, really like you. Always have done. You're not like the others; you mystify me. I don't know how to tread with you.' And he actually sounds sincere. Vincenzo can do sincere when he wants to.

If Sophia and Leonora could see me sitting here, being sweet-talked by this man, they'd be pulling me up by the scruff of my neck and whisking me out of this establishment before you could say '*Arrivederci*.'

I am determined not to fall for it.

'You're lovely, you are,' Vincenzo whispers drunkenly into my ear in the back of the taxi. He's been holding my hand since we left Monteriggioni, but now looks as though he's about to doze off, his eyelids doing battle to stay open, his head beginning to loll.

We had a very pleasant evening in the restaurant; he didn't try to declare his undying love for me any more, nor did he try to put his hand on my knee, up my skirt or anywhere else, or exhibit any other signs of worryingly over-friendly behaviour. In fact, he was very charming company throughout and we'd talked and laughed about everything and nothing.

The evening had stayed balmy, and we decided on a little walk around the town before jumping back in the taxi. He held my hand as we strolled along, neither of us speaking. Suddenly he pulled me to him and kissed me ever so gently, just for a short while, before releasing me, stroking my cheek and tucking a stray lock of hair tenderly behind my ear. All of which left me gasping for air and slightly dizzy. I know he's had a lot of practise, but that was some kiss, and I felt like the heroine of a romantic novel as I stood there panting and trying to pull myself together. If he noticed how flustered I was, he pretended not to notice.

Back in the taxi, I too feel like I've had enough to drink this time to pass out and let the entire terrifying return journey wash over me. I glance across at Vincenzo, who is now fast asleep, a few of his stray dark curls twirling onto the back of the seat. I am surprised at how little I am beating myself up over tonight's events – but then there is always the cold light of day of tomorrow in which to do that. Reality will no doubt dawn that I let Vincenzo kiss me, and I kissed him back! Oh no, what are the girls going to say?

Sophia is still up when I get back to the apartment, so I decide to bare all now and get it over with.

'Just be careful, Lydia,' is all she has to say, seeing my dreamy-eyed expression, 'you know what he's like.'

Yes, I do.

23

'Hi, Evie, how are you?' I enquire of my big sister. Unsociable as it might sound, I was a little loathe to call as I know Evie is desperate to come and see me out here, and ringing her now might just push her into booking a date to come over. Much as I'd love to spend some time with her and show her the sights, I don't need her – or any other member of my family – descending on me just yet; not until I've found out more about Maria and resolved the issues coming at me in the dreams. I could see myself blurting it all out to her if she came now, and I don't think this is something my family needs to know about for the moment.

I know my Dad's sister, Aunt Sarah, has been into family tree research for the past few years, since she retired, and that is my true reason for calling Evie. She's always been very close to Sarah, who took Evie to her heart just as much as my Dad did when he and Mum got together, and I'm kind of hoping that she will be able to wheedle some information out of Sarah, without me having to ask and therefore posing the question as to why I need it. I manage to convince Evie that it's for a project

I'm working on, that I need some links between art through the ages and my own personal history, and she doesn't take too much persuading to approach Sarah. It would just save me an awful lot of time and effort, and give me some kind of starting point, if I had some pre-researched stuff to be going on with.

Of course Sarah's research will only cover my Dad's side of the family, so what I do if my link to Titian is via my maternal side, I really don't know. And I can't believe for one minute that it will go back more than a century or so, but I have to start somewhere, and if Evie can email me Sarah's files then it's something, I suppose. Although 'needle in a haystack' would be a very appropriate term right now; what chance have I really got of stumbling across anything relevant, when there are so many centuries to trawl through? It's all quite daunting. I don't know what I'm looking for, when, where or why. It's an unsolved puzzle on a monumental scale.

So far today I've managed to put last night's events out of my mind and apply myself to the job in hand. But now I sit at my open window, smelling those roses and breathing in the warm air, and allow myself to think back over the whole evening What a fabulous night! Kissing Vincenzo aside, what a place Monteriggioni is, and that shop, that restaurant – wow! I suppose I was an easy conquest in the face of all that seduction of a material and aesthetic nature, and Vincenzo probably didn't have to try too hard to make me swoon and fall into his arms. It was not only him I was seduced by but the whole package. In any case, it was only a kiss – it wasn't like I'd jumped into bed with him or anything, was it?

My phone beeps with a message. Without even glancing at it I guess it will be Vincenzo, checking up on me and making sure I'm OK after last night. We'd both snoozed all the way back – how unromantic – so we hadn't talked about what happened, and I didn't stir until we were outside my apartment, at which point he'd woken me up with a light kiss on the cheek.

'*Siamo arrivati, bella Lydia*,' he'd said. '*Ci vediamo domani*.' I remembered how he'd said the same to me after that fateful meal out, months ago, when I'd first arrived. This time I get the feeling he really does want to see me tomorrow. After all, I mystify him, don't I? Instead of being the mad girl with the dreams, I am now mystifying, which has to be an improvement on crazy. I quite like the idea of that.

The message is from Vincenzo; just a quick one to check I'm OK (as expected) and asking if I can meet him for coffee later. I'm planning an afternoon in the library – after all the distractions this week I need to get on with some coursework – so I reply to say that I'll pop in on him at the end of the day and then we can go for a drink somewhere. With his tutor's hat on, hopefully he'll appreciate my dedication and not see it as a snub, as it isn't meant to be. I don't feel I need to go rushing over to see him right away; what happened last night was lovely, if unexpected, and I am surprisingly OK with it (which I also inform him of to put his mind at rest, adding a little smiley face to the end of the text). But I am behind with my studies and I can't afford to be.

The ancestry files from Aunt Sarah, via Evie, have just pinged through on my laptop – boy, she's a fast worker – so I resolve to spend what's left of the morning looking through those, and then knuckle down to some serious work in the afternoon, away from here and all distractions. Vincenzo will have to wait a little longer for the pleasure of my company. I'm sure he'll cope.

There's so much here to wade through. I've just spent the past couple of hours barely scratching the surface of Aunt Sarah's database, and I have to say that what I've seen so far looks fantastic. She's managed to trace some branches of the family right back to the eighteenth century; I can't begin to imagine how long she must have toiled over it. I know I can't really expect to stumble across something that might lead me to Titian so early on, it would be naïve of me to think that was likely, but I can't help myself from hoping. This first glance doesn't throw up any obvious names that might link through; nothing sounds remotely like it might have come from Italy, or from anywhere beyond the UK, come to that.

I just need to stumble across some little gem of information which will spark off a link. If only it were as easy as all that…

An afternoon in the library finds my coursework sufficiently caught up on and the nagging guilt for my lack of attention to my studies this week appeased, so I pop across town to meet Vincenzo as promised.

'*Bella Lydia*,' he says, greeting me enthusiastically with a kiss on the lips, his hands gently stroking my arms. His kiss doesn't linger though, and although he is smiling, his eyes give away the uncertainty he obviously feels, despite my reassurances by text this morning that I was fine about last night.

'Lydia-the-mysterious at your service,' I joke, kissing him again to try to dispel that uncertainty.

'You liked that tag, didn't you,' he replies, relaxing a little in the knowledge that I'm not about to tear him off a strip for pouncing on me last night. In any case, there was no pouncing involved, and for once I hadn't fought him off; I'd kissed him back. I suppose he imagined I'd only done that because I'd had too much to drink, and that in the cold light of day I would come to my senses and give him the boot. But no, he needn't worry. I'm happy to be at this point with him; at the start of a new relationship – possibly?

I must be turning native; what has happened to my complete disapproval of tutor-student relationships? I was so adamant at the start of the year that I'd never get embroiled in any such situation, and I'd still like to think I'm not doing anything morally wrong, but it does seem to be more acceptable over here, doesn't it? I find I don't have to try too hard to convince myself – and I'm amazed at just how easy it is to do that.

We decide to go for an *aperitivo* and then see how the mood takes us afterwards. I find myself really hoping we can spend the rest of the evening together; now that my wariness of his reputation seems to have miraculously deserted me, I really would like to get to know him better, on a personal level. I feel I know him quite well in the academic sense – we've spent a lot of time together over the past few months – but this is different. I want to know more about him the person, not the tutor, all the usual sort of early-date stuff. So is this a date? I suppose it has to be.

'Come to Bologna with me the weekend after next,' Vincenzo proposes as we linger over our desserts. We moved on post-aperitif to a little trattoria in the *centro*. It's a gorgeous little place; trattoria yes, but cheap and cheerful, no, in true Vincenzo style. It's what I'd have called 'authentically Italian' in the days before I came over here and knew any better; proper Italian food, not just pasta and not a pizza in sight, and fully staffed by Italians, not Eastern European students trained to sound Italian. It's also one of those rare places in Florence which isn't full of tourists. One of the advantages of going out with a local I suppose; they know where to go. Stefano and I used to go to some great places – in a lower price bracket, but still lovely. That's the first time I've thought about him for a while and it hits me with an icy blast. I wonder what he'd have to say about my dining companion this evening…

'I have to go up there and finalise the details for my commission this summer,' he continues. 'Come with me? Please?'

Bologna would be great, I have to admit. I'm not sure about spending a whole weekend with Vincenzo so early on in our relationship – if that's what it is turning into – but the opportunity to walk the same streets as Maria once did, see the churches, arches and palaces that she also set eyes on, is too much of an opportunity to miss, so I quickly agree to Vincenzo's proposition. He will be in meetings for a significant portion of the weekend, anyway, which will leave me free to wander around and do the tourist trail, get a real feel for the place where Maria spent her youth. It sounds too good an opportunity to miss.

24

I really could get used to this. Vincenzo has just checked us into our hotel, separate rooms, of course; I'm glad he didn't presume.

This place is unbelievably gorgeous, the Grand Hotel Majestic '*Già Baglioni*'. Now you have to realise that this is not the sort of place I have ever stayed at, or even dreamed that one day I might have the funds to do so – which I haven't. Holidays in the Irvine family never stretched much beyond a week on a caravan park in Dorset or Devon, which was lovely; we always had a fabulous time and the sun always shone, but until now I never knew such luxury existed. Or how much it costs to say somewhere like this; I have just spotted the tariff swinging innocently on the back of the door. I didn't realise you were expected to fork out the price of a small car to stay in one of their top suites for the night.

And something else I have to deal with is this strange notion that I am starting to feel like a kept woman. Vincenzo never lets me pay for anything, so much so that it got to the point in the middle of the week when I felt I needed to say something to try and redress the balance.

Not that I can reciprocate on the same scale, of course, but if he could at least let me pay for something small now and again it would really help. Even just treat him to a coffee once in a while.

That was when Vincenzo sat me down and told me all about his trust fund. He'd never spoken much about his family before, so I was amazed to discover that he is in fact descended from Italian aristocracy, and if the Italian Constitution of 1948 hadn't abolished the *Consulta Araldica*, or in other words the right to use a title of nobility, then he would also be a '*Nobile*'. His Grandfather was the last to use the title legally, and despite the dissolution of the aristocracy in this country, the families who once bore these titles are still highly regarded in current society. I find it all quite fascinating, as I'd always regarded Italians as much more of a nation without class, compared to us Brits. We are a country of royalists, still clinging to an outmoded class system and still in thrall to Kings and Queens, Dukes and Duchesses. The Italians don't have all that.

So anyway, back to the trust fund. As well as being 'nobility', the Tizzaro family is also extremely wealthy. Wealth and status don't always go hand in hand, of course, but in this case they do and Vincenzo's father, who is still alive and well and lives near Milan, settled a substantial portion of the family fortune on Vincenzo when he reached twenty-one. Vincenzo is entitled to the interest from the fund, but not to the capital, until his father dies. Not that it makes much difference by the sound of things. He certainly has enough cash at his disposal to live a more than comfortable existence; his salary from the University and commission from the sale of his paintings must seem like mere pin money to him. In fact, with that sort of money, I'm surprised he even bothers to work at all.

'I don't tell many people about the money,' Vincenzo added afterwards. 'And from the look on your face, I'm glad I don't.' I must have looked pretty shocked. I'd guessed he had to have more funds available to him than just an academic's salary, to facilitate the lifestyle he leads, but I wasn't expecting this.

'It's not every day you realise you're in the presence of landed gentry,' I'd replied, trying to sound light-hearted about the whole thing. 'Do I need to curtsey?'

He laughed. 'I don't tell people because I don't want them to change the way they think of me. In fact you're the first girlfriend I've told.'

Girlfriend. There it was, that word, and I found myself feeling snugly contented under that title.

'People already think I'm a bit flash, don't they?' he'd asked, and that had made me smile. As if! 'I don't want them thinking I throw my money around and also there are some girls who, well, you know, are only out for what they can get.'

'I really appreciate you telling me about your family,' I say to Vincenzo now, to convince him that I really am OK about discovering I'm going out with a millionaire, which I suppose he must be. I've only just recovered from the shock of seeing how much he paid for me to stay here. 'But I still want you to let me pay for something now and again. I could never fund this sort of thing, of course,' I say, waving my arm around at the opulence of the hotel bar, where we are having a drink together, 'but just let me buy the odd round of drinks, won't you? Let me feel useful?'

'OK I will. I hope it doesn't change anything, well, for us,' he replies.

'So we are an 'us' then, are we?' I bravely venture, needing to have my status confirmed. 'You referred to me as your girlfriend the other day. Does that mean we are 'officially dating?'' I waggle my fingers in the air to denote the speech marks.

'I think we are, don't you? I really, really like you, Lydia. You know that.' He reaches across the table and takes hold of my hand, raises it to his lips and kisses it gently, all the time looking into my eyes. A shiver runs up my spine. I have a boyfriend again, it would seem, and he is very, VERY rich. But that doesn't matter, because he is also very, very lovely. The money is a bonus – and a huge surprise – but I am not shallow enough to be swayed by it and I would like him just as much without it. I'm glad, and very relieved, to realise I feel that way. I'd hate to think I was also one of those mercenary, money-grabbing women he'd referred to.

We both go our separate ways for a while to freshen up and get ready for the evening ahead. Vincenzo is taking me to a restaurant he knows – is there any city in this country where he doesn't have the perfect venue for a date at his fingertips? So I retreat to my room to fill my vast Jacuzzi bath with bubbles and have a long soak. Having seen the room prices, I'm glad I'm not in a suite – why would I need all that space just for me, all for the price of a brand-new Punto? Nothing could justify that sort of expense, and given the choice, I think I'd go for the car. But now that this room is mine, I don't plan to waste this luxury, and I do plan to either use up all the gorgeous toiletries left in my bathroom, or pop them in my suitcase and take them home. A bit of both, probably.

I think my room must be classed as a 'Deluxe Kingsize', and it is pretty luxurious. The bed is massive and would comfortably sleep a family of six without them rolling over and the little one falling out. The high ceiling is lit with chandeliers, and the huge full-height windows offer a stunning view across the uniformly red roofs of the city to the Bolognese hills beyond.

The furniture is very French in its style; I sit in one of the luxurious Louis XV style armchairs and gaze around the room, trying to commit every little detail to memory. And then, like a five-year-old with an uncontrollable bubble of excitement building in their chest, I am seized by the urge to bounce on the bed, and so that is exactly what I do. As I leap up and down, sending plump cushions flying to the floor, arms waving, I let out a 'whoop' of sheer joy, feeling more exhilarated than I've felt in a very long time.

The next morning Vincenzo has to meet up with his client to discuss and plan the commission, so I am to be left to my own devices for most of the day. As we pass through the marbled foyer together, he asks the concierge to provide me with a map and a list of recommended places to visit, which I accept graciously, but actually what I want to do is just wander, get a feel for the place, see where I end up.

An hour later, having strolled briefly around the Piazza Maggiore and taken in some of the well-known sights, I find myself in a second-hand bookshop, flicking through the shelves for something, anything, that might bring me closer to Maria and her time here. I have no expectations of finding anything, but you just never know; you don't find unless you look.

There is an old, tattered book about Pope Paul III which I pick up and flick through. He was after all the reason Titian came to Bologna, bringing him to the city in which he would meet his lover; a moment in time which would define and shape the rest of his life. I look up Titian in the index and there are quite a few references to him, so I decide to buy it, and leave the shop. I can flick through it later, back at the hotel; right now I want to do some serious sight-seeing.

I join the hordes of tourists queuing to climb the five hundred steps up to the top of the Torre Asinelli. I'd paused a little while ago to grab a coffee and drink it on the steps of the Fontana di Nettuno, first picking up an English newspaper from a stand nearby. The vendor, clearly marking me out as just another tourist (how dare he, I consider myself semi-native now, and my Italian accent is almost perfect!) began to sing the praises of 'the best thing ever you can do in Bologna', so I decided bravely to give it a go.

Two hundred steps in and I am beginning to regret my decision. Three hundred and fifty steps in, and thoroughly bored of the view of the well-upholstered, ascending backside in front of me, I am hot and thirsty. Four hundred and seventy-something steps in and I am almost passing out from heat exhaustion. But now I have made it, I am at the top and I emerge suddenly into the dazzling sunshine, blinking and reaching quickly for my sunglasses and water bottle.

And I have to say, the newspaper vendor was right. The view is heavenly. I gaze down onto a sea of red roofs, interspersed with the Verdigris domes of churches, whose scale is reduced to model-village proportions by the altitude. Have I really climbed that high? The shadow cast by the tower throws a dark line across the city like a sundial, pointing in a westerly direction, which, once I have worked out my bearings, I realise is back towards the Piazza Maggiore, almost following the exact path I took to come here.

I move to the south side of the roof and try to identify more landmarks. It all looks so different from here; even the other towers seem insignificant in their size. I spot a further, smaller dome which must be that of San Domenico. That's where I plan to make for later, taking in San Petronio first, which is sort of en route. Today will be a day of churches and towers, I think, but that seems to be largely what Bologna is all about. I'm going to immerse myself in culture, then when that all gets a bit too much, do some shopping, buy a few souvenirs, that sort of thing. Vincenzo and I aren't meeting up until the early evening, so I have the whole day to do exactly as I want.

Despite an enormous blow-out breakfast at the hotel this morning, I don't quite make it as far as San Domenico before hunger strikes, so I head back into familiar territory, towards the Piazza Nettuno, in search of a café where I can grab a bite to eat. Gazing out of the window as I munch on my *panino* I spot the entrance to a library, the Biblioteca Salaborsa, and decide that this will be my next port of call. I need to find out more about what life was like in Bologna in those days, and what better place to start.

'This might sound like an odd request,' I nervously begin my question to the librarian, 'but I'm looking for information on brothels in Bologna in the sixteenth century.'

The librarian isn't fazed by my question at all, and instead beckons me to follow her poker-straight back towards the relevant section. Amazingly there are some books which contain such information, although she explains that I might have to do some digging, so she helps me to the nearest table with a selection of volumes and leaves me to it.

I soon become engrossed in a section on how syphilis was brought to Bologna – in 1495 by the French, apparently! – which is all fascinating stuff and goes some way to explaining why the brothels were set up, to try and contain the disease and reduce the spread, keep prostitution off the streets and all that. It says there was even a hospital dedicated to the treatment of it.

I am also interested to discover that Bologna was the only Italian city in those days which permitted women to take up a profession (other than prostitution, of course) and even allowed them to study at the university. For such a forward-thinking city, then, it was amazing that so many brothels existed, along with a record ninety-six convents, presumably with the intention of saving the souls whose ways had strayed from the path of righteousness. A city of two wild extremes, it would appear.

But how do I find out which brothel was the one where Maria lived and worked? And is there likely to be anything written about one such establishment, which has long since closed down? The only clue is the dream I had of the Pope's visit; she was able to see him pass by from her window, so what I need, if such thing exists, is something to tell me the route he took through the city on that visit in 1537. Huh, what likelihood is there of finding that?

I decide to stop trawling through books and return to the twenty-first century way of doing things instead, hitting the library's extensive website, which is being heavily plugged on all the walls around me. With little hope of finding anything I type 'Pope Paul Bologna 1537' into the search engine and sit back to wait and see what gems of information this throws up.

I am amazed to hit instantly on one or two articles which might possibly help. Apparently the Papal procession took the principal route through the city (well, I suppose that should have been obvious, really) along the Roman road, coincidentally called the Via Emilia. I scratch around for the Via Emilia in my guide book, only to discover that whilst this route still exists historically, the part that runs through the city now goes under several different street names, Maggiore, Rizzoli, Ugo Bassi and San Felice. I have already walked along those streets today, maybe passing the site, or even the actual building, where Maria used to live! Suddenly I feel a lot closer to her than ever, and a tiny shiver of excitement runs down my spine.

The article about the Pope's visit is fairly sketchy, but then it's bound to be. It's not like there was any newspaper reporting of such events in those days, no tabloid journalists hurriedly scribbling down details of outfits, routes, who said what to whom, what the crowd's reaction was, et cetera, snapping away on a jumble of cameras to secure 'the' shot of the day. It has merely been documented as an event that took place, for posterity and historical purpose, and nothing more. But then I scroll down to reveal a pencil sketch of the procession passing through town, which bears an uncanny resemblance to the sight that Maria saw from her window.

One of the articles refers to a document which has since been moved to the Archivio di Stato in Florence. There is very little information about what the document might reveal, but I have to fully investigate any link I can find, so I jot down the details and make a mental note to visit the state archives when I get back to Florence.

I decide to spend what remains of the afternoon – I look at my watch and there isn't much time left before I'm due to meet Vincenzo – strolling around on those four streets which follow the path of the Via Emilia. Just knowing that Maria could have lived around here somewhere is enough to inspire me to continue my search to find a link between us, should one exist. I gaze up at building after building, trying to will some images from my dreams to come back to me and help me identify the location.

I clearly remember how I, as Maria, gazed upon the Pope's procession from the window of Rosetta's. What was the view outside, beyond the pageantry? Which buildings could I see across the street? I wrack my brains but nothing further comes back to me. And in any case, although the bare bones of those buildings may or may not still be here, the scenery has to have changed dramatically over nearly five hundred years, doesn't it? I don't find the whole process disheartening, though, being so near and yet so far. It all just serves to strengthen the bond between Maria and me, and as I walk around I become more certain that this IS the area where she spent her youth.

'Race you to the top of those stairs,' Vincenzo challenges me, as we arrive back in the hotel foyer at the end of the evening.

'After three,' I propose, but only wait for the count of two before I start bounding up the staircase.

'Hey, you cheat!' he calls, starting his run a couple of seconds behind me, but sprinting up two stairs at a time and reaching the top only a split second after I do.

'Come on old man,' I joke. 'Shouldn't be too hard at your age!'

'I'd have beaten you if you'd played fair,' he replies, grabbing me gently by the wrist and pulling me to him, nuzzling into my neck.

'Your place or mine?' he asks, his hands starting to roam.

'Yours,' I reply, anticipating what is going to happen next, and knowing that, should I change my mind, it will then be easier to make an excuse and retreat to the sanctuary of my own room. Although I don't anticipate that I will change my mind; I'm ready for this.

We wake the next morning to another gorgeously blue sky, and brilliant sunshine streaming into the room, a long shaft of light reflecting off the chandeliers and twinkling across the dishevelled bed. In our haste last night we hadn't closed the shutters or the curtains, and now we lie here together, bathed in sunshine, awake at an earlier hour than we'd probably have chosen to be.

'Oahhhrrrrr,' Vincenzo emits as he rolls over lazily towards me, eyes barely open, reaching out one arm to pull me near. 'Do we have to get up yet?'

'Definitely not,' I reply, 'it's only six-thirty.'

'Oh well, in that case we have plenty of time,' he says, suddenly sounding more awake, and making his intentions on how he wants to spend the next few hours perfectly clear as he wraps himself around me again. We'd gravitated to our own sides of the bed during the night, but now there are barely millimetres between us again.

'Happy Birthday, bella Lydia,' he says, as he starts to kiss me again. 'I can't believe you're mine at last.'

This has to be the best birthday wake-up ever.

25

'So, Lydia, how did the weekend go?' Sophia asks me. She is perched on my bed as I unpack on Sunday evening, desperate for the low-down on my weekend with Vincenzo. 'How was it, waking up with him on your birthday?'

'How did you know that?' I swivel round suddenly to face her, feeling as though all my secrets from the weekend have been laid bare. I blush to my roots, which only serves to confirm her suspicions that the relationship has progressed to a more advanced level.

'Ah, well, you have that loved-up glow to you,' she laughs. 'I can always spot a woman who has been whipped off to a luxury hotel for the weekend and seduced by a handsome man. It's not hard to guess. And now you're bright pink, so you've given it away!'

I have to say that up till now I've been more than a little reluctant to discuss Vincenzo with Sophia and Leonora. Like me they'd had their doubts about him in the early days, but unlike me they haven't revised that opinion more recently, as they've never had the chance to get to know the real him, the kind, sensitive man who isn't all brash womaniser and really does care about me. If I still had any inkling that Vincenzo was just trying to charm me in order to get into my knickers, before casting me aside for the next pretty face to pop into his life, then I wouldn't be where I am now, and I certainly wouldn't have let things get as far as this. I was hurt too much by Ed to allow myself to fall for insincerity all over again; I'd have been the one to put a big stop to it long since.

But it's hard to make them see that, and I don't really know where to start. I know it's because they care about me and don't want to see me hurt again and all that, which is lovely, but really, I do trust Vincenzo, more now than ever. I know he genuinely cares for me and it's not just me falling for his charming spiel in the aftermath of post-coital endorphins. This is different. For both of us.

'What time are we meeting the others?' I ask, hoping she won't pry any more. The weekend was too special to dissect with a friend so soon, so I try to instigate a change of subject.

'In L'Incontro Bar at eight, and then on from there, to wherever you fancy!' she replies, taking the bait. 'A couple of rounds of birthday cocktails, followed by an evening of dancing, partying hard, or whatever you want!'

She has arranged for the old 'gang' to go out to celebrate my birthday. I do feel I've already done all the celebrating I need with Vincenzo, and I'm really tired. I could do with a whole night's sleep, in my own bed, alone, but I can't use that as an excuse and it is very sweet of her to sort it all out It will actually be lovely to go out with the whole gang again; it's something I've not really done since breaking up with Stefano, and I miss it.

I've been out with the girls plenty of times, and sometimes we've met up with one or other of the boys, but it isn't like it used to be, and quite frankly, I don't see how it ever can be. Not for me, anyway. They will always have each other, and that will continue long after I've left Florence, but it's nice to think that I might be able socialise with Stefano again without any hard feelings, and tonight will be the test of that.

As I get ready for the evening ahead I have to admit to being slightly nervous about it, but I am buoyed up with courage by the warm, fuzzy sensation still lingering from the weekend, plus a real 'birthday feeling', just like I used to get when I was a child. Today feels really special, and not just because it's my birthday AND the official start of a new relationship. I feel like nothing can touch me at the moment, as though I'm floating above my own charmed and lovely life, smiling down on it all and considering myself very lucky, with a self-satisfied nod of my head.

The bar is heaving when we arrive, but the boys have nabbed us a couple of tables outside, so we will have the added advantage of being able to people-watch on the Piazza della Repubblica whilst we drink and catch up on everyone's news.

I love this place; aside from the bar prices, it's a great place to meet, and all the beautiful people of the world seem to pass by, like a cat-walk of the more glamorous element of Florentine society. There's nothing really to compare to it back home, either in Sussex or up in Newcastle. And over here there's always this added magic of being outside in the evening, without sporting goose bumps or a heavy-duty coat. We Brits only get that for a handful of nights a year if we're lucky, and that's usually with the aid of a patio heater, pelting out enough energy to produce its own sizeable hole in the ozone layer.

Once again I realise I'm starting to feel wistful about my time here coming to an end. I know I still have a couple of months to go, but what then? I do have a degree to go back and finish, there's no denying that, but this place is a world away from Newcastle and all that goes with it. I'm really struggling to imagine myself slipping comfortably back into my old studenty ways as they were. Perfect days and evenings like this only serve to make it harder to imagine that it all has to end at some point. I know I'm here to work hard, and really I do, but despite that, the whole experience has the overriding feeling of a holiday to it. And what of Vincenzo and me? What happens to us when I have to go back home? Is this just a holiday romance or will our relationship stand up to the distance test? Too early to say, I think.

Stefano is leaning over the railing around the little terraced area in front of the bar, chatting to a girl who must have spotted him as she was passing by. I take in his back view, fully appreciating that it's still as gorgeous as ever, his bottom pert in those ever-present black jeans which the men of this country seem to wear so well.

There's a lump in my throat when I recognise the girl as Adriana, the one he was with the day I bumped into him. She spots me and waves, somewhat over-enthusiastically given our single meeting, and with a quick 'mwa-mwa' of double-cheeked kisses for Stefano and another wave to me she is off, swinging her designer handbag and glossy sheath of hair, her six-inch heels proving no impediment to her speed. There goes a girl who is confident that she has what she wants in life.

'Hi Stefano, how are you?' I begin, moving in and kissing him on both cheeks, which still harbour a faint aroma of their previous kisser. 'I hope I didn't scare her off? Isn't she joining us?' I consciously adopt what I hope is a smiling, bravado expression to show that I am perfectly fine about him and this new woman in his life.

'No, she's just off to meet her new boyfriend,' he replies, and sees the look of surprise on my face when I say:

'Oh, I thought…'

'Yes, so did she, for a while at least. But I wasn't ready. It was too soon after, well, you know…' he says, clearing his throat.

'I'm sorry,' I say, suddenly finding a tiny speck of dirt on my shoes fascinating and not being able to look him in the eye. 'She seems really nice.' A platitude, I know, and no, I don't think she's very nice actually, but I have to say something.

The thought of Stefano seeing someone else still bothers me, and I know that's unfair, especially now that I'm with Vincenzo. But neither do I like the thought that he's still hurting, and I feel the need to appease my conscience, somehow or other. But I don't quite know what to say to him. Trolling out an *Oh well, never mind, I'm sure the right woman is waiting for you just around the next corner*, seems a bit insipid, so I settle for rubbing him gently on the arm and giving it a sympathetic little squeeze, in the hope it conveys the right message. This time I manage to meet his gaze, and neither of us looks away.

The moment is broken when Stefano takes a deep breath and launches in with: 'I hear you and Vincenzo are together now. How are things going? Are you happy?' He says this last with something of a pinched smile and narrowed eyes. I didn't know he knew about us, but then news travels fast on the Florentine grapevine and I suspect he wasn't surprised to hear it; he'd always thought Vincenzo liked me, hence his defensive stance whenever Vincenzo came on the scene.

Dante butts in, hands me a cocktail menu and deposits two damply alcoholic birthday kisses on my cheeks, saving me from having to answer Stefano's question. I am very happy, ecstatically so, but I don't really want to have to tell him that and rub salt into a wound that's obviously still a little bit raw.

'I'll go for a Negroni, I think,' I tell Dante and he beckons to the bartender to come over and take our order.

Two hours later and we're still here. In the end we decided to stay and order food in the bar; I've not really got my dancing head on, and the others were happy to go with the flow, as long as I was having a good time and doing what I wanted. It's expensive in here, but it's not like we make a habit of it, and in any case it IS my birthday, and the gang have allowed me to buy some drinks for them all, so I don't feel too bad on behalf of their bank balances that we haven't moved off somewhere cheaper.

I'm tucking into my *Risotto con Fili di Zafferano* – delicious! – when an uninvited, but not unwelcome, guest appears beside me. It's Vincenzo. I think I might have told him in a text earlier on that we were coming here, but I hadn't really expected that he would show up. I just hope Stefano is OK with my new man's sudden appearance, and I look across at him for a reaction. Vincenzo notices me doing this and whispers quietly in my ear, as he pulls up a chair and squeezes in beside me.

'Don't worry about him, *cara*, you are with me now,' he murmurs, and his warm breath sends shivers up my spine.

'Yes, but he's my friend. It's hard for him,' I whisper in reply.

I think back to all those other times when we just seemed to stumble across Vincenzo on a night out, or rather he would stumble across us. In those days his presence wasn't always entirely welcome within our little circle, and I used to wish he would just go away. This time I'm glad he's here, despite any adverse reaction Stefano might have to him. As my boyfriend, he has every right to be at my birthday bash, whether invited or not.

'I hope you don't mind me joining you,' he offers to the rest of the group, making eye contact with each person around the table. Actually the lads – with the obvious exception of Stefano – welcome him wholeheartedly, shaking hands before passing him a menu and a wine list. Sophia and Leonora share a conspiratorial glance and Leonora looks over at Stefano to check he's OK.

'So, Vincenzo, I hear you are now the luckiest man in the world,' Stefano ventures, quite bravely I think. 'Look after her, she is very special.' Whilst he delivers this with a smile on his face, there is more than a tiny hint of a threat in his eyes. *Hurt her, and I will tear you limb from limb*, is his implied meaning, and I look across at Stefano and give him my hugest, most sincere smile, both to say thank you for his kind comment and to reassure him that I will be alright.

Vincenzo goes on to behave himself impeccably throughout the meal, making charming conversation with the girls, and fitting in companionably with the lads. Not surprisingly, Stefano is rather quiet, sitting back broodingly whilst the others chat, and studying Vincenzo intently, as though waiting for the one false move which could justify him pouncing.

I don't know why I might have expected Vincenzo NOT to behave tonight, but then I suppose I only have my experience of other nights out in his presence to base my opinions on, back in those days before we got together. On such occasions he'd generally arrive with a decorative partner on his arm, behave badly, drink too much, flirt with me and/or my friends, and leave very drunk. Tonight he is the model of a well-behaved boyfriend and is thoroughly charming company. I know he can be like this, but the others haven't seen this side of him very often, so I am glad he has broken free of his poor track record and set out to impress them all. Maybe Sophia and Leonora will stop stressing about us now.

The evening comes to a natural end and the others drift off, leaving Vincenzo and me alone. Stefano begrudgingly manages to shake Vincenzo's hand when he leaves, but not without whispering something quietly in his ear, which I don't catch.

'You don't mind me coming tonight, do you?' Vincenzo asks. 'It's your birthday, and I was missing you!'

'It's fine, really it is,' I reply, although I will have to get it through to him that sometimes I might just want to see my mates, without him. I'd hate him to turn into one of those possessive, jealous types who feel they have to follow their other half everywhere. Ed was a bit like that, well, till Jules came along, at least, and he no longer felt the need for us to be joined at the hip. Why didn't I spot the signs at the time?

'Your place or mine?' Vincenzo asks me for the second time in as many days, as we pour the last few dregs of wine into our glasses.

'No offence, but I really need to go back to mine. Alone,' I reply. I explain to him that I'm simply exhausted – he can take the credit for that, after all – and he doesn't seem to mind too much, interpreting it more as a sign of his prowess as a lover than a knock-back.

'I'll walk you home then,' he offers.

'That would be lovely,' I graciously accept. 'So what did Stefano whisper to you earlier?'

'Break her heart and I will kill you.'

'You'd better not, then!' I joke as we get up to leave.

26

'You're going to need a bit more than that,' Leonora says as I go to leave the apartment, carrying a small, collapsible umbrella, my only weapon of defence against the raging storm outside.

None of us slept well last night; the storm started in the early hours of the morning and, used only to the gentle chirruping of the local birdlife as night turns to day, the uncharacteristic crashing and banging of the wind, plus the clatter of torrential rain lashing the windows, had us all out of bed and drinking hot chocolate by five-thirty. We sat companionably yawning in our pyjamas for some time, contemplating whether we really had to go out today, or if anything we needed to do could be done from home instead. Sophia and Leonora sensibly decided to spend the morning indoors, as it surely must pass over at some time, but I really want to get across town this morning to the Archivio di Stato and so decide to stick to my Plan A.

I'm keen to unearth something that might lead me to Maria and Emilia as soon as I can; I'm not quite running out of time yet, but I'm conscious that I've got end of year assessments coming up, and as today is relatively free of lectures and tutorials, there is no time like the present…

However as I hesitate outside our apartment block, wearing Leonora's full-length oilskin coat, I wonder if I've made the right decision. I'm glad she offered me the use of it, but I never imagined someone living here would need, let alone own, a coat like this. It seems more English countryside than urban Italian wear, but Leonora informed me that when it rains here, there are no half measures. And taking shelter for a few moments under the small overhang of the building, I can see just what she means. It hasn't rained very often or very hard since I've been here, so today feels like quite a monsoon.

The Archivio di Stato is a fair way across town, beyond Santa Croce and the library, so I have quite a walk ahead of me, which on a fine day wouldn't bother me, but today I feel like I'm about to set off on a marathon trek into dangerous territory. I take a deep breath and venture forth.

The backstreets near the apartment are already awash, gutters full to overflowing and drains bubbling up with water that simply has nowhere to go. Hardly anyone is out and about, and who can blame them. A lone young man on a Piaggio scoots past, typically without a helmet, his dark hair plastered to his head, leather jacket shiny as the water runs off him, like a giant black beetle. His wheels send a jet of water from the gutter in my direction, and he looks across with a smile and a *'Scusi signorina!'*

I don't really know what to expect from today's visit. I've no idea why a document about the Pope's visit to Bologna should have been moved to the archives in

Florence, but whatever it is and however significant or otherwise, I have to go and have a look. I feel compelled to follow any lead I can, as, let's face it, there have been few leads so far.

I've a vague notion I might have stumbled across the area in Bologna where Maria lived, but that's about the extent of it, and even that's more of a feeling than a confirmed fact. So I'm not very optimistic about what today's findings will reveal, but you just never know. To rehash a tired cliché, I can leave no stone unturned.

Across the city, conditions are no better. I have never seen the Piazza della Signoria looking so forlorn, or so bereft of tourists. A few of the hardier ones are huddled under the arches of the Loggia dei Lanzi, cameras packed away for today into their waterproof holdalls, waiting for a break in the weather to return to their happy snapping. Tables are stacked up around the edge of the square and tied down with tarpaulins, businesses clearly taking a hit as their clientele stays at home or in warm and dry hotel bars.

I slosh across the square, past the 'looky-looky' men who today have swapped sunglasses and postcards for disposable pac-a-macs and cheap-and-cheerful umbrellas, guaranteed to blow inside out on first use. A few tourists, caught short in their lack of appropriate holiday garb are sporting these macs, bright red plastic cape-like things with a hood, and holes for the arms. I suspect I would be wearing one of those now, were it not for Leonora's coat. I am reminded of the Du Maurier book 'Don't Look Now,' as a red-caped child darts in front of me, attired in the miniature version of this fashion faux-pas, pointy hood concealing her face. I shudder, partly from the chill this weather has created, and partly from remembrance of that creepy tale. This place does feel more like Venice than Florence today.

As I pass the Uffizi I make a silent promise to Maria that I will be back soon. *I am trying to find out more about you, my dear friend,* I communicate to her in my head. *Give me time, I'm working on it.*

The archives are in an unprepossessing concrete monstrosity of a building, whose complete lack of anything architecturally pleasing is not enhanced by the weather. I shake off the worst of the rain from my coat and head inside, feet squelching in boots which feel like they might never recover from being so thoroughly soaked through.

I am directed to the appropriate room by a very nice – dry – lady on the reception desk whose hair looks too perfect for her to have arrived in this weather. Perhaps she has a kindly other half who dropped her right outside the door this morning, avoiding the need for heavy duty rainwear or a bad-hair-day situation.

'*Andate nella Sala Studio al primo piano, e firmate il registro,*' she informs me in her brusque, head-mistressy way, and I do just that, up to the first floor, and sign my name in the book. The Sala Studio looks more like an exam hall; row upon row of desks, about two thirds of which are taken up with what appear to be students, industriously working away. I walk over to a free desk, conscious of the soggy squelch emanating from my feet in the deathly silence, dump my things and go in search of someone who can help me with my request.

At the enquiries counter I find a very kind-faced lady of close to retirement age, whose name badge reads Antonella Pasi. I explain to her that I was directed here from a web search I did in the Biblioteca Salaborsa in Bologna, showing her the printout with the reference number, and she disappears into a room behind her counter, instructing me to wait a few moments.

Signora Pasi returns several minutes later looking somewhat apologetic.

'*Mi dispiace molto, signorina,*' she begins, '*ma questo documento non è qui. È stato distrutto durante l'alluvione.*'

I try to avoid collapsing into a squelchy heap of mush in my disappointment. How ironic on a day as soggy as today, that the one piece of paper which might have helped me find a small lead to Maria, has been destroyed by flooding.

Signora Pasi goes on to explain that the document hasn't actually been here for several decades; it was destroyed in the great flood of 1966, that very famous event which obliterated, not just what feels like my only hope of ever tracing Maria, but thousands of works of art in some of the major institutions across the city. I know my loss is a small one in relation to all that, and that piece of paper might not even have proved useful, but it was my one hope, and now it has gone.

I slump down onto a seat by the enquiries desk. Signora Pasi looks concerned as I turn a whiter shade of pale and start shivering. She comes out from behind her counter, and very kindly and concernedly puts an arm around my shoulders.

'You are frozen,' she says. 'Come through to my back office, there's a comfortable chair in there and a fan heater. Here, take off your shoes and socks, I'll soon have those dried out for you. You can sit and recover for a moment. I'll make you something warm to drink. I can't believe how cold it is today, this rain chills you to the bone.'

What a lovely lady. She takes over completely and ushers me into her office, where within minutes I am provided with a steaming cup of hot chocolate and a fluffy blanket to cover my bare feet. Being mothered and fussed over is a great elixir, and her constant stream of friendly chit-chat picks me up no end, so much so that I begin to feel embarrassed and start to apologise for my loss of composure.

'I'm sorry, I seemed to lose it there for a moment. I don't know what came over me.'

'Don't worry about it, you'll be fine now. Was it something really important to you?' she asks.

'I don't know really.' I want to explain to her, after all she has been so kind, but I don't want to reveal too much. How silly would my story seem to an outsider?

'Just something I thought might lead me to an ancestor.' There, I said it. Maria is my ancestor. But still it's only an assumption; I need that proof that links me to her, need to know how we are related, need to have a piece of concrete evidence in my possession that proves there is a reason for her telling me her story.

'I was an *'Angelo del Fango'* in 1966, you know. A 'Mud Angel,'' Signora Pasi tells me. I quickly sit up and take notice, wanting to hear more. 'I was a student here when the floods came. Really, I have never seen anything like it. It was heart-breaking to see so many treasures damaged, so many things completely destroyed. At the time we were more concerned for the works of art than for our own safety, not afraid of drowning. The recklessness of youth, I suppose. What else could we have done but help? We had to save these things, it's our heritage, it's what Florence is all about, isn't it? It wasn't so much the water that was the problem in many cases; it was the mud.'

She goes on to tell me more about her efforts. Apparently she worked solidly for a year, cleaning, disinfecting and scraping mud and slime off books and paintings, learning about the painstaking restoration process as she went along, and working with experts from the field of conservation.

'Mud mixed with oil from all the broken heating tanks around the city, not to mention the pollution from the river. Well, you can imagine. All that muck over all those beautiful things. I'm so glad I did it, though,' she goes on. 'Glad I got involved. And it's how I met my husband.' At this point she giggles and blushes, like a little girl with her first crush. Clearly he's a special one and they are still madly in love. Lucky her.

She really is an angel, my Signora Pasi. I feel like I've known her forever, and when I finally leave her office an hour later, not only do I have dry feet and a warm glow inside, but I have made a new friend, and as I kiss her on both cheeks, I vow to come back and see her before I return to England.

'I promise,' I say. Her stories have put things into perspective for me. My loss – if it had indeed turned out to be a useful document, and that I will never know – is so insignificant in the face of all that Florence lost in 1966. It's thanks to people like her that these treasures are still around in the museums, galleries and churches of this great city. Even so, I am still bitterly disappointed, and I know there is only one person who will fully understand, Antonio Di Girolamo, my friend and tutor. I need to pay him a visit.

'Lydia, *cara*, I think you know in your heart of hearts why Maria talks to you like this, so don't upset yourself,' he says, in an attempt to console me.

I'd amazed myself by breaking down in tears as soon as I saw him. I thought I'd sorted it all out in my head on the way there, but I think the lack of sleep last night has magnified this situation into something bigger than it is, turning me into a blubbing wreck in the process.

'I think I knew in my own mind that I had some kind of link to Tiziano, well before I discovered some evidence to prove it,' he goes on. 'And you know, that document you were looking for in the archives might have been completely useless to you. Somehow, Lydia, I doubt it would have thrown any more light on Maria's life. It was probably just a report on the Papal visit, at best. Keep your chin up, my dear, and keep going with your family research; you just never know what you might happen across. But even if you don't find anything, I think you know in your heart that Maria chose you for a reason, don't you? I was lucky enough to find something, but you have a much harder task ahead of you. You've no idea how the link reaches all the way to England, for one thing, so where are you supposed to start looking? At least my family has always lived in much the same part of Italy, so I had something to be going on with.'

It does make me feel a bit better, I suppose, but I so want to find something which proves Maria's existence, other than the 'facts' inside my head.

I need your help, Maria, I plead. *You have to give me something more in the dreams. Tell me where I can find you.*

27

'So you will do it? Really?' Vincenzo had asked me as we sat enjoying a prosecco together on the Piazza della Signoria. 'I really can paint you?'

Shoot me if you will, and think what you like, but yes, I've succumbed. I am going to pose for Vincenzo, and yes, I'm going to pose for him without my clothes on. I am about to become, dare I say it, another one of his nudes, and yes, there are a fair few of them, and no, I'm not threatened by that, really I'm not.

The whole process leading up to me agreeing to it has been quite amusing though. For me, at least. I knew exactly what Vincenzo was getting at when he asked me initially, even though he didn't once refer to me being nude. My English sense of humour couldn't stop me from having some fun, so I pretended I was going to be in some costume or other, getting all excited about 'which style of period dress' I was going to be wearing, or 'choosing a hat' to suit the outfit. I knew full well he didn't actually want me with any clothes on at all, apart from maybe a carefully placed scarf, or some flowers or jewellery, a bit like Maria. He just didn't quite have the courage to come out and say it, which was quite sweet, really.

So there was plenty of wind-up value to be had from stringing it out this week, until I finally admitted to knowing what he'd wanted all along.

'You mean, with no clothes on? Naked?' I'd said, pretending to look shocked and horrified that he should dare ask such a thing of his girlfriend. I put my hand over my mouth to feign horror but couldn't keep the twinkle of mischief from my eyes, and at that point he knew I'd been winding him up.

'Of course I will,' I said, much to his relief, and slight disbelief that he hadn't seen through me. Spot the difference between the Italian and English sense of humour – ours is way too warped for them.

So here I am, posed and at the ready. And slightly nervous, too. Vincenzo has seen me lots of times without my clothes on, but this somehow just feels more… naked, I suppose, which must seem daft, but there you go. Something to do with feeling like I'm laid out on a slab – a corpse awaiting a post mortem.

I've also given some brain time to the fact that people, REAL LIVE PEOPLE, with whom I don't have the sort of relationship that involves removal of clothing, will actually see me in this painting WITH MY CLOTHES OFF. They will know what I look like naked. Arghh. What if my Dad sees it? I banish that thought quickly, or I will be off this couch and fully clothed again before Vincenzo has even picked up a brush.

Vincenzo's nudes, or at least the ones that I've seen, have generally been pretty contemporary in their style. So there is nothing of the Renaissance Maria in my pose, none of the detailed background or general air of sumptuousness and suggestiveness as in her paintings. But on the whole they are tastefully done, I have to admit. Bar one or two, but I made it quite clear to Vincenzo that my painting was going to be tasteful, or simply not happen. So I have a plain white background behind me, and am lying on one side on a grey, modern chaise-longue type thing. The whole effect will be 'pale but luminous', as Vincenzo puts it. He can see the painting in his head already, he tells me. I am going to look beautiful, he also tells me, as I gulp back something akin to stage fright.

As Vincenzo starts to sketch and I gaze around the room (with my eyeballs only, of course, as I'm not allowed to move a hair on my head) I feel some empathy with Maria, and all those hours upon hours she must have sat still like this for Titian. She had a lifetime of it, and made it a labour of love, but I know now that this single sitting will be quite enough for me. I don't see my future as an artist's muse, somehow. Life's too short for this level of inactivity.

So, what am I going to think about for the next few hours, now that I have a bit of time on my hands…? Mmmm, work? End of year assessments? No, too dull. Where I'm going to live when I go back to Newcastle? How I'm going to feel about leaving Florence and everyone and everything about this place that I love? No, too depressing. I don't want to go there at the moment. Plenty of time to deal with it all later in the year, when I really need to…

Actually, just managing to stay awake could be a problem, I think, as my eyelids droop and I yawn for the second time – and am reprimanded by Vincenzo for it.

I clench Clara's hand tightly and see her wince with pain as my fingernails dig into her flesh. I am caught in the grip of the most extreme agony I have ever known. 'Clara, help me, I am dying!' I scream as this latest contraction seizes my body and grips it in its devil's clutch for those few brief but never-ending seconds.

'No, Maria, you are not dying, you have a life inside you! You are going to live, and bring this child safely into the world,' she whispers softly and calmly, my wonderful Clara. How I wish my Tito could be with me now, but this is no place for a man; childbirth is women's work. Better that he should come later, when all is done. Then I can present his daughter to him. For I feel now, stronger than ever, that this child is female.

I come to with a small judder, and realise I'd started to doze off. I look at Vincenzo for a reaction, expecting to be scolded again, but he is engrossed, so much so that I wonder if he actually needs me here at all, or if he's just making up my image on canvas from the memories in his head.

A dream. I started to have a dream, didn't I? About Maria, I think? I'm pretty sure it was. A tiny snapshot of a Maria dream. But I only dream in the Uffizi, so how could it happen here? Maybe just a coincidence; it has to be that.

Lovely smell in here. Must be those roses on Vincenzo's desk. Can't look round at them now. Too tired. He'll be cross. Smell nice though. Pink, I think. Love pink roses…

'It hurts so much Clara, help me!' I scream again as another contraction grips. 'I do swear this child will cleave me in two! If I should die, swear to me you will look after her? Promise me, Clara?' I yell, seizing her wrist, in case she should not fully have understood my plea.

'You will not die, Maria, I will not let you,' she says, stroking my hair back from my face with a cool cloth, as the midwife examines my belly for the umpteenth time. But I am witness to the brief flash of fear which graces her gentle features.

'It is still not time, Mistress,' the midwife says, and this I cannot comprehend. How long must it take for this child to come out of my body? I can bear it no more.

The roses. Oh, yes, I can smell them once more. Did I nod off again for a moment? Vincenzo is none the wiser, his face a picture of utter concentration as he scribbles hard and fast.

'Those roses, Vincenzo, can you move them closer, somewhere I can see them?' I ask, interrupting him. 'I need something to focus on here, or I think I'm going to fall asleep. How's it going, anyway? You've been at it for a while now.'

'It's only been half an hour, Lydia,' he replies. 'I'm going to need you for a bit longer than that, yet, I'm afraid. Are you OK? Another half hour or so and we'll have a break, get you something to eat. Can't have you falling asleep on the job, can we?' He gives me one of his dazzling smiles, then remembers my request for the roses, and leaps up to grab the vase from his desk, placing it on a small table to the side of him before returning to his canvas.

'Funny, it feels like I've been here for hours already,' I say, breathing in the scent of the roses, and trying to recall where I've seen that particular variety before. Oh yes, in the hospital when Leonora was there, and… with Maria, of course. They are just like the ones she is always surrounded by. Funny, they don't seem to smell in the dreams, or if they do, that particular sense has never survived as a memory. Smelling in dreams, is that possible? We can touch, hear and feel in dreams; can we smell and taste too? Or is smell something which creeps into a dream from the real world, like dreaming you can smell bacon frying, only to wake up and find someone has made your breakfast?

I did start to dream about Maria, didn't I? How odd. I do think about her a lot, but I've never had a dream anywhere but in room twenty-eight.

Sleepy again. Roses are gorgeous. Petal just dropped off. Whoops…

'Where is Tito, I need him here with me,' I bleat to Clara, who stands to one side as the midwife again examines me. How I have had enough of people touching me, prodding me, feeling they have some right to my body! Please, God, let this baby come out of my belly soon; let me reclaim this body as my own.

'She is nearly ready,' the midwife says to Clara, 'keep on with the cold compresses, she is very warm and I do not want her to distress herself too much. She will need her strength when the time comes to push.'

'Very well,' Clara replies, and returns to my side, mopping my brow and gently stroking my hair back from my face.

'Is the baby coming soon?' I ask, hoping they will consider me still capable of understanding what is happening. I am not stupid; I

am in pain! This child is taking a lifetime to emerge from my body, and I know I am physically very weak, but I have not lost my mind. They should not discuss my situation behind my back. How rude of them to do so!

'Does she know?' I hear the midwife whisper to Clara. How indiscreet they are! No sense in whispering if I am still to hear what they say!

'What is it that I should know?' I demand of Clara, suddenly lucid and clear of thought again, finding the strength to pull myself up on the bed.

'Lydia, wake up? Lydia, are you OK?' I can hear someone calling to me. Is it Vincenzo? I suppose it must be. Maybe I dozed off again, but I don't know what he's getting so worked up about.

'Yes,' I go to reply, but it seems my lips won't form the words. Someone seems to have glued them together and the words won't come. Why can't I open my eyes? Too sleepy, can't do this, can't answer any more questions…

'Clara, what is it that I should know? Where is Tito? Is he awaiting news of us downstairs?' I beg. 'I know it is not usual, but please send for him. Ask him to come up, I have to see him. Just for a few moments. I simply need to see him; it will help me so much. Please?'

A glance passes between Clara and the midwife, such that I know something has happened. Something they do not want to share with me.

'Is he ill? Is that why he is not here?' I ask but then concern gives way to anger: 'I am giving birth to his child and he promised to look after us. Why is he not here?'

'Lydia, my love. Oh God, what's happening to you?' I can hear the alarm in Vincenzo's voice. Why is he panicking? I'm just having a little nap, that's all. What's the fuss about? He has wrapped me up in something furry and warm, and I can hear him frantically jabbing at buttons on his phone, his voice higher pitched than normal as he makes a call. 'The ambulance will be here soon,' he says. 'Stay with me Lydia.' Well, I'm not going anywhere am I? I'm way too tired to even get myself off this sofa. Nothing seems to want to work. Limbs are all floppy, I'm so tired. But I'm fine. I'm just having a rest. If only Vincenzo would stop flapping.

There is a rush of air as someone joins us in the room and starts fiddling with me. Get off! Who are you and what are you doing to me?

Why can't I tell them I'm OK? I'm trying to speak, but they can't hear me. I don't know who this person is, touching my neck, lifting my eyelids, feeling my wrist. Who are you? Go away, will you, I'm having a little snooze…

'Where is Tito? Why isn't he here?' I ask again, frantic with worry now.

'He is gone,' Clara says simply, and the way she says that word denotes its finality.

'Why is he gone? Does he no longer love me?' I begin to sob. 'He promised to take care of us. We were to return to Venice and live as a family once the child is born. What do you mean, 'gone'?'

'Do not distress yourself, Madam, it is not good for the baby,' begs the midwife, gently stroking my arm and trying to make me lie down. But I sit up again and find an inner strength to go on.

'Get this baby out of me! I need to find Tito. Get this baby out of me now so that I can go after him!' And then I do lie back on the bed, spent after my outburst, desolate tears of bitter sadness rolling from my eyes.

'Why has he left us, Clara? Why now?'

We seem to be in a fast-moving vehicle. Vincenzo carried me to it in his arms, all wrapped up in this lovely furry throw, although why he wouldn't let me walk, I really don't know. He could at least have let me stand up and put my clothes back on. Although I think I might be a bit too sleepy to manage that.

It's making some sort of noise, like a police car, or something. We're going so fast! If I could ask why or where we are going then I would, but it seems I just have to lie here and let them do what they want. I wonder where they're taking me? But I just want to go back to sleep, so I don't mind where I am as long as I'm horizontal…

Vincenzo keeps talking to me in a really funny voice. It's all kind of high and squeaky, not like him at all. I can feel him holding my hand, and he keeps stroking it and squeezing it. He's made a lot of phone calls too. I hope he's not driving, AND talking to me, AND making all those calls. I know he's Italian and they drive like, well… But there's a limit. So who's driving then? Where are they taking me? Don't we need to get back and let him finish that painting? He won't be too happy about the interruption, will he? Why can't everyone just calm down and let me sleep? I'll wake up in my own good time…

'His wife knows of you, Maria,' Clara replies. 'And of the child, too. That is why he brought you here to Bologna for your confinement. Back to your home town in all its familiarity. And he hoped to take you both back to Venice with him, despite his wife's wrath. But I'm afraid he left at first light this morning. There is a letter for you. Would you like me to read it to you?'

'No! I will read it. Fetch it to me now!' I yell again in agony as another contraction seizes me. But the midwife pushes Clara to one side.

'She cannot read the letter now, it is time.'

What are these wires all over me? Why are they plugging me into the mains like this? I must look like Frankenstein's monster. What is this place? I can hear lots of hushed voices as what feels like an army of people buzzes and fusses around me. Just take me back to Vincenzo's office, will you? We were fine there; I was having a little lie-down on the sofa, and he was painting me, so what's all the sudden fuss? But still I don't seem able to tell them. I can't make them hear me, and I can't see who they are. Still can't open my eyes. Hold on Maria, I'm here for you…

'My Darling Maria,' the letter begins.

'It is with a great pain in my heart that I write to you now. I know that by this time, my love, you will likely have been delivered of our child. I hope with God's blessing all has passed well, and this communication finds you in good health.

Maria, my darling, before I say anything else, you must know this truth. You are the one and only love of my life. Never before has a woman brought such emotion, such love, such happiness into the very depths of my heart and soul. I knew from the moment I first set eyes on you that it would be so, and you have been a veritable gift from God, an inspiration to me.

Thus it pains me to tell you this: it is no longer possible for me to bring you and our child back to Venice, and I know you will consider me weak for giving into the powers which seek to keep us apart. My wife has for some time known of our love, but as loyal wives do, has been prepared to overlook my indiscretion for the sake of propriety. However of late she has been informed of the child you carry, and this has thrown her into a fit of paroxysm such as I have never seen.

You will be aware that I am in some difficulties at present in my relationship with the ducal palace and the work I have been appointed to undertake there. I have today been ordered to repay the commission received thus far, and Pordenone, that vile man who has for so long been my rival, is appointed to take my place. This is a huge misfortune and I must therefore proceed with care if I am to maintain any vestige of professional standing within the city.

I wish for nothing more than to bring you and our son back to live with me in Venice, but this cannot happen. My wife has threatened me with exposure should I bring this to bear, and I can ill afford such a denunciation at this time. Her father has great influence with the Council of Ten, and hence my future depends on her continued goodwill towards me.

Do not fear for the safety of the child, for I have made provision for him. He is to be taken to France by a genteel man and his wife, who are of my sound acquaintance. He too is an artist and is commissioned to paint in Paris. They are a very fine couple who will make their way well in the world. Sadly lacking children of their own, they have vowed to bring up our child as though he were their flesh and blood, and I have provided them with the means to do this. Rest assured that he will be safe and happy with them. I have asked that they give him the family name of Urbino, to guarantee his anonymity but also in remembrance of that wonderful painting, one of many, for which you were my inspiration, and during whose creation he was within your belly. They will come for him before the week is out.

I know this will be hard for you, but I am certain that you will see it is for the best, if not now, then as you pass through life, for you are young, with many years, and opportunities, ahead of you. You have no need of the encumbrance a child born out of wedlock will bring. I do hope that, in a year or so, once the scandal has passed over and all is returned to normal, we shall be reunited and it will be possible for you to join me in Venice, albeit in secret. We can never publicly declare our love, my dear, but the thought that I might never see you again tears at my very soul, so I hold this hope for the future within my heart. Please remain in Bologna and I will send news when it is safe for you to come.

Forgive my clumsy words and the sorry news they convey, for I am no writer. Please kiss my darling child for me and give him my blessing. I hope he is endowed with your beauty and grace, and not my cowardice.

Forever yours,

Tito.'

My eyes won't open, but they seem perfectly able to cry. Maria's story is unfolding inside my head, and it is the saddest thing ever. I hear Vincenzo exclaim when he sees my tears.

'She must be waking up! Look, she's crying! Doctor, look! Lydia, my love, can you hear me?'

She is here! Emilia is here! The child who for so long I had felt move inside me is here! And, oh, what beauty! I have never before seen such perfection in so tiny a face. But then.... I cannot bear it.

I cannot put into words the pain inside me, for it is far, far worse than that searing, never-ending pain of childbirth. Nor can I find the strength to describe the events which have unfolded here, these past few hours.

Suffice to say, they came for her, and she is gone. She, too, is gone. And I have never felt so alone.

How could Tito do this to us, when I thought he loved me so? I never believed him capable of such cowardice. I know I would fight to the death for him and for our child, but it seems that strength of conviction is not reciprocated.

It has been several days, and now I am well of body again, but I have been sane of mind throughout this ordeal, and I am resolute in what I must do.

I love Tito still, but what life is there here for me now, with him gone and with no child to love and care for? I know I must leave this place and my dear Clara. She, along with my darling Bella, is all I have left. I shall seek a new life elsewhere, but where that will be, I do not yet know.

The carriage is waiting for me and I leave the house before Clara awakes. She cannot see me leave, or she would try to stop me. My poor, dear, Clara, who has been everything to me.

Tito will not see me again, but I have left a letter for Clara to send to him in Venice, informing him he that has a daughter, and that I have named her Emilia. I know the prospects for a child born out of wedlock, and a mere girl at that, are few. But how terrible only to set eyes on my most precious daughter for a few brief moments before she was taken from me. I fear I shall die of a broken heart. I know she is safe; the family he has chosen for her was chosen wisely, and will cherish her and raise her as their own, I am certain of that. I should not fear for her safety, but how will I live without her? Again my heart aches unbearably and the agony threatens to cleave me in two. But she is not here, she is long gone, and I have nothing to keep me in this city.

We speed through the Piazza Maggiore and I permit myself one last glance up at the church of San Petronio, its huge campanile cutting the shadows of the square firmly in two. A sudden spear of moonlight illuminates a stained glass window, and the image of Our Lord is revealed to me. Am I worthy of looking upon his face? I feel I should deflect my gaze, lower my head in shame, but I am drawn to see his visage one last time. As I glance upwards, his enigmatic smile is sufficient to bestow upon me his blessing and forgiveness.

And then at this very moment I know what I must do. As though struck by a bolt of lightening, I realise He is calling to me, and I must go to Him. I had believed that leaving Bologna would be sufficient to rid myself of these dark, dark days, but what is there left for me on God's earth? I am alone in the world; no mortal has need of me now. My Lord is calling to me….

As the carriage makes a sharp turn into the Via d'Azeglio I pull my cloak tightly around me and throw myself onto the street below.

'Lydia, *cara*, can you hear me?' Vincenzo asks.

'Yes,' I reply in a whisper.

28

'She's dead,' I sob. 'Maria is dead.'

'Lydia, you're awake. Thank God for that!' Vincenzo sighs, and I open my eyes to find him standing by my side, tears streaming down his face.

'Maria, died,' I say again, but he doesn't seem to be listening, clearly too caught up in the emotion of the moment. But I've only been asleep.

'She killed herself because the man she loved wasn't brave enough to do what he should have done.' Then I look around and register where I am, no longer in the sixteenth century, but back in the twenty-first, in a high-tech hospital suite, with wires and beepers all around me.

'Why am I in here? What's happened with your painting? What's all this for?' I ask, pulling at the wires which pin me to the bed as I try to haul myself into a sitting position.

Vincenzo moves to open the door and calls out 'She's awake!' and then it seems it's party-time, as Sophia and Leonora, Dante, Lanzo and Stefano, plus Antonio Di Girolamo all pile in, a real frenzy of friends. I am overwhelmed as they all come across to my bed and plaster me with kisses and hugs, with 'We were so worried,' and 'What happened to you, Lydia?' and 'We thought we were losing you,' flying around everywhere, until a young, female doctor, a nurse trailing in her wake, comes into the room and calls order, sending them back outside so that she can check me over.

'You had us worried there for a moment, Signorina Irvine,' she says, standing back from the bed once she has finished prodding and poking at me. 'But you seem to have come round very quickly. We thought you were in danger of going into a coma, as your vital signs were very weak when Signore Tizzaro brought you in, but amazingly you now seem to be showing no symptoms at all. Your body is returning to normal very quickly. It's quite unheard of.'

'I was asleep,' I reply, simply. 'I don't know what all the fuss was about.'

'I think it was a little more than that, Signorina,' she chuckles condescendingly, considering herself, as she rightly would, the better qualified to pass judgement on my health.

'I feel fine, just like I've had a long, long sleep,' I say, but don't add out loud that I also feel deeply sad, remembering the dreams and Maria's fate.

'How long was I out for?' I ask.

'A little under an hour,' the doctor replies, and I am surprised at that.

'But it felt like a lifetime,' Vincenzo says, slumping back into his chair, looking thoroughly exhausted. 'You really scared me, you know.'

'I'm sorry,' I say. The doctor excuses herself, once more expressing her amazement at my rapid recovery, and promising to return in fifteen minutes to carry out further observations.

'Where did you go to?' Vincenzo asks, panic subsiding and curiosity taking hold.

'I was dreaming about Maria,' I reply. 'I've never done that before outside the gallery, so to start with I just felt a bit sleepy and didn't give too much thought to it. I think those roses sent me off, you know, those ones on your desk. Maria always had roses like that around her. Such a strong smell. She's dead,' I say again, as the pain of memory hits once more.

'Of course she's dead,' he laughs, 'she lived nearly five hundred years ago.'

'No, you know what I mean,' I say impatiently. 'She died in the dream. Can you bring Antonio in? I want him to hear all this.'

Antonio comes into the room clutching a small bunch of flowers. Not roses, I'm glad to say. Bless him, he must have nipped to the hospital shop at break-neck speed after I woke up.

'How are you, my dear?' he asks in his gentle, fatherly way.

'I'm fine, thank you,' I reply, smiling in confirmation.

'Well, I must say you look remarkably well for one whom we considered in such grave health mere moments ago.'

'I dreamt about Maria,' I tell him. 'She gave birth to Emilia. And Titian sent the baby away. To live in France. With a couple who were going there. They went to Paris. Then she killed herself. Maria, I mean.' I blurt out the bare facts in short, sharp sentences, wanting to tell him everything all at once, and knowing he will want to hear it, as it is the resolution of his own story, too.

'Slow down, slow down, my dear,' he says, taking hold of my hand and patting it with his other. 'It sounds like you have a lot to tell us, but there is no rush.'

'How could he do that to her?' I ask, once I've recounted pretty much everything I can remember to Vincenzo and Antonio. 'They were so in love, they meant everything to each other, and he threw it away so easily. He always thought he was having a son, but Maria wrote him a letter to tell him about Emilia, after she'd been taken away. She had nothing to live for, poor girl.'

'That would be why my story ended so abruptly,' says Antonio, and I have to say he almost looks relieved, not at the outcome obviously, which is a tragic one, but that he now knows there is a valid reason for his own dreams coming to an end as they did. They ceased at the moment in time when Tiziano Vecellio pushed Maria Rossi and their daughter, Emilia, from his life. There was nothing more for Antonio to dream about, as the love of Titian's life was no longer with him. Titian wouldn't have known what had then become of Maria, I should imagine.

'Things were very different in those days,' Vincenzo says. 'There must have been a huge stigma attached to having a child out of wedlock, and Maria probably would have fared better in life on her own, had she chosen life. And it was a very brave decision she took, not to.'

'And the child would have been well taken care of, too. Raised as though she were their own.' Antonio says.

'But with Titian asking the painter to give the child the name of Urbino, surely everyone would know she wasn't theirs?' I ask.

'Yes, but she could have been a poor orphan that they took in,' Antonio replies. 'Don't forget they moved hundreds of miles away from their home. No one would have known them in Paris, least of all asked questions about their child's origins. 'Urbino,' you say. What a fortunate choice of name for her, especially as you had your dreams in front of that painting! You must be so relieved to find out what happened to Maria, even though it's not the ending you might have hoped for?'

'It's a horrible ending for her, poor girl, but at least I know what happened now. It's no wonder she wanted me to know her story. Things like that just don't make it to the history books, do they? But it still doesn't explain why I had the dreams,' I say. 'I still have no evidence that I might be related to them, I'm just assuming I am, like with you and your relationship to Titian. And calling the child Urbino just complicates things, doesn't it? I can't follow down the Rossi or Vecellio lines of investigation any more.'

'Urbino is a very unusual name,' Antonio says. 'It's a place, and not a commonly used surname in Italy, really. Would you like me to look into it for you? Let's see what else we can find out. I'll go and do that now for you. You just concentrate on getting better.'

'There goes a man with a mission,' Vincenzo laughs, as Antonio leaves the room, intent on his next piece of historical detective work. 'If anyone can find out something, then he's the one.' And he turns back to me. 'This is all great stuff, and I know you're pleased to have a resolution to the dreams and all that, but I'm just so relieved you're OK.'

'Can we go home now?' I ask, impatiently tearing at the covers and looking around. 'Where are my clothes?'

'Oh, they're probably still in my study, sorry. I didn't think to bring them in all the panic. I'll call in that bossy doctor to start the discharge process and I'll nip back and get them for you. We'll have you out of here soon, don't worry.'

Vincenzo has tucked me up in bed back at the apartment, despite my protestations that I feel absolutely fine, and that there was never anything medically wrong with me in the first place.

'But that doctor insisted,' he says. 'She wasn't very happy about you going home so soon, but I promised I'd take care of you, so that's exactly what I'm going to do, whether you like it or not.'

At that moment Sophia sticks her head round the door, checking it's OK for her to come in. She is bearing a tray with some fruit juice and a Panino.

'Room service!' she announces, popping the tray down on the table beside my bed. 'How are you feeling?'

'I'm fine, and really, all this is lovely, but I'm not ill. Honestly. I'll be back on my feet tomorrow, you'll see. In fact, I'd be back on my feet now if this man here would let me get out of bed,' I add, jabbing Vincenzo affectionately in the ribs. 'But thank you, you're all doing a great job of looking after me.'

'My pleasure,' she says, leaving us to it, but then, 'Oh, someone else to see you,' and Antonio's head appears round the door.

'Are you feeling better?' he asks, and I try not to sound impatiently cross when I reply:

'Yes. Fine. Really. Thank you.' It's lovely that they're all so concerned about me, but really, they don't need to be. 'That was quick. Did you manage to find anything out?'

'Well, it's interesting,' he begins, perching on the side of the bed. 'I did some research into the origins of surnames, and Urbino isn't a very common one, so there aren't many references to it. But there is evidence of a small cluster of D'Urbino's in Paris in the sixteenth and seventeenth centuries, one of which may or may not be your Emilia. If she had married of course, then her name could have changed, and none of these might be her, but on the other hand, perhaps her adoptive parents told her who she was when she came of age and she decided to keep her name throughout her life as a reference to her heritage? But that of course, my dear, we shall never know. All we do know is that the Urbino name surfaces in Paris, where we know Emilia went, so that has to be encouraging news, doesn't it?

'And… and this is the really interesting part,' he goes on. 'Urbino and your name, Irvine, are actually from the same 'family', as it were, of names. Urbino kind of evolved into Irvine, as the 'b' sound isn't terribly French when it occurs in the middle of a word. They can make the 'v' sound much easier in their native tongue, you see.'

I try not to leap out of bed with excitement at this news. Vincenzo has to practically hold me down.

Antonio continues: 'So Urbino evolved into Urvino and then lost the Italianate 'o' from the end. Urvine and Irvine sound the same, and to all intents and purposes are the same name. Spellings were easily confused over the centuries, particularly when only a small proportion of the population could actually write their own names. So there you go. Irvine equals Urbino! Perhaps that is your link?'

He sees the look of utter excitement on my face and smiles.

'I think it's more than a 'perhaps', Antonio,' I reply. 'And actually, rumour has it that my family is of French origin. You never really know, do you, as these stories get passed down through the generations, and you're never sure quite how much truth there is in them, but I think you have just confirmed things for me! I have to be related to Emilia! I am Lydia Irvine, otherwise known as Lydia D'Urbino! Hey, that has quite a ring to it! I like it!'

Antonio leans in and gives me a big hug. 'I'm so pleased for you, Lydia,' he says. 'I know there's still nothing concrete as such to prove your link to Emilia, but I think this is as close as you are going to get, don't you? As long as you are certain in your own mind, then that's all that matters. And I think you are now, aren't you?'

'Yes, I am. Very. Thank you so much Antonio,' I say. 'I have a feeling there won't be any more dreams now. Maria's all done with me, isn't she? Her story is complete. Although I might have to pop back to the gallery at some point, just to check…' I look across to Vincenzo to gauge his reaction.

'No you don't, not yet!' Vincenzo laughs.

29

'James, darling, we need a photo,' Evie says, thrusting her phone into her husband's hands. 'Here, in front of David. Hang on, wait a sec until there's a gap in the crowds, will you? We don't want everyone's heads getting in the way of David and his lovely body, do we?!' She turns to me and giggles. We both produce a perfectly-timed cheesy grin and point to the statue as James clicks the button and the photo is a done deal. 'I must send that one to my friend, Grace, back home. Her new bloke looks just like him. It'll make her laugh.'

'Just let me get one with my camera, too,' James says, pulling an expensive-looking piece of kit with an enormous lens from its special padded case. 'Takes a much better quality of photo than these phone camera things,' he mutters, handing Evie's back to her.

'What is it they say about a man with a big lens?' I giggle to Evie, as James twiddles the lens and instructs us to pose again, but sensibly this time. Nothing should ruin his shot, and certainly not two mad sisters pointing to David's private parts. Heaven forbid it should turn into a tourist snapshot, and not a piece of art.

'No, that's big cars. But hey, maybe it applies to lenses, too,' she laughs. 'Not so, in James' case, dear sister, I hasten to add.'

'Too much information!' I reply, putting my hands over my ears before she reveals any more intimate details.

My mad sister and her husband have come to stay, making their long-promised visit to see me, and I have to say, their timing couldn't be better. I'd managed to persuade Vincenzo not to call my family after the hospital incident; I wasn't ill as such, anyway, and the last thing I wanted was my parents jumping on a plane and dragging me back to the UK with them. I need to enjoy my last few weeks here in peace. God knows it's going to be hard enough to leave when I do have to.

So I can relax and enjoy Evie's visit. I've had my results for this year – and passed with flying colours, the dreams are all over and done with, and so the rest of the time here is my own, to soak up this wonderful place as much as I can before I have to leave it behind.

It helps to have someone to show round, as it makes me realise just how intimately I know Florence now, plus it forces me to visit places I haven't been to for a while, one last time. Typically for Evie, she insisted on shopping before sightseeing, and so we have done the smarter shopping quarters this morning, followed by a beautiful little restaurant for lunch. It was well outside my price bracket, so I've never been there before, not even with Vincenzo – but James was picking up the tab – and now we're planning a few touristy bits and pieces before I introduce them to Vincenzo, later on this evening. I'm a little nervous about that; I so want Evie to love Vincenzo.

I don't see why she wouldn't, but it's a little scary introducing the love of your life to your family.

We have an Uffizi tour planned for this afternoon, with me acting as guide. I've been back to the gallery just the once since the dream I had in Vincenzo's office, and although I didn't linger in room twenty-eight, there was no feeling, as I passed the painting, that Maria had anything else to tell me. She doesn't, I know that; her story is complete and her spirit is gone, but I have to admit I feel kind of bereft, as though it were a final acknowledgment that that period of my life is over. I was very privileged to have those dreams, I think, to have been the chosen one for Maria to tell her story to. In a way I'm glad it's all over, but part of me misses her deeply.

Evie has a novel approach to taking in the gallery, whizzing through some rooms like a whirling dervish, and lingering in others, when her attention happens to be caught by a particular piece.

'Uh, she's just like this round the shops,' James bemoans, deliberately holding back as she tries to drag him through to the next room at her pace. He seems rather taken with the busts and statues in the First Corridor, pausing to read the inscriptions and standing back to fully admire them. Evie gives him a chance to catch up when she reaches the Second Corridor at the end of the gallery, overlooking the Arno, stopping to admire the view, up-river towards the Ponte Vecchio. Then she switches sides and people-watches the swarming crowds below, her second favourite hobby after retail therapy.

'So, this new man of yours,' she starts, plopping her designer handbag on the plinth of a statue (not allowed, I'm sure – must keep an eye out for guards) and swiftly parking her bottom next to it. 'Tell me more. He's a lecturer you say. Handsome? Sexy? Rich? And more importantly, does he treat you well?'

Evie, bless her, is never backwards in coming forwards when it comes to my boyfriends, hence my slight trepidation about this evening. When Ed and I broke up and I filled her in on the details, it was as much as I could do to prevent her from seeking him out and disembowelling him on the spot. I suppose it's something to do with the age difference between us; she feels protective of me, like a surrogate mother sort of thing. And in the absence of parental presence, I think she feels it's her job to carry out the Spanish Inquisition of my new lover. I just hope Vincenzo's shoulders are broad enough to cope with it. I go on to extol his virtues, in the hope that she will start the evening with good expectations of him.

'Hey, I know this one,' Evie says a little later, pulling me away from the Bronzino painting in room twenty-seven and through the archway into room twenty-eight. I know exactly which painting she is referring to; after all, Venus of Urbino is one of those paintings everyone wants to see in the Uffizi, hence the crowds milling around it on a pretty constant basis. Although there are quieter moments, I know that…

'I love this one,' she goes on. 'Isn't she gorgeous? Just look at that hair, oh, and I'd never noticed that little dog before. Sweet! Come and sit over here with me for a mo, will you? We can wait till the crowds have gone and have a proper look. Do you know, I always thought the painting would be bigger than that.'

'No, it's OK thanks, I'm just going to carry on over here,' I protest, not wanting to take up my regular place on the bench. 'I… er… I spent a lot of time in here doing… er… research, so I know that one pretty well. But you go for it, I'll just be over here. She is lovely, though, isn't she?' I can't help throwing a backwards glance at Maria as I move to the other side of the room.

I'd decided before Evie arrived that I wasn't going to tell her about the dreams. She's always been a 'face value' sort of person, not a dreamer by any means, and much more of a practical 'doer', so the notion of her little sister being transported back to the sixteenth century in her mind just wouldn't wash with her. I'd asked Vincenzo what he thought, and even though he's never met her, he too thought it probably best just to keep it amongst those who already knew and understood.

Maybe one day I'll get round to writing about it; I have so many notes, after all, I'm sure I could knock up a volume of a similar size to Antonio's in no time. One day, when I have some time on my hands. Maybe then I'll tell my family how I came by the knowledge…

Anyway, here I am gazing at Flora instead – also Maria, I know, but I've never had the same pull to this or any of Titian's many other works of art. Strange really, but I do feel quite safe looking this way whilst Evie gets her fill of Venus. There she is now, muscling in on a tour guide – an English-speaking one at that – and staring interestedly as the woman recounts the history of the painting in great length. *Huh that's what you think*, I chuckle to myself as the guide explains how the exact identity of the model is still a mystery. Oh no it's not…

Sneaking another quick glance at Venus, I can't help wondering what happened to Bella, Maria's little dog. I hope she ended up with Clara; I'm pretty sure she would have taken care of her when her mistress left. Despite that final snippet of unfinished business I can't see Maria wanting to summon me back to dreamland to tell me about her dog's fate, much as I'd love to go there again, just for one last time.

I needn't have worried about introducing Vincenzo to my sister. Half an hour in, Evie is chatting to him as though they have known each other for years. I suppose it helps that Vincenzo has called upon his huge reserve of suave, Italian charm, and as I glance across the table at them, he has her pretty much eating out of his hand.

James is trying to have a serious conversation about art with me, so I have one ear on that, making sure I nod and make a few noises in the right places, occasionally contributing with an interesting fact that he probably wouldn't have known, and the other ear on what my boyfriend and sister are talking about, just to make sure they don't stray into dangerous territory. But what likelihood is there that I might have to leap to Vincenzo's defence and rescue him from my sister's clutches? Let's face it, this is a man who has been brought up on a diet of charm, and somehow I don't think he'll need my help.

I used to wonder if there was some sort of secret Italian charm school that adolescent boys got whisked off to for a couple of years. Or maybe it's just passed down from generation to generation: a lifetime spent watching your elders behave around women and learning to emulate them. Either way, our lads back home could certainly learn a thing or two from them, that's for sure.

After best part of a year here, I know now that this charm stems from a deep-rooted admiration and respect for women, and has nothing whatsoever to do with disrespect or finding women easy prey. At first glance, the amount of attention they pay to women might seem sleazy, but Italian men grow up with a deep respect for their Mamma and their sisters, which they never lose as the Italian family unit is so strong. This coupled with the fact that they simply adore women for their beauty and grace and the fact that they are so different from them, gives them the ability to make women feel as special as we know we are.

Vincenzo certainly makes me feel like that. I look over at him and pass him a look with an implicit 'You OK?' and he smiles back, twisting round in his seat to include me in the conversation once more, his body language letting me know he's missing me all the way across from the other side of the table. He reaches across and takes hold of my hand.

'Your sister, she is as lovely as you,' he says in perfect English, with the aforementioned bucket of Italian charm. 'Almost as lovely,' he adds with a giggle, glancing at James to make sure he hasn't overstepped the mark.

Later as we are saying our goodbyes, Evie and James heading back to their hotel, and Vincenzo and I to his apartment, Evie pulls me to one side.

'He's lovely,' she says, and I smile at her with relief. 'Mad about you, too. Totally head over heels.'

30

England, One Year Later

My parents are glowing with pride. The smile on Dad's face as I leave King's Hall says it all: 'My clever girl, graduating from university with a First Class Honours Degree.' He couldn't look more proud if he was at Buckingham Palace, receiving a knighthood from the Queen.

Mum fusses around me, adjusting my mortar board and gown, and squeezing in a few quick snaps as I stroll across the lawn to meet up with the others, who hadn't been allowed into the graduation ceremony. They are all here: Sophia, Leonora, Dante, Stefano and Lanzo. All of them have made the journey to see me graduate, wanting to support me on my big day; it was just a shame I couldn't get enough tickets for them all to come inside. But still, they're here for the party afterwards, and that's the most important part. It's lovely to have them here. All of them, even Stefano. Despite what happened between us, I can safely say we have remained firm friends, which I'm so pleased about.

They are all quite taken with Newcastle, these sophisticated Italian friends of mine, and for some of them it's their first taste of UK life. They'd arrived yesterday afternoon, and I'd managed to shirk a quiet meal with my parents in favour of showing my friends a few of the sights. And some of the nightlife too, which I have to say I'm regretting slightly this morning. Although it could be the level of euphoria and general feeling that the rest of my life begins today which is making my head spin.

They've all fallen for this quaint old northern city with its grey skies, rows of terraced houses – and amazingly – stotties. I'd tried to explain Newcastle's answer to the focaccia to them, but there is no substitute for popping into a little corner café and ordering one stuffed to overflowing with bacon, egg and sausage. Blissful, especially on the back of the teensy weensy hangovers we all have today. I think it's safe to say they are all converts already; they appreciate good food when they see it, after all.

Stefano hands me a little parcel. 'From Antonio,' he says.

I rip off the paper to reveal a tiny book, with a perfect reproduction of a Titian painting on each page. It's beautiful. The label reads, 'To my dearest Lydia on your graduation day. Much love as always, your cousin Antonio Di Girolamo.'

My cousin. Yes, he is, however many times removed, which is something we will never be able to calculate. All that matters is that we are two members of the same huge family who have been privileged to share in the same story from five hundred years ago.

I stroll over to Vincenzo, who is looking gorgeous in his dark suit and designer sunglasses, kiss him on the cheek and take hold of his hand. Oh yes, here's here too, of course. This day wouldn't be complete without him, would it? In fact, he's been staying with me for the past week, as we finalise our plans for our return to Florence together.

Yes, I'm going back. For good this time. England is still my home, and I have to keep reminding my parents of that, to help them deal with the fact that I'm going; they're struggling a little bit to come to terms with their baby daughter leaving them to live overseas. But Italy isn't far away, is it? They can quite easily hop on a plane and come and see me any time they like. And vice versa.

Vincenzo has been across to see me whenever he can during this past year, which has been fantastic to help ease the pain of having to leave behind not just him but my beloved Florence. Every time he came over it was like he brought a little bit of Florentine life with him. I'm pleased to say our love has survived the test of time and distance – but then we both knew it would.

I've also secured myself a job. With a little influence from my lovely friend Antonella Pasi, who I met that wet day at the archives, and the contacts she has in the world of galleries and museums, I have managed to land the grand position of Junior Curator, Sixteenth Century Art, at the Uffizi, of all places. It sounds very grand, but really it's a very junior position and there are loads of us. Still, it's a start, a foot in the door of my career in art, and therefore just what I want and need. I'm going to do a Masters alongside it, I think. I need to carry on my academic studies, particularly in the light of what I learnt from, and about, Maria. There's more to Renaissance life than just the paintings, I know that now.

The best thing of all about getting the job is that it gives me a valid reason for going to Florence to be with Vincenzo. He's always said I could come out and he would support me, job or no job, but I need a reason to be there, other than him, and I think he understands that. He knows I love him and I want us to be together, but I need to think of the me in all this, and not lose sight of what I want for myself and my career too.

We've bought a little house, Vincenzo and I, a tiny, picturesque villa high on the hill overlooking the centre of Florence, up near the Piazzale Michelangelo. This has to be the scariest, most grown-up thing I've ever done! It's a gorgeous little place – it needs a lot of work doing to it but it's going to be our home. Vincenzo has already bought me something to hang on the walls – a print of the Venus of Urbino, just a small one, beautifully framed. When the renovations are finished it will take pride of place on the wall in the loo; Vincenzo fails to understand this quirky element of British interior design which can lead to an Old Master hanging in the smallest room of the house.

And I am planning to write that book about Maria. Life's going to be busy, isn't it? My book is going to be available to the wider public straight away – I'm not going to keep it under wraps like Antonio did – provided I'm lucky enough to secure a publishing deal of course, although both Vincenzo and Antonio have several contacts in that area, so here's hoping...

Actually, Antonio is thinking of doing a third edition of his book and braving the outside world with it. I'm going to publish mine as a historical novel, then there will be no worries in the future about my reputation as a serious art scholar (a reputation I have yet to earn) being called into question.

I've chosen a title for it already, *Urban Venus, A Renaissance Love Story*.

Author's Note & Acknowledgements

The Venus of Urbino painting first 'hooked me in' on a writing course back in 2009. Under the tutelage of the lovely Allegra Taylor, we aspiring writers were tasked with selecting a postcard and writing about it in the first person. I chose Venus, and hastily scribbled two pages about a girl who dozed off in front of the painting, and dreamt she was the artist's model.

From then on, I felt there was an awful lot more I wanted to write about the painting. On a trip to Florence later the same year – including a tour of the Uffizi – a full-length story started to form in my head. When a little early research revealed that Titian had an illegitimate daughter whose name was Emilia – also my daughter's name – then it felt like fate, and I knew I had to carry on.

But I don't profess to be a historian, even an amateur one, and I have used artistic licence by the bucket-load to put this story together. Whilst Titian and Emilia are of course real historical figures, most of the events surrounding them – and many of the dates – come entirely from my imagination, as does the padded bench in room twenty-eight where Lydia has her dreams. If only that bench really existed!

Titian was born around 1491 and painted the Venus of Urbino in 1538, but it is 1540-41 before my Maria sits for the painting, whilst pregnant with Emilia, and to make her young enough to be the girl in the painting, I have assumed she was born in 1519. This would have given the lovers a couple of years of blissful existence in Venice, after that chance meeting at the brothel in Bologna in 1537, before their daughter was conceived.

The real Emilia was born much later, some time in the 1550's, by which time Titian would have been in his sixties. I didn't want him to be too old in this story, and I wanted the Pope's visit to Bologna (a real historical event, during which Titian actually did paint the Pope) to be the occasion which brought Titian and Maria together. So I brought this papal visit forward from 1543 to 1537, which would have made Titian a quite elderly (by sixteenth century standards only!) forty-six, but still young enough to be attractive to a girl like Maria.

Florence continues to fascinate and amaze me more than any other city I've been to; I've learnt so much about it, as well as Venice, Bologna and the Renaissance era, in carrying out the research for this book. I am indebted to the following publications for their insight into the life and times of that richly exciting period of history:

Italy in the Age of the Renaissance – John M. Najemy

Titian – National Gallery Company

At Home in Renaissance Italy – Marta Ajmar Wollheim & Flora Dennis

Thanks are due too to my posse of supportive friends and family: to my readers Alli Neal and Ginny Getting for their valued input, to Manuela Cherchi for her checking of my sometimes dubious Italian, to Liz Bryan for another wonderful cover design, and to Wadham for his unerring belief that I can do this writing thing. And, of course, to my children, just for being lovely.

saradowningwriter.co.uk

SaraDowningWriter

@sarawritesbooks

30317141R00177

Printed in Poland
by Amazon Fulfillment
Poland Sp. z o.o., Wrocław